P9-EDF-014

The Devil All the Time

The Devil All the Time

A NOVEL

DONALD RAY POLLOCK

DOUBLEDAY

NEW YORK LONDON TORONTO SYDNEY AUCKLAND

All rights reserved. Published in the United States by Doubleday, a division of Random House, Inc., New York, and in Canada by Random House of Canada Limited, Toronto.

www.doubleday.com

DOUBLEDAY and the portrayal of an anchor with a dolphin are registered trademarks of Random House, Inc.

A portion of this work previously appeared in slightly different form in the *Washington Square Review*.

Jacket photographs: Dog © Christie's Images/SuperStock/Getty Images; Logs © Mark Hooper/UpperCut Images/Getty Images; Car © Jena Ardell/Flickr/Getty Images

Jacket design by Michael J. Windsor

LIBRARY OF CONGRESS CATALOGING-IN-PUBLICATION DATA
Pollock, Donald Ray
The devil all the time / Donald Ray Pollock. — 1st ed.
p. cm.
1. Ohio—Rural conditions—Fiction. I. Title.
PS3616.O5694D48 2011
813'.6—dc22
2010053322

ISBN 978-0-385-53504-5

46500046 8/11

PRINTED IN THE UNITED STATES OF AMERICA

10 9 8 7 6 5 4 3 2 1

First Edition

ONCE AGAIN
FOR
PATSY

The Devil All the Time

ON A DISMAL MORNING near the end of a wet October, Arvin Eugene Russell hurried behind his father, Willard, along the edge of a pasture that overlooked a long and rocky holler in southern Ohio called Knockemstiff. Willard was tall and raw-boned, and Arvin had a hard time keeping up with him. The field was overgrown with brier patches and fading clumps of chickweed and thistle, and ground fog, thick as the gray clouds above, reached to the nine-year-old boy's knees. After a few minutes, they veered off into the woods and followed a narrow deer path down the hill until they came to a log lying in a small clearing, the remains of a big red oak that had fallen many years ago. A weathered cross, fitted together out of boards pried from the back of the ramshackle barn behind their farmhouse, leaned a little eastward in the soft ground a few yards below them.

Willard eased himself down on the high side of the log and motioned for his son to kneel beside him in the dead, soggy leaves. Unless he had whiskey running through his veins, Willard came to the clearing every morning and evening to talk to God. Arvin didn't know which was worse, the drinking or the praying. As far back as he could remember, it seemed that his father had fought the Devil all the time. Arvin shivered a little with the damp, pulled his coat tighter. He wished he were still in bed. Even school, with all its miseries, was better than this, but it was a Saturday and there was no way to get around it.

Through the mostly bare trees beyond the cross, Arvin could see wisps of smoke rising from a few chimneys half a mile away. Four hundred or so people lived in Knockemstiff in 1957, nearly all of them connected by blood through one godforsaken calamity or another, be it lust or necessity or just plain ignorance. Along with the tar-papered shacks and cinder-block houses, the holler included two general stores and a Church of Christ in Christian Union and a joint known throughout the township as the Bull Pen. Though the Russells had rented the house on top of the Mitchell Flats for five years now, most of the neighbors down below still considered them outsiders. Arvin was the only kid on the school bus who wasn't somebody's relation. Three days before, he'd come home with another black eye. "I don't condone no fighting just for the hell of it, but sometimes you're just too easygoing," Willard had told him that evening. "Them boys might be bigger than you, but the next time one of 'em starts his shit, I want you to finish it." Willard was standing on the porch changing out of his work clothes. He handed Arvin the brown pants, stiff with dried blood and grease. He worked in a slaughterhouse in Greenfield, and that day sixteen hundred hogs had been butchered, a new record for R. J. Carroll Meatpacking. Though the boy didn't know yet what he wanted to do when he grew up, he was pretty sure he didn't want to kill pigs for a living.

They had just begun their prayers when the sharp crack of a branch breaking sounded behind them. As Arvin started to turn around, Willard reached over and stopped him, but not before the boy caught a glimpse of two hunters in the pale light, dirty and ragged men whom he'd seen a few times slouching in the front seat of an old sedan scabbed with rust in the parking lot of Maude Speakman's store. One carried a brown burlap sack, the bottom stained a bright red. "Don't pay them no mind," Willard said quietly. "This here is the Lord's time, not nobody else's."

Knowing that the men were close by made him nervous, but Arvin settled back down and closed his eyes. Willard considered the log as holy as any church built by man, and the last person in the world the boy wanted to offend was his father, even though that seemed like a losing battle at times. Except for the dampness dripping from the leaves and a squirrel cutting in a tree nearby, the woods were still again. Arvin was just beginning to think the men had moved on when one of them said in a raspy voice, "Hell, they havin' them a little revival meeting."

"Keep it down," Arvin heard the other man say.

"Shit. I'm thinking now would be a good time to pay his old lady a visit. She probably laying over there in bed right now keeping it warm for me."

"Shut the fuck up, Lucas," the other said.

"What? Don't tell me you wouldn't take a piece of that. She's a looker, damned if she ain't."

Arvin glanced over uneasily at his father. Willard's eyes remained shut, his big hands woven together on top of the log. His lips moved rapidly, but the words he said were too faint for anyone but the Master to hear. The boy thought about what Willard had told him the other day, about standing up for yourself when someone gave you some shit. Evidently, those were just words, too. He had a sinking feeling that the long ride on the school bus was not going to get any better.

"Come on, you dumb sonofabitch," the other man said, "this thing's getting heavy." Arvin listened as they turned and made their way back across the hill in the direction from which they'd come. Long after their footsteps faded away, he could still hear the mouthy one laughing.

A few minutes later, Willard stood up and waited for his son to say his amens. Then they walked back to the house in silence, scraped the mud off their shoes on the porch steps, and entered the warm kitchen. Arvin's mother, Charlotte, was frying slices of bacon in an iron skillet, beating eggs with a fork in a blue bowl. She poured Willard a cup of coffee, set a glass of milk down in front of Arvin. Her black, shiny hair was pulled back in a ponytail, secured with a rubber band, and she wore a faded pink robe and a pair of fuzzy socks, one with a hole in the heel. As Arvin watched her move about the room, he tried to imagine what might have happened if the two hunters had come on to the house instead of turning around. His mother was the prettiest woman he'd ever seen. He wondered if she would have invited them in.

As soon as Willard finished eating, he pushed back his chair and went outside with a dark look on his face. He hadn't said a word since he'd finished his prayers. Charlotte got up from the table with her coffee and stepped over to the window. She watched him stomp across the yard and go into the barn. She considered the possibility that he had an extra bottle hid out there. The one he kept under the sink hadn't been touched in several weeks. She turned and looked at Arvin. "Your daddy mad at you for something?"

Arvin shook his head. "I didn't do nothing."

"That ain't what I asked you," Charlotte said, leaning against the counter. "We both know how he can get."

For a moment, Arvin considered telling his mother what had happened at the prayer log, but the shame was too great. It made him sick to think that his father would listen to a man talk about her that way and just ignore it. "Had a little revival meeting, that's all," he said.

"Revival meeting?" Charlotte said. "Where did you get that from?"

"I don't know, just heard it somewhere." Then he got up and walked down the hallway to his bedroom. He closed the door and lay down on the bed, pulling the top blanket over him. Turning on his side, he stared at the framed picture of the crucified Jesus that Willard had hung above the scratched and battered chest of drawers. Similar pictures of the Savior's execution could be found in every room of the house except the kitchen. Charlotte had drawn the line there, the same as she'd done when he started taking Arvin over to the woods to pray. "Only on the weekends, Willard, that's it," she'd said. The way she saw it, too much religion could be as bad as too little, maybe even worse; but moderation was just not in her husband's nature.

An hour or so later, Arvin was awakened by his father's voice in the kitchen. He jumped off the bed and smoothed the wrinkles out of the wool blanket, then went to the door and pressed his ear against it. He heard Willard ask Charlotte if she needed anything from the store. "I got to gas up the truck for work," he told her. When he heard his father's footsteps in the hall, Arvin moved quickly away from the door and across the room. He was standing by the window pretending to study an arrowhead he'd picked up from the small collection of treasures he had lying on the sill. The door opened. "Let's take a ride," Willard said. "No sense you sitting in here like a house cat all day."

As they walked out the front door, Charlotte yelled from the kitchen, "Don't forget the sugar." They got in the pickup and drove out to the end of their rutted lane and then turned down Baum Hill Road. At the stop sign, Willard made a left onto the stretch of paved road that cut through the middle of Knockemstiff. Though the trip to Maude's store never took more than five minutes, it always seemed to Arvin as if he had entered another country when they came off the Flats. At the Patterson place, a group of boys, some younger than himself, stood in the open doorway of a dilapidated garage passing cigarettes back and forth and taking turns punching a gutted deer carcass that hung from a joist. One of the boys whooped and took a couple of swings at the chilly air as they drove past, and Arvin scooted down in his seat a little. In front of Janey Wagner's house, a pink baby crawled around in the yard under a maple tree. Janey was standing on the sagging porch pointing at the baby and yelling through a broken window patched with cardboard at someone inside. She was wearing the same outfit she wore to school every day, a red plaid skirt and a frayed white blouse. Though she was only a grade ahead of Arvin in school, Janey always sat in the rear of the bus with the older boys on the way home. He'd heard some of the other girls say that they allowed her back there because she'd spread her legs and let them play stink finger with her snatch. He hoped that maybe someday, when he was a little older, he would find out exactly what that meant.

Instead of stopping at the store, Willard made a sharp right up the gravel road called Shady Glen. He gave the truck some gas and whirled into the bald, muddy yard that surrounded the Bull Pen. It was littered with bottle caps and cigarette butts and beer cartons. An ex-railroader spotted with warty skin cancers named Snooks Snyder lived there with his sister, Agatha, an old maid who sat in an upstairs window all day dressed in black and pretending to be a grieving widow. Snooks sold beer and wine out of the front of the house, and, if your face was even vaguely familiar, something with a lot more kick out the back. For his customers' convenience, several picnic tables were set up under some tall sycamores off to the side of the house, along with a horseshoe pit and an outhouse that always appeared on the verge of collapse. The two men that Arvin had seen in the woods that morning were sitting on top of one of the tables drinking beer, their shotguns leaning against a tree behind them.

With the truck still rolling to a stop, Willard pushed the door open and leaped out. One of the hunters stood up and threw a bottle that glanced off the truck's windshield and landed with a clatter in the road. Then the man turned and started running, his filthy coat flapping behind him and his bloodshot eyes looking around wildly at the big man chasing him. Willard caught up and shoved him down into the greasy slop pooled in front of the outhouse door. Rolling him over, he pinned the man's skinny shoulders with his knees and began pounding his bearded face with his fists. The other hunter grabbed one of the guns and hurried to a green Plymouth, a brown paper sack under his arm. He sped away, bald tires slinging gravel all the way past the church.

After a couple of minutes, Willard stopped beating the man. He shook the sting out of his hands and took a deep breath, then walked over to the table where the men had been sitting. He picked up the shotgun propped against the tree, unloaded two red shells, then swung it like a ball bat against the sycamore until it shattered into several pieces. As he turned and started for the truck, he glanced over and saw Snooks Snyder standing in the doorway with a stubby pistol pointed at him. He took a few steps toward the porch. "Old man, you want some of what he got," Willard said in a loud voice, "you just step on out here. I'll stick that gun clear up your ass." He stood waiting until Snooks closed the door.

When he got back inside the pickup, Willard reached under the seat for a rag and wiped the traces of blood off his hands. "You remember what I told you the other day?" he asked Arvin.

"About them boys on the bus?"

"Well, that's what I meant," Willard said, nodding over at the hunter. He tossed the rag out the window. "You just got to pick the right time."

"Yes, sir," Arvin said.

"They's a lot of no-good sonofabitches out there."

"More than a hundred?"

Willard laughed a little and put the truck in gear. "Yeah, at least that many." He started to ease the clutch out. "I'm thinking it best if we keep this between us, okay? No sense gettin' your mom all upset."

"No, she don't need that."

"Good," Willard said. "Now how about I buy you a candy bar?"

For a long time, Arvin would often think of that as the best day he ever spent with his father. After supper that evening, he followed Willard back over to the prayer log. The moon was rising by the time they got there, a sliver of ancient and pitted bone accompanied by a single, shimmering star. They knelt down and Arvin glanced over at his father's skinned knuckles. When she'd asked, Willard had told Charlotte that he'd hurt his hand changing a flat tire. Arvin had never heard his father lie before, but he felt certain that God would forgive him. In the still, darkening woods, the sounds traveling up the hill from the holler were especially clear that night. Down at the Bull Pen, the clanging of the horseshoes against the metal pegs sounded almost like church bells ringing, and the wild hoots and jeers of the drunks reminded the boy of the hunter lying bloody in the mud. His father had taught that man a lesson he'd never forget; and the next time somebody messed with him, Arvin was going to do the same. He closed his eyes and began to pray.

Sacrifice

PART ONE

I

IT WAS A WEDNESDAY AFTERNOON in the fall of 1945, not long
after the war had ended. The Greyhound made its regular stop in
Meade, Ohio, a little paper-mill town an hour south of Columbus
that smelled like rotten eggs. Strangers complained about the stench,
but the locals liked to brag that it was the sweet smell of money. The
bus driver, a soft, sawed-off man who wore elevated shoes and a limp
bow tie, pulled in the alley beside the depot and announced a forty-
minute break. He wished he could have a cup of coffee, but his ulcer
was acting up again. He yawned and took a swig from a bottle of pink
medicine he kept on the dashboard. The smokestack across town, by
far the tallest structure in this part of the state, belched forth another
dirty brown cloud. You could see it for miles, puffing like a volcano
about to blow its skinny top.

Leaning back in his seat, the bus driver pulled his leather cap
down over his eyes. He lived right outside of Philadelphia, and he
thought that if he ever had to live in a place like Meade, Ohio, he'd
go ahead and shoot himself. You couldn't even find a bowl of lettuce
in this town. All that people seemed to eat here was grease and more
grease. He'd be dead in two months eating the slop they did. His wife
told her friends that he was delicate, but there was something about
the tone of her voice that sometimes made him wonder if she was
really being sympathetic. If it hadn't been for the ulcer, he would have
gone off to fight with the rest of the men. He'd have slaughtered a
whole platoon of Germans and shown her just how goddamn delicate he was. The biggest regret was all the medals he'd missed out on.
His old man once got a certificate from the railroad for not missing a
single day of work in twenty years, and had pointed it out to his sickly
son every time he'd seen him for the next twenty. When the old man

finally croaked, the bus driver tried to talk his mother into sticking the certificate in the casket with the body so he wouldn't have to look at it anymore. But she insisted on leaving it displayed in the living room as an example of what a person could attain in this life if he didn't let a little indigestion get in his way. The funeral, an event the bus driver had looked forward to for a long time, had nearly been ruined by all the arguing over that crummy scrap of paper. He would be glad when all the discharged soldiers finally reached their destinations so he wouldn't have to look at the dumb bastards anymore. It wore on you after a while, other people's accomplishments.

Private Willard Russell had been drinking in the back of the bus with two sailors from Georgia, but one had passed out and the other had puked in their last jug. He kept thinking that if he ever got home, he'd never leave Coal Creek, West Virginia, again. He'd seen some hard things growing up in the hills, but they didn't hold a candle to what he'd witnessed in the South Pacific. On one of the Solomons, he and a couple of other men from his outfit had run across a marine skinned alive by the Japanese and nailed to a cross made out of two palm trees. The raw, bloody body was covered with black flies. They could still see the man's heart beating in his chest. His dog tags were hanging from what remained of one of his big toes: Gunnery Sergeant Miller Jones. Unable to offer anything but a little mercy, Willard shot the marine behind the ear, and they took him down and covered him with rocks at the foot of the cross. The inside of Willard's head hadn't been the same since.

When he heard the tubby bus driver yell something about a break, Willard stood up and started toward the door, disgusted with the two sailors. In his opinion, the navy was one branch of the military that should never be allowed to drink. In the three years he'd served in the army, he hadn't met a single swabby who could hold his liquor. Someone had told him that it was because of the saltpeter they were fed to keep them from going crazy and fucking each other when they were out to sea. He wandered outside the bus depot and saw a little restaurant across the street called the Wooden Spoon. There was a piece of white cardboard stuck in the window advertising a meat loaf special for thirty-five cents. His mother had fixed him a meat loaf the day before he left for the army, and he considered that a good sign. In a booth by the window, he sat down and lit a cigarette. A shelf ran around the room, lined with old bottles and antique kitchenware and cracked black-and-white photographs for the dust to collect on. Tacked to the wall by the booth was a faded newspaper account of a Meade police officer who'd been gunned down by a bank robber in front of the bus depot. Willard looked closer, saw that it was dated February 11, 1936. That would have been four days before his twelfth birthday, he calculated. An old man, the only other customer in the diner, was bent over at a table in the middle of the room slurping a bowl of green soup. His false teeth rested on top of a stick of butter in front of him.

Willard finished the cigarette and was just getting ready to leave when a dark-haired waitress finally stepped out of the kitchen. She grabbed a menu from a stack by the cash register and handed it to him. "I'm sorry," she said, "I didn't hear you come in." Looking at her high cheekbones and full lips and long, slender legs, Willard discovered, when she asked him what he wanted to eat, that the spit had dried in his mouth. He could barely speak. That had never happened to him before, not even in the middle of the worst fighting on Bougainville. While she went to put the order in and get him a cup of coffee, the thought went through his head that just a couple of months ago he was certain that his life was going to end on some steamy, worthless rock in the middle of the Pacific Ocean; and now here he was, still sucking air and just a few hours from home, being waited on by a woman who looked like a live version of one of those pinup movie angels. As best as Willard could ever tell, that was when he fell in love. It didn't matter that the meat loaf was dry and the green beans were mushy and the roll as hard as a lump of #5 coal. As far as he was concerned, she served him the best meal he ever had in his life. And after he finished it, he got back on the bus without even knowing Charlotte Willoughby's name.

Across the river in Huntington, he found a liquor store when the bus made another stop, and bought five pints of bonded whiskey that he stuck away in his pack. He sat in the front now, right behind the driver, thinking about the girl in the diner and looking for some indication that he was getting close to home. He was still a little drunk. Out of the blue, the bus driver said, "Bringing any medals back?" He glanced at Willard in the rearview mirror.

Willard shook his head. "Just this skinny old carcass I'm walking around in."

"I wanted to go, but they wouldn't take me."

"You're lucky," Willard said. The day they'd come across the marine, the fighting on the island was nearly over, and the sergeant had sent them out looking for some water fit to drink. A couple of hours after they buried Miller Jones's flayed body, four starving Japanese soldiers with fresh bloodstains on their machetes came out of the rocks with their hands up in the air and surrendered. When Willard and his two buddies started to lead them back to the location of the cross, the soldiers dropped to their knees and started begging or apologizing, he didn't know which. "They tried to escape," Willard lied to the sergeant later in the camp. "We didn't have no choice." After they had executed the Japs, one of the men with him, a Louisiana boy who wore a swamp rat's foot around his neck to ward off slant-eyed bullets, cut their ears off with a straight razor. He had a cigar box full of ones he'd already dried. His plan was to sell the trophies for five bucks apiece once they got back to civilization.

"I got an ulcer," the bus driver said.

"You didn't miss nothing."

"I don't know," the bus driver said. "I sure would have liked to got me a medal. Maybe a couple of them. I figure I could have killed enough of those Kraut bastards for two anyway. I'm pretty quick with my hands."

Looking at the back of the bus driver's head, Willard thought about the conversation he'd had with the gloomy young priest on board the ship after he confessed that he'd shot the marine to put him out of his misery. The priest was sick of all the death he'd seen, all the prayers he'd said over rows of dead soldiers and piles of body parts. He told Willard that if even half of history was true, then the only thing this depraved and corrupt world was good for was preparing you for the next. "Did you know," Willard said to the driver, "that the Romans used to gut donkeys and sew Christians up alive inside the carcasses and leave them out in the sun to rot?" The priest had been full of such stories.

"What the hell's that got to do with a medal?"

"Just think about it. You're trussed up like a turkey in a pan with just your head sticking out a dead donkey's ass; and then the maggots eating away at you until you see the glory."

The bus driver frowned, gripped the steering wheel a little tighter. "Friend, I don't see what you're getting at. I was talking about coming home with a big medal pinned to your chest. Did these Roman fellers give out medals to them people before they stuck 'em in the donkeys? Is that what you mean?"

Willard didn't know what he meant. According to the priest, only God could figure out the ways of men. He licked his dry lips, thought about the whiskey in his pack. "What I'm saying is that when it comes right down to it, everybody suffers in the end," Willard said.

"Well," the bus driver said, "I'd liked to have my medal before then. Heck, I got a wife at home who goes nuts every time she sees one. Talk about suffering. I worry myself sick anytime I'm out on the road she's gonna take off with a purple heart."

Willard leaned forward and the driver felt the soldier's hot breath on the back of his fat neck, smelled the whiskey fumes and the stale traces of a cheap lunch. "You think Miller Jones would give a shit if his old lady was out fucking around on him?" Willard said. "Buddy, he'd trade places with you any goddamn day."

"Who the hell is Miller Jones?"

Willard looked out the window as the hazy top of Greenbrier Mountain started to appear in the distance. His hands were trembling, his brow shiny with sweat. "Just some poor bastard who went and fought in that war they cheated you out of, that's all."

WILLARD WAS JUST GETTING READY to break down and crack open one of the pints when his uncle Earskell pulled up in his rattly

Ford in front of the Greyhound station in Lewisburg at the corner of Washington and Court. He had been sitting on a bench outside for almost three hours, nursing a cold coffee in a paper cup and watching people walk by the Pioneer Drugstore. He was ashamed of the way he'd talked to the bus driver, sorry that he'd brought up the marine's name like he did; and he vowed that, though he would never forget him, he'd never mention Gunnery Sergeant Miller Jones to anyone again. Once they were on the road, he reached into his duffel and handed Earskell one of the pints along with a German Luger. He'd traded a Japanese ceremonial sword for the pistol at the base in Maryland right before he got discharged. "That's supposed to be the gun Hitler used to blow his brains out," Willard said, trying to hold back a grin.

"Bullshit," Earskell said.

Willard laughed. "What? You think the guy lied to me?"

"Ha!" the old man said. He twisted the cap off the bottle, took a long pull, then shuddered. "Lord, this is good stuff."

"Drink up. I got three more in my kit." Willard opened another pint and lit a cigarette. He stuck his arm out the window. "How's my mother doing?"

"Well, I gotta say, when they sent Junior Carver's body back, she went a little off in the head there for a while. But she seems pretty good now." Earskell took another hit off the pint and set it between his legs. "She just been worried about you, that's all."

They climbed slowly into the hills toward Coal Creek. Earskell wanted to hear some war stories, but the only thing his nephew talked about for the next hour was some woman he'd met in Ohio. It was the most he'd ever heard Willard talk in his life. He wanted to ask if it was true that the Japs ate their own dead, like the newspaper said, but he figured that could wait. Besides, he needed to pay attention to his driving. The whiskey was going down awful smooth, and his eyes weren't as good as they used to be. Emma had been waiting on her son to return home for a long time, and it would be a shame if he wrecked and killed them both before she got to see him. Earskell chuckled a little to himself at the thought of that. His sister was one of the most God-fearing people he'd ever met, but she'd follow him straight into hell to make him pay for that one.

"WELL, WHAT IS IT EXACTLY you like about this girl?" Emma Russell asked Willard. It had been near midnight when he and Earskell parked the Ford at the bottom of the hill and climbed the path to the small log house. When he came through the door, she carried on for quite a while, grabbing onto him and soaking the front of his uniform with her tears. He watched over her shoulder as his uncle slipped into the kitchen. Her hair had turned gray since Willard had seen her last. "I'd ask you to get down with me and thank Jesus," she said, wiping the tears from her face with the hem of her apron, "but I can smell liquor on your breath."

Willard nodded. He'd been brought up to believe that you never talked to God when you were under the influence. A man needed to be sincere with the Master at all times in case he was ever really in need. Even Willard's father, Tom Russell, a moonshiner who'd been hounded by bad luck and trouble right up to the day he died of a diseased liver in a Parkersburg jail, ascribed to that belief. No matter how desperate the situation—and his old man had been caught in plenty of those—he wouldn't ask for help from on High if he had even a spoonful in him.

"Well, come on back to the kitchen," Emma said. "You can eat and I'll put on some coffee. I made you a meat loaf."

By three in the morning, he and Earskell had killed four pints along with a cupful of shine and were working on the last bottle of store-bought. Willard's head was fuzzy, and he was having a hard time putting his words together, though evidently he'd mentioned to his mother the waitress he'd seen in the diner. "What was that you asked me?" he said to her.

"That girl you was talkin' about," she said. "What is it you like about her?" She was pouring him another cup of boiling coffee from a pan. Though his tongue was numb, he was sure he'd already burned it more than once. A kerosene lamp hanging from a beam in the ceiling lit the room. His mother's wide shadow wavered on the wall.

He spilled some coffee on the oilcloth that covered the table. Emma shook her head and reached behind her for a dishrag.

"Everything," he said. "You should see her."

Emma figured it was just the whiskey talking, but her son's announcement that he'd met a woman still made her uneasy. Mildred Carver, as good a Christian woman as ever there was in Coal Creek, had prayed for her Junior every day, but they'd still sent him home in a box. Right after she heard that the pallbearers doubted that there was even anything in the casket, as light as it was, Emma started looking for a sign that would tell her what to do to guarantee Willard's safety. She was still searching when Helen Hatton's family burned up in a house fire, leaving the poor girl all alone. Two days later, after much deliberation, Emma got down on her knees and promised God that if He would bring her son home alive, she'd make sure that he married Helen and took care of her. But now, standing in the kitchen looking at his dark, wavy hair and chiseled features, she realized she'd been crazy to ever pledge such a thing. Helen wore a dirty bonnet tied under her square chin, and her long, horsey face was the spitting image of her grandmother Rachel's, considered by many the homeliest woman who ever walked the ridges of Greenbrier County. At the time, Emma hadn't considered what might happen if she couldn't keep her promise. If only she had been blessed with an ugly son, she thought. God had some funny ideas when it came to letting people know He was displeased.

"Looks ain't everything," Emma said.

"Who says?"

"Shut up, Earskell," Emma said. "What's that girl's name again?"

Willard shrugged. He squinted at the picture of Jesus carrying the cross that hung above the door. Ever since entering the kitchen, he had avoided looking at it, for fear of ruining his homecoming with more thoughts of Miller Jones. But now, just for a moment, he gave himself over to the image. The picture had been there as long as he could remember, spotty with age in a cheap wooden frame. It seemed almost alive in the flickering light from the lantern. He could almost hear the cracks of the whips, the taunts of Pilate's soldiers. He glanced down at the German Luger lying on the table by Earskell's plate.

"What? You don't even know her name?"

"Didn't ask," Willard said. "I left her a dollar tip, though."

"She won't forget that," Earskell said.

"Well, maybe you ought to pray about it before you go traipsing back up to Ohio," Emma said. "That's a long ways off." All her life, she had believed that people should follow the Lord's will and not their own. A person had to trust that everything turns out just as it's supposed to in this world. But then Emma had lost that faith, ended up trying to barter with God like He was nothing more than a horse trader with a plug of chew in his jaw or a ragged tinker out peddling dented wares along the road. Now, no matter how it turned out, she had to at least make an effort to uphold her part of the bargain. After that, she would leave it up to Him. "I don't think that would hurt none, do you? If you prayed on it?" She turned and started covering what was left of the meat loaf with a clean towel.

Willard blew on his coffee, then took a sip and grimaced. He thought about the waitress, the tiny, barely visible scar above her left eyebrow. Two weeks, he figured, and then he'd drive up and talk to her. He glanced over at his uncle trying to roll a cigarette. Earskell's hands were gnarled and twisted with arthritis, the knuckles big around as quarters. "No," Willard said, pouring a little whiskey into his cup, "that never hurt none at all."

2

WILLARD WAS HUNGOVER and shaky and sitting by himself on
one of the back benches in the Coal Creek Church of the Holy Ghost
Sanctified. It was nearly seven thirty on a Thursday evening, but
the service hadn't started yet. It was the fourth night of the church's
annual weeklong revival, aimed mostly at backsliders and those who
hadn't been saved yet. Willard had been home over a week, and this
was the first day he'd drawn a sober breath. Last night he and Earskell
had gone to the Lewis Theater to see John Wayne in *Back to Bataan*.
He walked out halfway through the movie, disgusted with the phoni-
ness of it all, ended up in a fight at the pool hall down the street. He
roused himself and looked around, flexed his sore hand. Emma was
still up front visiting. Smoky lanterns hung along the walls; a dented
wood stove sat halfway down the aisle off to the right. The pine
benches were worn smooth by over twenty years of worship. Though
the church was the same humble place it had always been, Willard
was afraid that he had changed quite a bit since he had been overseas.

Reverend Albert Sykes had started the church in 1924, shortly
after a coal mine collapsed and trapped him in the dark with two
other men who'd been killed instantly. Both of his legs had been
broken in several places. He managed to reach a pack of Five Brothers chewing tobacco in Phil Drury's pocket, but he couldn't stretch
far enough to grab hold of the butter and jam sandwich he knew Burl
Meadows was carrying in his coat. He said he was touched by the
Spirit on the third night. He realized he was going to soon join the
men beside him, already putrid with the smell of death, but it didn't
matter anymore. A few hours later, the rescuers broke through the
rubble while he was asleep. For a moment, he was convinced that the
light they shined in his eyes was the face of the Lord. It was a good
story to tell in church, and there were always a lot of Hallelujahs when

he came to that part. Willard figured he'd heard the old preacher tell
it a hundred times over the years, limping back and forth in front
of the varnished pulpit. At the end of the story, he always pulled
the empty Five Brothers pack out of his threadbare suit coat, held it
up toward the ceiling cradled in the palms of his hands. He carried
it with him everywhere. Many of the women around Coal Creek,
especially those who still had husbands and sons in the mines, treated
it like a religious relic, kissing it whenever they got a chance. It was a
fact that Mary Ellen Thompson, on her deathbed, had asked for it to
be brought to her instead of the doctor.

Willard watched his mother talking to a thin woman wearing
wire-rim glasses set crooked on her long, slender face, a faded blue
bonnet tied under her pointy chin. After a couple of minutes, Emma
grabbed the woman's hand and led her back to where Willard was
sitting. "I asked Helen to sit with us," Emma told her son. He stood
up and let them in, and as the girl passed by him, the odor of old
sweat made his eyes water. She carried a worn leather Bible, kept her
head down when Emma introduced her. Now he understood why his
mother had been going on for the last few days about why good looks
were not all that important. He would agree that was true in most
cases, that the spirit was more important than the flesh, but hell, even
his uncle Earskell washed his armpits once in a while.

Because the church had no bell, Reverend Sykes went to the open
door when it was time for the service to start and shouted to those
still loitering outside with their cigarettes and gossip and doubts. A
small choir, two men and three women, stood up and sang "Sinner,
You'd Better Get Ready." Then Sykes went to the pulpit. He looked
out over the crowd, wiped the sweat off his brow with a white handkerchief. There were fifty-eight people sitting on the benches. He'd
counted twice. The reverend wasn't a greedy man, but he was hoping
on the basket bringing in maybe three or four dollars tonight. He and
his wife had been eating nothing but hardtack and warbled squirrel
meat for the past week. "Whew, it's hot," he said with a grin. "But
it's bound to get hotter, ain't that right? Especially for them that ain't
right with the Lord."

"Amen," someone said.

"Surely is," said another.

"Well," Sykes went on, "we gonna take care of that shortly. They's two boys from over around Topperville gonna lead the service tonight, and from what everyone tells me, they got a good message." He glanced at the two strangers sitting in the shadows off to the side of the altar, hidden from the congregation by a frayed black curtain. "Brother Roy and Brother Theodore, get on over here and help us save some lost souls," he said, motioning them forward with his hand.

A tall, skinny man stood up and pushed the other, a fat boy in a squeaky wheelchair, out from behind the curtain and near the center of the altar. The one with the good legs wore a baggy black suit and a pair of heavy, broken-down brogans. His brown hair was slicked back with oil, his sunken cheeks pitted and scarred purple from acne. "My name is Roy Laferty," he said in a quiet voice, "and this here is my cousin, Theodore Daniels." The cripple nodded and smiled at the crowd. He held a banged-up guitar in his lap and sported a soup-bowl haircut. His overalls were mended with patches cut from a feed sack, and his thin legs were twisted up under him at sharp angles. He had on a dirty white shirt and a brightly flowered tie. Later, Willard said that one looked like the Prince of Darkness and the other like a clown down on his luck.

In silence Brother Theodore finished tuning a string on his flattop. A few people yawned, and others began whispering among themselves, already fidgety with what seemed to be the beginning of a boring service by a couple of shy and wasted newcomers. Willard wished he'd slipped out to the parking lot and found someone with a jug before things got started. He had never felt comfortable worshipping God around strangers packed together inside a building. "We ain't passing no basket tonight, folks," Brother Roy finally said after the cripple nodded that he was ready. "Don't want no money for doing the Lord's work. Me and Theodore can get by on the sweetness of the air if we have to, and, believe me, we've done it a many a time. Savin' souls ain't about the filthy dollar." Roy looked to the old preacher, who managed a sick smile and nodded in reluctant agreement. "Now we gonna summon the Holy Ghost to this little church tonight, or, I swear to you all, we gonna die trying." And with that, the fat boy hit a lick on the guitar and Brother Roy leaned back and let out a high, awful wail that sounded as if he was trying to shake the very gates of heaven loose. Half the congregation nearly jumped out of their seats. Willard chuckled when he felt his mother jerk against him.

The young preacher started pacing up and down the center of the aisle asking people in a loud voice, "Now what is it you most afraid of?" He waved his arms and described the loathsomeness of hell—the filth, horror, and despair—and the eternity that stretches out in front of everyone forever and ever without end. "If your worst fear is rats, then Satan will make sure you get your fill of 'em. Brothers and sisters, they'll chew your face off while you lay there unable to lift a single finger against them, and it won't ever cease. A million years in eternity ain't even an afternoon here in Coal Creek. Don't even try and figure that up. Ain't no human head big enough to calculate misery like that. Remember that family over in Millersburg got murdered in their beds last year? The ones had their eyes cut out by that lunatic? Imagine that for a trillion years—that's a million million, people, I looked it up—being tortured like that, but never dying. Having your peepers plucked out of your head with a bloody ol' knife over and over again, forever. I hope them poor people was right with the Lord when that maniac slipped in their window, I surely do. And really, brothers and sisters, we can't even picture the ways the Devil's got to torment us, ain't no man ever been evil enough, not even that Hitler feller, to come up with the ways Satan is gonna make the sinners pay come the Judgment Day."

While Brother Roy preached, Theodore kept up a rhythm on the guitar that matched the flow of the words, his eyes following the other's every movement. Roy was his cousin on his mother's side, but sometimes the fat boy wished they weren't so closely related. Though he was satisfied with just being able to spread the Gospel with him, he'd had feelings for a long time that he couldn't pray away. He knew what the Bible said, but he couldn't accept that the Lord thought such a thing a sin. Love was love, the way Theodore saw it. Heck, hadn't he proved that, showed God that he loved him more than anyone? Taking that poison until he wound up a cripple, showing the Lord that he had the faith, even though sometimes now he couldn't help thinking that maybe he'd been a little too enthusiastic. But for now, he had God and he had Roy and he had his guitar, and that was all he needed to get by in this world, even if he never did get to stand up straight again. And if Theodore had to prove to Roy how much he loved him, he'd gladly do that, too, anything he asked. God was Love; and He was everywhere, in everything.

Then Roy hopped back up on the altar, reached under Brother Theodore's wheelchair, and brought out a gallon jar. Everyone leaned forward a bit on the benches. A dark mass seemed to be boiling inside it. Someone called out, "Praise God," and Brother Roy said, "That's right, my friend, that's right." He held up the jar and gave it a violent shake. "People, let me tell you something," he went on. "Before I found the Holy Ghost, I was scared plumb to death of spiders. Ain't that right, Theodore? Ever since I was a little runt hiding under my mother's long skirts. Spiders crawled through my dreams and laid eggs in my nightmares, and I couldn't even go to the outhouse without someone holding my hand. They was hanging in their webs everywhere waiting on me. It was an awful way to live, in fear all the time, awake or asleep, it didn't matter. And that's what hell is like, brothers and sisters. I never got no rest from them eight-legged devils. Not until I found the Lord."

Then Roy dropped to his knees and gave the jar another jiggle before he twisted the lid off. Theodore slowed the music down until all that was left was a sad, ominous dirge that chilled the room, raised the short hairs on the backs of necks. Holding the jar above him, Roy looked out over the crowd and took a deep breath and turned it over. A variegated mass of spiders, brown ones and black ones and orange-and-yellow-striped ones, fell on top of his head and shoulders. Then a shiver ran through his body like an electric current, and he stood up and slammed the jar to the floor, sending shards of glass flying everywhere. He let out that awful screech again, and began shaking his arms and legs, the spiders falling off onto the floor and scurrying away in all directions. Some lady wrapped in a knitted shawl jumped up and

hurried toward the door and several more screamed, and in the midst
of the commotion, Roy stepped forward, a few spiders still clinging to
his sweaty face, and yelled, "Mark my word, people, the Lord, He'll
take away all your fears if you let Him. Look what He's done for me."
Then he gagged a little, spit something black out of his mouth.

Another woman started beating at her dress, crying out that she'd
been bit, and a couple of children started blubbering. Reverend Sykes
ran back and forth attempting to restore some order, but by then people were scrambling toward the narrow door in a panic. Emma took
Helen by the arm, trying to lead her out of the church. But the girl
shook her off and turned and walked into the aisle. She held her Bible
against her flat chest as she stared at Brother Roy. Still strumming his
guitar, Theodore watched his cousin nonchalantly brush a spider off
his ear, then smile at the frail, plain-looking girl. He didn't stop playing until he saw Roy beckon the bitch forward with his hands.

ON THE DRIVE HOME, WILLARD SAID, "Boy, them spiders was
a nice touch." He slipped his right hand over and began moving his
fingers lightly up his mother's fat, jiggly arm.

She squealed and swatted at him. "Quit that. I won't be able to
sleep tonight as it is."

"You ever heard that boy preach before?"

"No, but they do some crazy stuff at that church over in Topperville. I'll bet Reverend Sykes is regrettin' he ever invited them.
That one in the wheelchair drank too much strychnine or antifreeze
or something is why he can't walk. It's just pitiful. Testing their faith,
they call it. But that's taking things a little bit too far, the way I see it."
She sighed and leaned her head back against the seat. "I wish Helen
had come with us."

"Well, wasn't nobody slept through that sermon, I'll give him
that."

"You know," Emma said, "she might have if you'd paid a little
more attention to her."

"Oh, the way it looked to me, Brother Roy's gonna give her about
as much of that as she can handle."

"That's what I'm afraid of," Emma said.

"Mother, I'm going back up to Ohio in a day or two. You know that."

Emma ignored him. "She'd make someone a good wife, Helen would."

SEVERAL WEEKS AFTER WILLARD LEFT for Ohio to find out about the waitress, Helen knocked on Emma's door. It was early in the afternoon on a warm November day. The old woman was sitting in her parlor listening to the radio and reading again the letter she'd received that morning. Willard and the waitress had gotten married a week ago. They were going to stay in Ohio, at least for now. He'd gotten a job at a meatpacking plant, said he had never seen so many hogs in his life. The man on the radio was blaming the unseasonable weather on the fallout from the atomic bombs unleashed to win the war.

"I wanted to tell you first because I know you been worried about me," Helen said. It was the first time Emma had ever seen her without a bonnet on her head.

"Tell me what, Helen?"

"Roy asked me to marry him," she said. "He said God give him a sign we was meant for each other."

Standing in the doorway with Willard's letter in her hand, Emma thought about the promise she'd been unable to keep. She'd been dreading a violent accident, or some horrible disease, but this was good news. Maybe things were going to turn out all right after all. She felt her eyes start to blur with tears. "Where you all going to live?" she asked, unable to think of anything else to say.

"Oh, Roy's got a place behind the gas station in Topperville," Helen said. "Theodore, he'll be staying with us. At least for a little while."

"That's the one in the wheelchair?"

"Yes'm," Helen said. "They been together a long time."

Emma stepped out onto the porch and hugged the girl. She smelled faintly of Ivory soap, as if she'd had a bath recently. "You want to come in and sit for a while?"

"No, I got to go," Helen said. "Roy's waiting on me." Emma looked past her down over the hill. A dung-colored car shaped like a turtle was sitting in the pull-off behind Earskell's old Ford. "He's preaching over in Millersburg tonight, where them people got their eyes carved out. We been out gathering spiders all morning. Thank God, with the way this weather's been, they're still pretty easy to find."

"You be careful, Helen," Emma said.

"Oh, don't worry," the girl said, as she started down off the porch, "they ain't too bad once you get used to them."

3

IN THE SPRING OF 1948, Emma got word from Ohio that she was finally a grandmother; Willard's wife had given birth to a healthy baby boy named Arvin Eugene. By then, the old woman was satisfied that God had forgiven her for her brief loss of trust. It had been nearly three years, and nothing bad had happened. A month later, she was still thanking the Lord that her grandson hadn't been born blind and pinheaded like Edith Maxwell's three children over on Spud Run when Helen showed up at her door with an announcement of her own. It was one of the few times Emma had seen her since the girl married Roy and switched to the church over in Topperville. "I wanted to stop by and let you know," Helen said. Her arms and legs were pale and thin, but her belly was swollen big with a baby.

"My goodness gracious," Emma said, opening the screen door. "Come on in, honey, and rest awhile." It was late in the day, and gray-blue shadows covered the weedy yard. A chicken clucked quietly under the porch.

"I can't right now."

"Oh, don't be in such a hurry. Let me fix you something to eat," the old woman said. "We haven't talked in ages."

"Thank you, Mrs. Russell, but maybe some other time. I got to get back."

"Is Roy preaching tonight?"

"No," Helen said. "He ain't preached in a couple of months now. Didn't you hear? One of them spiders bit him real bad. His head puffed up big as a pumpkin. It was awful. He couldn't open his eyes for a week or better."

"Well," the old woman said, "maybe he can get on with the power company. Someone said they was hiring. They supposed to be running the electric through here before long."

"Oh, I don't think so," Helen said. "Roy ain't give up preaching, he's just waiting for a message."

"A message?"

"He ain't sent one in a while, and it's got Roy worried."

"Who ain't sent one?"

"Why, the Lord, Mrs. Russell," Helen said. "He's the only one Roy listens to." She started to step down off the porch.

"Helen?"

The girl stopped and turned around. "Yes'm?"

Emma hesitated, not quite knowing what to say. She looked past the girl, down the hill at the dung-colored car. She could see a dark figure sitting behind the steering wheel. "You'll make a good mother," she said.

AFTER THE SPIDER BITE, Roy stayed shut up in the bedroom closet most of the time waiting on a sign. He was convinced that the Lord had slowed him down in order to prepare him for something bigger. As far as Theodore was concerned, Roy knocking the bitch up was the last straw. He began drinking and staying out all night, playing in private clubs and illegal joints hid back in the sticks. He learned dozens of sinful songs about cheating spouses and cold-blooded murders and lives wasted behind prison bars. Whoever he ended up with usually just dumped him drunk and piss-stained in front of the house; and Helen would have to go out at dawn and help him inside while he cursed her and his ruined legs and that pretend preacher she was fucking. She soon grew afraid of them both, and she traded Theodore rooms, let him sleep in the big bed beside Roy's closet.

One afternoon a few months after the baby was born, a little girl they named Lenora, Roy walked out of the bedroom convinced that he could raise the dead. "Shit, you're just a loony," Theodore said. He was drinking a can of warm beer to settle his stomach. A small metal file and a Craftsman screwdriver lay in his lap. The night before, he'd played for eight hours straight at a birthday party over on Hungry Holler for ten dollars and a fifth of Russian vodka. Some bastard had made fun of his affliction, tried to pull him up out of his wheelchair and make him dance. Theodore set the beer down and started working on the head of the screwdriver again. He hated the whole god-damn world. The next time someone fucked with him like that, the sonofabitch was going to end up with a hole in his guts. "You ain't got it no more, Roy. The Lord done left you, just like He left me."

"No, Theodore, no," Roy said. "That ain't true. I just talked to Him. He was sitting right in there with me a minute ago. And He don't look like the pictures say, either. Ain't got no beard for one thing."

"Loony as hell," Theodore said.

"I can prove it!"

"How you gonna do that?"

Roy paced back and forth a couple of minutes, moving his hands around like he was trying to stir inspiration up out of the air. "We'll go kill us a cat," he said, "and I'll show you I can bring it back." Next to spiders, cats were Roy's biggest fear. His mother had always claimed that she caught one trying to suck his breath away when he was a baby. He and Theodore had slaughtered dozens of them over the years.

"You're kidding me, right?" Theodore said. "A fuckin' cat?" He laughed. "No, you gonna have to get a little more serious than that before I'll believe you now." He pressed his thumb against the end of the screwdriver. It was sharp.

Roy wiped the sweat from his face with one of the baby's dirty diapers. "What then?"

Theodore glanced out the window. Helen was standing in the yard with the pink-faced brat in her arms. She'd gotten huffy with him again this morning, said she was getting tired of him waking the baby up. She had been bitching a lot lately, too damn much in his opinion. Hell, if it wasn't for the money he brought home, they'd all starve to death. He gave Roy a sly look. "How about you bring Helen back to life? Then we'll know for sure you ain't just talkin' crazy."

Roy shook his head violently. "No, no, I can't do that."

Theodore smirked, picked up the can of beer. "See? I knew you was full of shit. You always have been. You ain't no more a preacher than them drunks I play for every night."

"Don't say that, Theodore," Roy said. "Why you want to say things like that?"

"Because we had it good, goddamn it, and then you had to go and get married. It's drained the light right out of you, and you too dumb to see it. Show me you got it back, and we'll start spreading the Gospel again."

Roy recalled the conversation he'd had in the closet, God's voice clear as a bell in his head. He looked out the window at his wife standing by the mailbox singing softly to the baby. Maybe Theodore was onto something. After all, he told himself, Helen was right with the Lord, and always had been as far as he knew. That could only help matters when it came to a resurrection. Still, he'd like to try it out on a cat first. "I'll have to think on it."

"Can't be no tricks," Theodore said.

"Only the Devil needs them." Roy took a sip of water from the kitchen sink, just enough to wet his lips. Refreshed, he decided to pray some more, and started toward the bedroom.

"If you can pull this off, Roy," Theodore said, "there won't be a church in West Virginia big enough to hold all the people that will want to hear you preach. Shit, you'll be more famous than Billy Sunday."

A few days later, Roy asked Helen to leave the baby with her friend, the Russell woman, while they took a drive. "Just to get out of the stinking house for a while," he explained. "I promise you, I'm done with that closet." Helen was relieved; Roy had suddenly started acting like his old self again, was talking about getting back into preaching. Not only that, Theodore had quit going out at night, was practicing some new religious songs and sticking to coffee. He even held the baby for a few minutes, something he had never done before.

After they dropped off Lenora at Emma's house, they drove thirty minutes to a woods a few miles east of Coal Creek. Roy parked the car and asked Helen to go for a walk with him. Theodore was in the backseat pretending to be asleep. After going just a few yards, he said, "Maybe we ought to pray first." He and Theodore had argued about this, Roy saying he wanted it to be a private moment between just him and his wife while the cripple insisted that he needed to see the Spirit leave her firsthand to make sure they weren't faking it. When they knelt down under a beech tree, Roy pulled Theodore's screwdriver from beneath his baggy shirt. He put his arm around Helen's shoulder and gripped her close. Thinking he was being affectionate, she turned to kiss him just as he plunged the sharp point deep into the side of her neck. He let go of her and she fell sideways, then rose up, grabbing frantically for the screwdriver. When she jerked it out of her neck, blood sprayed from the hole and covered the front of Roy's shirt. Theodore watched out the window as she tried to crawl away. She went only a few feet before falling forward into the leaves and flopping about for a minute or two. He heard her call out Lenora's name several times. He lit a cigarette and waited a few minutes before he hauled himself out of the car.

Three hours later, Theodore said, "It ain't gonna happen, Roy." He sat in his wheelchair a few feet from Helen's body holding the screwdriver. Roy was down on his knees beside his wife, holding her hand, still trying to coax her back to life. At first his supplications had rung through the woods with faith and fervor, but the longer he went without even a twitch from her cold body, the more garbled and deranged they had become. Theodore could feel the onslaught of a headache. He wished he had brought something to drink.

Roy looked up at his crippled cousin with tears running down his face. "Jesus, I think I killed her."

Theodore pushed himself closer and pressed the back of his dirty hand against her face. "She's dead, all right."

"Don't you touch her," Roy yelled.

"I'm just trying to help."

Roy struck the ground with his fist. "It wasn't supposed to be this way."

"I hate to say it, but if they catch you for this, them ol' boys in Moundsville will fry you like bacon."

Roy shook his head, wiped the snot from his face with his shirtsleeve. "I don't know what went wrong. I thought for sure . . ." His voice dwindled away, and he let go of her hand.

"Shit, you just miscalculated, that's all," Theodore said. "Anybody could have done that."

"What the hell am I gonna do now?" Roy said.

"You could always run," Theodore said. "That's the only smart thing to do in a situation like this. I mean, fuck, what you got to lose?"

"Run where?"

"I been sitting here thinking on it, and I figure that old car would probably make it to Florida if you babied it."

"I don't know," Roy said.

"Sure you do," Theodore said. "Look, once we get there, we sell the car and start preaching again. That's what we should have been doing all along." He looked down at pale, bloody Helen. Her whining days were over with. He almost wished he had killed her himself. She had ruined everything. By now, they might have had their own church, maybe even been on the radio.

"We?"

"Well, yeah," Theodore said, "you gonna need a guitar player, ain't you?" For a long time he had dreamed of going to Florida, living by the ocean. It was hard to live the crippled life surrounded by all these lousy hills and trees.

"But what about her?" Roy said, pointing at Helen's body.

"You gonna have to bury her deep, brother," Theodore said. "I put a shovel in the boot just in case things didn't turn out like you expected."

"And Lenora?"

"Believe me, that baby will be better off with the old lady," Theodore said. "You don't want your kid growing up running from the law, do you?" He looked up through the trees. The sun had disappeared behind a wall of dark clouds, and the sky had turned the color of ash. The damp smell of rain was in the air. From over around Rocky Gap came a slow, faint rumble of thunder. "Now you better start digging before we get soaked."

WHEN EARSKELL CAME IN THAT NIGHT, Emma was sitting in a chair by the window rocking Lenora. It was nearly eleven o'clock, and the storm was just starting to ease off. "Helen told me they wouldn't be gone but a couple hours," the old woman said. "She only left one bottle of milk."

"Aw, you know them preachers," Earskell said. "They probably went out and got on a good one. Hell, from what I hear, that crippled boy could drink me under the table."

Emma shook her head. "I wish we had a phone. There's something about this just don't feel right to me."

The old man peered down at the sleeping infant. "Poor little thing," he said. "She looks just like her mother, don't she?"

4

WHEN ARVIN WAS FOUR YEARS OLD, Willard decided that he didn't want his son growing up in Meade around all the degenerates. They had been living in Charlotte's old apartment above the dry cleaners ever since they had gotten married. It seemed to him as if every pervert in southern Ohio was located in Meade. Lately, the newspaper was filled with their sick shenanigans. Just two days ago a man named Calvin Claytor had been arrested in the Sears and Roebuck with a foot of Polish sausage tied to his thigh. According to the *Meade Gazette*, the suspect, dressed only in ripped coveralls, was caught brushing up against elderly women in what the reporter described as a "lewd and aggressive manner." As far as Willard was concerned, that Claytor sonofabitch was even worse than the retired state representative the sheriff caught parked along the highway on the outskirts of town with a chicken stuck to his privates, a Rhode Island Red that he'd purchased for fifty cents from a nearby farm. They'd had to take him to the hospital to cut it off. People said that the deputy, out of respect for the other patients or maybe the victim, had covered the hen with his uniform jacket when they marched the man into the ER. "That's somebody's mother the bastard was doing that to," Willard told Charlotte.

"Which one?" she asked. She was standing at the stove stirring a pot of spaghetti.

"Jesus, Charlotte, the sausage man," he said. "They oughta cram that thing down his throat."

"I don't know," his wife said. "I don't see that being as bad as someone messing with animals."

He looked over at Arvin, sitting on the floor rolling a toy truck back and forth. From all indications, the country was going to hell in a hurry. Two months ago, his mother had written him that they had finally found Helen Laferty's body, what little was left of it anyway, buried in the woods a few miles from Coal Creek. He had read the letter every night for a week. Charlotte had noticed that Willard started becoming increasingly upset about the news in the paper right after that. Though Roy and Theodore were the prime suspects, there hadn't been a sign of them anywhere for almost three years, so the sheriff still couldn't rule out that they might have also been murdered and dumped elsewhere. "We don't know, could have been the same one butchered them people in Millersburg that time," the sheriff told Emma when he came with the news that Helen's grave had been found by a couple of ginseng hunters. "He might have killed the girl, then cut them boys up and scattered them. The one in the wheelchair would have been easy pickings, and everybody knows that other one didn't have sense enough to pour piss out of a boot."

Regardless of what the law said, Emma was convinced that the two were alive and guilty, and she wouldn't rest easy until they were locked up or dead. She told Willard she was raising the little girl as best she could. He had sent her a hundred dollars to help pay for a proper burial. Sitting there watching his son, Willard suddenly had an intense desire to pray. Though he hadn't talked to God in years, not a single petition or word of praise since he'd come across the crucified marine during the war, he could feel it welling up inside him now, the urge to get right with his Maker before something bad happened to his family. But looking around the cramped apartment, he knew he couldn't get in touch with God here, no more than he'd ever been able to in a church. He was going to need some woods to worship his way. "We got to get out of this place," he told Charlotte, laying the newspaper down on the coffee table.

THEY RENTED THE FARMHOUSE on top of the Mitchell Flats for thirty dollars a month from Henry Delano Dunlap, a plump, girlish lawyer with shiny, immaculate fingernails who lived over by the Meade Country Club and dabbled in real estate as a hobby. Though at first Charlotte had been against it, she soon fell in love with the leaky, run-down house. She didn't even mind pumping her water from the well. Within a few weeks after they moved in, she was talking about someday buying it. Her father had died of tuberculosis when she was just five years old, and her mother had succumbed to a blood infection just after Charlotte entered the ninth grade. All her life, she'd lived in gloomy, roach-infested apartments rented by the week or month. The only family member she still had living was her sister, Phyllis, but Charlotte didn't even know where she was anymore. One day six years ago, Phyllis had walked into the Wooden Spoon wearing a new hat and handed Charlotte her key to the three rooms they shared above the dry cleaners on Walnut Street. "Well, Sis," she said, "I got you raised and now it's my turn," and out the door she went. Owning the farmhouse would finally mean some stability in her life, something she craved more than anything, especially now that she was a mother. "Arvin needs to have somewhere he can always call home," she told Willard. "I never did have that." Every month they struggled to put another thirty dollars away for a down payment. "You just wait and see," she said. "This place will be ours someday."

They discovered, however, that dealing with their landlord about anything was no easy matter. Willard had always heard that most lawyers were crooked, conniving pricks, but Henry Dunlap proved to be first-class in that regard. As soon as he found out that the Russells were interested in buying the house, he started playing games, raising the price one month, reducing it the next, then turning around and hinting that he wasn't sure he wanted to sell at all. Too, whenever Willard turned in the rent money at the office, money he'd worked his ass off for at the slaughterhouse, the lawyer liked to tell him exactly what he was going to spend it on. For whatever reason, the rich man felt the need to make the poor man understand that those few wadded-up dollars didn't mean a thing to him. He'd grin at Willard with his liver-colored lips and blow off about how it barely covered the cost of a couple of nice cuts of meat for Sunday dinner, or ice cream for his son's pals at the tennis club. The years passed by, but Henry never tired of taunting his renter; every month there was a new insult, another reason for Willard to kick the fat man's ass. The only thing that held him back was thinking about Charlotte, sitting at the kitchen table with a cup of coffee, waiting nervously for him to return home without getting them evicted. As she reminded him time and time again, it didn't really matter what the windbag said. Rich people always thought you wanted what they had, though that wasn't true, at least not in Willard's case. As he sat across from the lawyer at the big oak desk and listened to him prattle on, Willard thought about the prayer log he'd fixed up in the woods, about the peace and calm it would bring him once he got home and ate supper and made his way over there. Sometimes he even rehearsed in his head a prayer he always said at the log after his monthly visit to the office: "Thank you, God, for giving me the strength to keep my hands off Henry Dunlap's fat fucking neck. And let the sonofabitch have everything he wants in this life, though I got to confess, Lord, I sure wouldn't mind seeing him choke on it someday."

WHAT WILLARD DIDN'T KNOW was that Henry Dunlap used his big talk to hide the fact that his life was a shameful, cowardly mess. In 1943, right out of law school, he'd married a woman who, he discovered not too long after their wedding night, couldn't get enough of strange men. Edith had fucked around on him for years—paper boys, auto mechanics, salesmen, milkmen, friends, clients, his former partner—the list went on and on. He'd put up with it, had even grown to accept it; but not too long ago, he'd hired a colored man to take care of the lawn, a replacement for the white teenager whom she'd been screwing, believing that even she wouldn't stoop that low. But within a week, he'd come home in the middle of the day without warning and saw her bent over the couch in the family room with her ass up in the air and the tall, skinny gardener pounding it for all it was worth. She was making sounds that he'd never heard before. After watching for a couple of minutes, he slipped quietly away and returned to his office, where he finished off a bottle of scotch and ran the scene over and over in his head. He pulled a silver-plated derringer out of his desk and contemplated it for a long time, then put it back in the drawer. He thought it best first to consider other ways to solve his problem.

No sense in blowing his brains out if he didn't have to. After practicing law in Meade for nearly fifteen years, he'd made the acquaintance of several men in southern Ohio who probably knew people who would get rid of Edith for as little as a few hundred dollars, but there wasn't one of them he felt could be trusted. "Don't get in a hurry now, Henry," he told himself. "That's when people fuck up."

A couple of days later, he hired the black man full-time, even gave him a quarter raise on the hour. He was assigning him a list of jobs to do when Edith pulled in the driveway in her new Cadillac. They both stood in the yard and watched her get out of the car with some shopping bags and walk into the house. She was wearing a tight pair of black slacks and a pink sweater that showed off her big, floppy tits. The gardener looked over at the lawyer with a sly smile on his flat, pocked face. After a moment, Henry smiled back.

"DUMB AS GOATS," Henry told his golfing buddies. Dick Taylor had asked him about his renters out in Knockemstiff again. Other than listening to Henry brag and make a fool of himself, the other rich men around Meade didn't have much use for him. He was the biggest joke in the country club. Every single one of them had fucked his wife at one time or another. Edith couldn't even swim in the pool anymore without some woman trying to scratch her eyes out. Rumor had it she was after the black meat now. Before long, they joked, she and Dunlap would probably move up to White Heaven, the colored section on the west side of town. "I swear," Henry went on, "I think that ol' boy married his own goddamn sister, the way they favor each other. By God, you should see her, though. She wouldn't be half bad if you cleaned her up some. They ever get behind in the rent, maybe I'll take it out in trade."

"What would you do to her?" Elliot Smitt asked, winking at Dick Taylor.

"Shit, I'd bend that sweet little thing over, and I'd . . ."

"Ha!" Bernie Hill said. "You ol' dog, I bet you've already busted it open."

Henry picked a club from his bag. He sighed and looked dreamily down the fairway, placing one hand over his heart. "Boys, I promised her I wouldn't tell."

Later, after they'd returned to the clubhouse, a man named Carter Oxley walked up to the fat, sweating lawyer in the bar and said, "You might want to watch what you say about that woman."

Henry turned and frowned. Oxley was a new man at the Meade Country Club, an engineer who had worked himself up to the #2 position at the paper mill. Bernie Hill had brought him along to be part of their foursome. He hadn't said two words the entire game. "What woman?" Henry said.

"You were talking about a man named Willard Russell out there, right?"

"Yeah, Russell's his name. So?"

"Buddy, it's no skin off my back, but he damn near killed a man with his fists last fall for talking trash about his wife. The one he beat up still ain't right, sits around with a coffee can hanging from his neck to catch his slobbers. You might want to think about that."

"You sure we're talking about the same guy? The one I know wouldn't say shit if he had a mouthful."

Oxley shrugged. "Maybe he's just the quiet type. Those are the ones you got to watch."

"How do you know all this?"

"You're not the only one who owns land out in Knockemstiff."

Henry pulled a gold cigarette case from his pocket and offered the new man a smoke. "What else do you know about him?" he asked. That morning Edith had told him that she thought they should buy the gardener a pickup truck. She was standing at the kitchen window eating a fluffy pastry. Henry couldn't help noticing that the top of it was covered with chocolate icing. How appropriate, he thought, the fucking whore. He was glad, though, to see that she was putting on weight. Before long, her ass would be as wide as an ax handle. Let the grass-cutting bastard pound it then. "It doesn't have to be a new one," she told him. "Just something he can get around in. Willie's feet are too big for him to be walking to work all the time." She reached in the bag for another pastry. "My God, Henry, they're twice as long as yours."

5

EVER SINCE THE FIRST OF THE YEAR, Charlotte's insides had been giving her fits. She kept telling herself it was just the flux, maybe indigestion. Her mother had suffered greatly from ulcers, and Charlotte remembered the woman eating nothing but plain toast and rice pudding the last few years of her life. She cut back on the grease and pepper, but it didn't seem to help. Then in April, she began bleeding a little. She spent hours lying on top of the bed when Arvin and Willard were gone, and the cramps eased considerably if she curled up on her side and stayed still. Worried about hospital bills and spending all the money they had saved for the house, she kept her pain a secret, foolishly hoping that whatever ailed her would go away, heal itself. After all, she was only thirty years old, too young for it to be anything serious. But by the middle of May, the spotty bleeding had become a steady trickle, and to dull the pain she'd taken to sneaking drinks from the gallon of Old Crow that Willard kept under the kitchen sink. Near the end of that month, right before school let out for the summer, Arvin found her passed out on the kitchen floor in a puddle of watery blood. A pan of biscuits was burning in the oven. They didn't have a phone, so he propped her head up with a pillow and cleaned up the mess as best he could. Sitting down on the floor beside her, he listened to her shallow breathing and prayed it wouldn't stop. She was still unconscious when his father came home from work that evening. As the doctor told Willard a couple of days later, it was too late by that time. Someone was always dying somewhere, and in the summer of 1958, the year that Arvin Eugene Russell counted himself ten years old, it was his mother's turn.

AFTER TWO WEEKS IN THE HOSPITAL, Charlotte raised up in her bed and said to Willard, "I think I had a dream."

"A good one?"

"Yeah," she said. She reached out and squeezed his hand a little. She glanced over at the white cloth partition that separated her from the woman in the next bed, then lowered her voice. "I know it sounds crazy, but I want to go home and pretend we own the house for a while."

"How you gonna do that?"

"With this stuff they got me on," she said, "they could tell me I was the Queen of Sheba and I wouldn't know any different. Besides, you heard what the doctor said. I sure as hell don't want to spend what's left of my time in this place."

"Is that what the dream was about?"

She gave him a puzzled look. "What dream?" she said.

Two hours later, they were pulling out of the hospital parking lot. As they headed out Route 50 toward home, Willard stopped and bought her a milk shake, but she couldn't keep it down. He carried her into the back bedroom and made her comfortable, then gave her some morphine. Her eyes glazed over and she went to sleep within a minute or so. "You stay here with your mother," he told Arvin. "I'll be back in a little bit." He walked across the field, a cool breeze against his face. He knelt down at the prayer log and listened to the small, peaceful sounds of the evening woods. Several hours passed while he stared at the cross. He viewed their misfortune from every conceivable angle, searching for a solution, but always ended up with the same answer. As far as the doctors were concerned, Charlotte's case was hopeless. They had given her five, maybe six weeks at the most. There were no other options left. It was up to him and God now.

By the time he returned to the house, it was turning dark. Charlotte was still sleeping and Arvin was sitting beside her bed in a straight-backed chair. He could tell the boy had been crying. "Did she ever wake up?" Willard asked, in a low voice.

"Yeah," Arvin said, "but, Dad, why don't she know who I am?"

"It's just the medicine they got her on. She's gonna be fine in a few days."

The boy looked over at Charlotte. Just a couple of months ago, she was the prettiest woman he had ever seen, but most of the pretty was gone now. He wondered what she would look like by the time she got well.

"Maybe we better eat something," Willard said.

He fixed egg sandwiches for him and Arvin, then heated up a can of broth for Charlotte. She threw it up, and Willard cleaned up the mess and held her in his arms, feeling her heart beat rapidly against him. He turned out the light and moved to the chair beside her bed. Sometime during the night he dozed off, but woke up in a sweat dreaming of Miller Jones, the way the man's heart had kept on throbbing as he hung on those palm trees skinned alive. Willard held the alarm clock close to his face, saw that it was nearly four in the morning. He didn't go back to sleep.

A few hours later, he poured all his whiskey out on the ground and went to the barn and got some tools: an ax, a rake, a scythe. He spent the rest of the day expanding the clearing around the prayer log, hacking away at the briers and smaller trees, raking the ground smooth. He began tearing boards off the barn the next day, had Arvin help him carry them to the prayer log. Working into the night, they erected eight more crosses around the clearing, all the same height as the original. "Them doctors can't do your mom any good," he told Arvin, as they made their way back to the house in the dark. "But I got hopes we can save her if we try hard enough."

"Is she gonna die?" Arvin said.

Willard thought a second before he answered. "The Lord can do anything if you ask Him right."

"How we do that?"

"I'll start showing you first thing in the morning. It won't be easy, but there ain't no other choice."

Willard took a leave of absence from work, told the foreman that his wife was sick, but that she'd soon be better. He and Arvin spent hours praying at the log every day. Every time they started across the field toward the woods, Willard explained again that their voices had to reach heaven, and that the only way that would happen was if they were absolutely sincere with their pleas. As Charlotte grew weaker, the prayers grew louder and began to carry down the hill and across the holler. The people of Knockemstiff woke up to the sound of their entreaties every morning and went to bed with them every night. Sometimes, when Charlotte was having a particularly bad spell, Willard accused his son of not wanting her to get better. He'd strike and kick the boy, and then later sink into remorse. Sometimes it seemed to Arvin as if his father apologized to him every day. After a while, he stopped paying attention and accepted the blows and harsh words and subsequent regrets as just part of the life they were living now. At night, they would go on praying until their voices gave out, then stumble back to the house and drink warm water from the well bucket on the kitchen counter and fall into bed exhausted. In the morning, they'd start all over again. Still, Charlotte grew thinner, closer to death. Whenever she came out of the morphine slumber, she begged Willard to stop this nonsense, just let her go in peace. But he wasn't about to give up. If it required everything that was in him, then so be it. Any moment, he expected the spirit of God to come down and heal her; and as the second week of July came to an end, he could take a little comfort in the fact that she'd already lasted longer than the doctors had predicted.

It was the first week of August and Charlotte was out of her head most of the time now. While he was trying to cool her off with wet cloths one sweltering evening, it occurred to Willard that maybe something more was expected of him than just prayers and sincerity. The next afternoon he came back from the stockyards in town with a lamb in the bed of the pickup. It had a bad leg and cost only five dollars. Arvin jumped off the porch and ran out into the yard. "Can I give it a name?" he asked as his father brought the truck to a stop in front of the barn.

"Jesus Christ, this ain't no goddamn pet," Willard yelled. "Get in the house with your mother." He backed the truck into the barn and got out and hurriedly tied the animal's hind legs with a rope, then hoisted the lamb in the air upside down with a pulley attached to one of the wooden beams that supported the hayloft. He moved the truck a few feet forward. Then he lowered the terrified animal until its nose was a couple of feet from the ground. With a butcher knife, he slit its throat and caught the blood in a five-gallon feed bucket. He sat on a bale of straw and waited until the wound stopped dripping. Then he carried the bucket to the prayer log and carefully poured the sacrifice over it. That night, after Arvin went to bed, he hauled the furry carcass to the edge of the field and shoved it off into a ravine.

A couple of days later, Willard began picking up animals killed along the road: dogs, cats, raccoons, possums, groundhogs, deer. The corpses that were too stiff and too far gone to bleed out, he hung from the crosses and the tree limbs around the prayer log. The heat and humidity rotted them quickly. The stench made Arvin and him choke back vomit as they knelt and called out for the Savior's mercy. Maggots dripped from the trees and crosses like squirming drops of white fat. The ground around the log stayed muddy with blood. The number of insects swarming around them multiplied every day. Both were covered with bites from the flies and mosquitoes and fleas. Despite it being August, Arvin took to wearing a long-sleeved flannel shirt and a pair of work gloves and a handkerchief over his face. Neither of them bathed anymore. They lived on lunch meat and crackers bought at Maude's store. Willard's eyes grew hard and wild, and it seemed to his son that his matted beard turned gray almost overnight.

"This is what death is like," Willard said somberly one evening as he and Arvin knelt at the putrid, blood-soaked log. "You want such as this for your mother?"

"No, sir," the boy said.

Willard struck the top of the log with his fist. "Then pray, goddamn it!"

Arvin pulled the filthy handkerchief from his face and breathed deeply of the rot. From then on, he quit trying to avoid the mess, the endless prayers, the spoiled blood, the rotten carcasses. But still, his mother kept fading. Everything smelled of death now, even the hallway leading back to her sickroom. Willard started locking her door, told Arvin not to disturb her. "She needs her rest," he said.

6

AS HENRY DUNLAP WAS GETTING READY to leave the office one afternoon, Willard showed up, over a week late on the rent. For the last few weeks, the lawyer had been slipping home in the middle of the day for a few minutes and watching his wife and her black lover go at it. He had a feeling that it was an indication of some kind of sickness on his part, but he couldn't help himself. His hope, though, was that he could somehow pin Edith's murder on the man. God knows the bastard deserved it, fucking his white employer's wife. By then, sled-footed Willie was getting cocky, reporting for work in the mornings smelling of Henry's private stock of imported cognac and his French aftershave. The lawn looked like hell. He was going to have to hire a eunuch just to get the grass cut. Edith was still pestering him about buying the sonofabitch a vehicle.

"Jesus Christ, man, you don't look so good," Henry said to Willard when the secretary let him in.

Willard pulled out his wallet and laid thirty dollars on the desk. "Neither do you, for that matter," he said.

"Well, I've had a lot of things on my mind lately," the lawyer said. "Grab a chair, sit down a minute."

"I don't need none of your shit today," Willard said. "Just a receipt."

"Oh, come on," Henry said, "let's have a drink. You look like you could use one."

Willard stood staring at Henry for a moment, not sure he had heard him right. It was the first time Dunlap had ever offered him a drink, or acted the least bit civil since right after he'd signed the lease six years ago. He had come in ready for the lawyer to give him hell about being late with the rent money, had already made up his mind to knock the fuck out of him today if he got too mouthy. He glanced at the clock on the wall. Charlotte needed another prescription filled, but the drugstore was open until six. "Yeah, I reckon I could," Willard said. He sat down in the wooden chair across from the lawyer's soft leather one while Henry got two glasses and a bottle of scotch from a cabinet. He poured the drinks, handed the renter one.

Taking a sip from his drink, the lawyer leaned back in his chair and gazed at the money lying on top of the desk in front of Willard. Henry's stomach was sour from worrying about his wife. He'd been thinking for several weeks about what the golfer had told him about his renter beating the fuck out of that man. "You still interested in buying the house?" Henry asked.

"Ain't no way I can come up with that kind of money now," Willard said. "My wife's sick."

"I hate to hear that," the lawyer said. "About your wife, I mean. How bad is it?" He pushed the bottle toward Willard. "Go ahead, help yourself."

Willard poured two fingers from the bottle. "Cancer," he said.

"My mother died from it in her lungs," Henry said, "but that was a long time ago. They've come a long way with treating it since then."

"About that receipt," Willard said.

"There's damn near forty acres goes with that place," Henry said.

"Like I said, I can't get the money right now."

The lawyer turned in his chair and looked at the wall away from Willard. The only sound was a fan swiveling back and forth in the corner, blowing hot air around the room. He took another drink. "A while back I caught my wife cheating on me," he said. "I ain't been worth a shit since." Admitting to this hillbilly that he was a cuckold was harder than he thought.

Willard studied the fat man's profile, watched a trickle of sweat run down his forehead and drip off the end of his lumpy nose onto his white shirt. It didn't surprise him, what the lawyer said. After all, what sort of woman would marry a man like that? A car went by in the alley. Willard picked up the bottle and poured his glass full. He reached in his shirt pocket for a cigarette. "Yeah, that would be hard to take," he said. He didn't give a damn about Dunlap's marital problems, but he hadn't had a good drink since he'd brought Charlotte home, and the lawyer's whiskey was top shelf.

The lawyer looked down into his glass. "I'd just go ahead and divorce her, but, goddamn it, the man she's fucking is black as the ace of spades," he said. He looked over at Willard then. "For my boy's sake, I'd rather the town didn't know about that."

"Hell, man, what about kicking his ass?" Willard suggested. "Take a shovel to the bastard's head, he'll get the message." Jesus, Willard thought, rich people did fine and dandy as long as things were going their way, but the minute the shit hit the fan, they fell apart like paper dolls left out in the rain.

Dunlap shook his head. "That won't do any good. She'd just get her another one," he said. "My wife's a whore, been one all her life." The lawyer pulled a cigarette from the case lying on the desk and lit it. "Oh, well, that's enough of that shit." He blew a cloud of smoke toward the ceiling. "Now about that house again. I've been thinking. What if I told you there was a way you could own that place free and clear?"

"Ain't nothing free," Willard said.

The lawyer smiled slightly. "There's some truth to that, I guess. But still, would you be interested?" He set his glass on the desk.

"I'm not sure what you're getting at."

"Well, neither am I," Dunlap said, "but how about you call me next week here at the office and maybe we can talk about it. I should have things worked out by then."

Willard stood up and drained his glass. "That depends," he said. "I'll have to see how my wife's doing."

Dunlap pointed at the money Willard had laid on the desk. "Go ahead and take that with you," he said. "Sounds like you might need it."

"No," Willard said, "that's yours. I still want that receipt, though."

THEY KEPT PRAYING AND SPILLING BLOOD on the log and hanging up twisted, mashed roadkill. All the while, Willard was considering the conversation he'd had with the fat-ass landlord. He'd run it through his head a hundred times, figured Dunlap probably wanted him to kill the black man or the wife or maybe both of them. There wasn't anything else in the world he could think of that would be worth signing over the land and the house. But he also couldn't help but wonder why Dunlap would think that he would do something like that; and the only thing Willard could come up with was that the lawyer considered him stupid, was playing him for a fool. He'd make sure his renter's ass was sitting in jail before the bodies cooled off. For a brief spell, he had thought after talking to Dunlap that maybe there was a chance he could fulfill Charlotte's dream. But there wasn't any way they were ever going to own the house. He could see that now.

One day in the middle of August, Charlotte seemed to rally, even ate a bowl of Campbell's tomato soup and held it down. She wanted to sit on the porch that evening, the first time she'd been out in the fresh air for weeks. Willard took a bath and trimmed his beard and combed his hair, while Arvin heated some popcorn on the stove. A breeze blew in from the west and cooled things off a bit. They drank cold 7-Up and watched the stars slowly cross the sky. Arvin sat on the floor next to her rocking chair. "It's been a rough summer, hasn't it, Arvin?" Charlotte said, running her bony hand through his dark hair. He was such a sweet, gentle boy. She hoped Willard would realize that when she was gone. That was something they needed to talk about, she reminded herself again. The medicine made her so forgetful.

"But now you're getting better," he said. He stuck another handful of popcorn in his mouth. He hadn't had a hot meal in weeks.

"Yeah, I feel pretty good for a change," she said, smiling at him.

She finally went to sleep in the rocker around midnight and Willard carried her to bed. In the middle of the night, she woke up thrashing around with the cancer eating another hole through her. He sat beside her until morning, her long fingernails digging deeper and deeper into the meat of his hand with each new wave of the pain. It was her worst episode yet. "Don't worry," he kept telling her. "Everything's going to get better soon."

He spent several hours the next morning driving along the back roads searching in the ditches for new sacrifices, but came up empty. That afternoon, he went to the stockyards, reluctantly bought another lamb. But even he had to admit, they didn't seem to be working. On his way out of town, already in a foul mood, he passed by Dunlap's office. He was still thinking about that sonofabitch when he suddenly jerked the truck over and stopped along the berm of Western Avenue. Cars drove by honking their horns, but he didn't hear them. There was one thing that he hadn't tried yet. He couldn't believe that he hadn't thought of it earlier.

"I'D ALMOST GIVEN UP ON YOU," Dunlap said.

"I been busy," Willard said. "Look, if you still want to talk, how about you meet me at your office at ten o'clock tonight?" He was standing in a phone booth in Dusty's Bar on Water Street, just a couple of blocks north of the lawyer's office. According to the clock on the wall, it was almost five. He'd told Arvin to stay in the sickroom with Charlotte, said he might be getting in late. He'd made the boy a pallet on the floor at the foot of her bed.

"Ten o'clock?" the lawyer said.

"That's as early as I can get there," Willard said. "It's up to you."

"Okay," the lawyer said. "I'll see you then."

Willard bought a pint of whiskey from the bartender and drove around for the next couple of hours listening to the radio. He passed by the Wooden Spoon as it was closing, saw some skinny teenage girl walking out the door with the bowlegged old cook, the same one who had been working the grill there when Charlotte was waiting tables. He probably still couldn't fix a meat loaf worth a shit, Willard thought. He stopped and filled the truck with gas, then went to the Tecumseh Lounge on the other side of town. Sitting at the bar, he drank a couple of beers, watched a guy wearing thick glasses and a dirty yellow hard hat run the pool table four times in a row. When he walked back out into the gravel lot, the sun was starting to go down behind the paper mill smokestack.

At nine thirty, he was sitting in his truck on Second Street, a block east of the lawyer's office. A few minutes later, he watched

Dunlap park in front of the old brick building and go inside. Willard drove around to the alley, backed up against the building. He took a few deep breaths before getting out of the truck. Reaching behind the seat, he got a hammer and stuffed the handle down his pants, pulled his shirt over it. He looked up and down the alley, then went to the rear door and knocked. After a minute or so, the lawyer opened the door. He was wearing a wrinkled blue shirt and a pair of baggy gray slacks held up by red suspenders. "That's smart, coming in the back like that," Dunlap said. He had a glass of whiskey in his hand and his bloodshot eyes indicated that he'd already had a few. As he turned toward his desk, he staggered a bit and farted. "Sorry about that," he said, just before Willard struck him in the temple with the hammer, a sickening crack filling the room. Dunlap fell forward without a sound, knocking over a bookcase. The glass he'd been holding shattered on the floor. Willard bent over the body and hit him again. When he was sure the man was dead, he leaned against the wall and listened carefully for a while. A couple of cars drove by on the street out front and then nothing.

Willard put on a pair of work gloves he had in his back pocket and dragged the lawyer's heavy body to the door. He straightened up the bookcase and picked up the broken glass and wiped up the spilled whiskey with the sport coat that was slung over the back of the lawyer's chair. He checked the lawyer's pants pockets, found a set of keys and over two hundred dollars in his wallet. He put the money in a desk drawer, stuck the keys in his overalls.

Opening the office door, he stepped into the small reception room and checked the front door to make sure it was locked. He went into the lavatory and ran some water on Dunlap's jacket and went back to wipe the blood off the floor. Surprisingly, there wasn't that much. After tossing the sport coat on top of the body, he sat down at the desk. He looked around for something that might have his name on it, but found nothing. He took a pull from the bottle of scotch on the desk, then capped it and stuck it in another drawer. On the desk was a photo in a gold frame of a chubby teenage boy, the spitting image of Dunlap, holding a tennis racket. The one of the wife was gone.

Turning out the lights in the office, Willard stepped into the alley and laid the jacket and the hammer in the front seat of the truck. Then he let the tailgate down and started the truck and backed it up to the open doorway. It took only a minute to drag the lawyer into the bed of the truck and cover him with a tarp, weigh the corners down with cement blocks. He shoved the clutch in on the truck and coasted a couple of feet, then got out and shut the office door. As he drove out Route 50, he passed by a sheriff's cruiser parked in the empty store lot at Slate Mills. He watched in the rearview and held his breath until the illuminated Texaco sign faded from view. At Schott's Bridge, he stopped and tossed the hammer into Paint Creek. By three AM, he was finishing up.

The next morning when Willard and Arvin got to the prayer log, fresh blood was still dripping off the sides into the rancid dirt. "This wasn't here yesterday," Arvin said.

"I run over a groundhog last night," Willard said. "Went ahead and bled him out when I got home."

"A groundhog? Boy, he must have been a big one."

Willard grinned as he dropped to his knees. "Yeah, he was. He was a big fat bastard."

7

EVEN WITH THE SACRIFICE OF THE LAWYER, Charlotte's bones began breaking a couple of weeks later, little sickening pops that made her scream and claw gashes in her arms. She passed out from the pain whenever Willard tried to move her. A festering bedsore on her backside spread until it was the size of a plate. Her room smelled as rank and fetid as the prayer log. It hadn't rained in a month, and there was no letup from the heat. Willard purchased more lambs at the stockyard, poured buckets of blood around the log until their shoes sank over the tops in the muddy slop. One morning while he was out, a lame and starving mutt with soft white fur ventured up to the porch timidly with its tail between its legs. Arvin fed it some scraps from the refrigerator, had already named it Jack by the time his father got home. Without a word, Willard walked into the house and came back out with his rifle. He shoved Arvin away from the dog, then shot it between the eyes while the boy begged him not to do it. He dragged it into the woods and nailed it to one of the crosses. Arvin stopped speaking to him after that. He listened to the moans of his mother while Willard drove around looking for more sacrifices. School was getting ready to start again, and he hadn't been off the hill a single time all summer. He found himself wishing that his mother would die.

A few nights later, Willard rushed into Arvin's bedroom and jerked him awake. "Get over to the log now," he said. The boy sat up, looked around with a confused look. The hall light was on. He could hear his mother gasping and wheezing for breath in the room across the hall. Willard shook him again. "Don't you quit praying until I come and get you. Make Him hear you, you understand?" Arvin threw on his clothes and started jogging across the field. He thought about wishing her dead, his own mother. He ran faster.

By three in the morning, his throat was raw and blistered. His father came once and dumped a bucket of water on his head, implored him to keep praying. But though Arvin kept screaming for the Lord's mercy, he didn't feel anything and none came. Some of the people down in Knockemstiff closed their windows, even with the heat. Others kept a light on the rest of the night, offered prayers of their own. Snook Haskins's sister, Agnes, sat in her chair listening to that pitiful voice and thinking of the ghost husbands that she had buried in her head. Arvin looked up at the dead hound, its vacant eyes staring across the dark woods, its belly bloated and near bursting. "Can you hear me, Jack?" he said.

Right before dawn, Willard covered his dead wife with a clean white sheet and walked across the field, numb with loss and despair. He slipped up behind Arvin silently, listened to the boy's prayers for a minute or two, barely a choked whisper now. He looked down, realized with disgust that he was gripping his open penknife in his hand. He shook his head and put it away. "Come on, Arvin," he said, his voice gentle with his son for the first time in weeks. "It's over. Your mom's gone."

Charlotte was buried two days later in the little cemetery outside of Bourneville. On the way home from the funeral, Willard said, "I'm thinking we might take us a little trip. Go down and visit your grandma in Coal Creek. Maybe stay for a while. You can meet Uncle Earskell, and that girl they got living with them would be just a little younger than you. You'll like it there." Arvin didn't say anything. He still hadn't gotten over the dog, and he was certain there was no way to get over his mother. All along, Willard had promised that if they prayed hard enough, she would be all right. When they arrived home, they found a blueberry pie wrapped in newspaper on the porch by the door. Willard wandered off into the field behind the house. Arvin went inside and took off his good clothes and lay down on the bed.

When he woke several hours later, Willard was still gone, which suited the boy fine. Arvin ate half the pie and put the rest in the icebox. He went out on the porch and sat in his mother's rocking chair and watched the evening sun sink behind the row of evergreens west of the house. He thought about her first night under the ground. How dark it must be there. He'd overheard an old man standing off under a tree leaning on a shovel telling Willard that death was either a long journey or a long sleep, and though his father had scowled and turned away, Arvin thought that sounded all right. He hoped for his mother's sake that it was a little of both. There had been only a handful of people at the funeral: a woman his mother used to work with at the Wooden Spoon, and a couple of old ladies from the church in Knock-emstiff. There was supposed to be a sister somewhere out west, but Willard didn't know how to get in touch with her. Arvin had never been to a funeral before, but he had a feeling that it hadn't been much of one.

As the darkness spread across the overgrown yard, Arvin got up and walked around the side of the house and called out for his father several times. He waited a few minutes, thought about just going back to bed. But then he went inside and got the flashlight from the kitchen drawer. After looking in the barn, he started toward the prayer log. Neither of them had been there in the three days since his mother had passed. The night was coming on quick now. Bats swooped after insects in the field, a nightingale watched him from its nest beneath a bower of honeysuckle. He hesitated, then entered the woods and followed the path. Stopping at the edge of the clearing, he shined the light around. He could see Willard kneeling at the log. The rotten stench hit him, and he thought he might get sick. He could taste the pie starting to come up in his throat. "I'm not doing that no more," he told his father in a loud voice. He knew it was bound to cause trouble, but he didn't care. "I ain't praying."

He waited a minute or so for a reply, and then said, "You hear me?" He stepped closer to the log, kept the light shining on Wil-lard's kneeling form. Then he touched his father's shoulder and the penknife dropped to the ground. Willard's head lolled to one side and exposed the bloody gash he'd cut from ear to ear across his throat. Blood ran down the side of the log and dripped onto his suit pants. A slight breeze blew down over the hill and cooled the sweat on the back of Arvin's neck. Branches creaked overhead. A tuft of white fur floated through the air. Some of the bones hanging from the wires and nails gently tapped against one another, sounding like some sad, hollow music.

Through the trees, Arvin could see a few lights glimmering in Knockemstiff. He heard a car door slam somewhere down there, then a single horseshoe clang against a metal peg. He stood waiting for the next pitch, but none came. It seemed like a thousand years had passed since the morning the two hunters had come up behind Willard and him here. He felt guilty and ashamed that he wasn't crying, but there were no tears left. His mother's long dying had left him dry. Not knowing what else to do, he stepped around Willard's body and pointed the flashlight ahead of him. He began making his way down through the woods.

8

AT EXACTLY NINE O'CLOCK THAT EVENING, Hank Bell stuck the
CLOSED sign in the front window of Maude's store and turned off the
lights. He went behind the counter and got a six-pack of beer from
the bottom of the meat case, then stepped out the back door. In his
front shirt pocket was a little transistor radio. He sat down in a lawn
chair and opened a beer and lit a cigarette. He had lived in a camper
behind the concrete-block building for four years now. Reaching into
his pocket, he turned the radio on just as the announcer reported
that the Reds were down by three runs in the sixth inning. They
were playing out on the West Coast. Hank estimated it was just after
five o'clock there. The way time worked, that was a funny thing, he
thought.

He looked over at the little cigar tree he'd planted the first year he
worked at the store. It had grown nearly five feet since then. It was
a start he'd gotten from the tree that stood in the front yard of the
house he and his mother had lived in before she passed, and he lost
the place to the bank. He wasn't sure why he'd planted it. A couple
more years at the most, and he was planning on leaving Knockemstiff.
He talked about it to any customer who would listen. Every week, he
saved back a little bit from the thirty dollars Maude paid him. Some
days he thought he'd move up north, and other times he decided the
South might be best. But there was plenty of time to decide where to
go. He was still a young man.

He watched a silvery-gray mist a couple of feet high move slowly
up from Black Run Creek and cover the flat, rocky field behind the
store, part of Clarence Myers's cow pasture. It was his favorite part
of the day, right after the sun went down and right before the long
shadows disappeared. He could hear some boys whooping and yell-

ing on the concrete bridge out in front of the store whenever a car drove by. A few of them hung there almost every night, regardless of the weather. Poor as snakes, every one of them. All they desired out of life was a car that would run and a hot piece of ass. He thought that sounded nice in a way, just going through your entire life with no more expectations than that. Sometimes he wished he weren't so ambitious.

The praying on top of the hill had finally stopped three nights ago. Hank tried not to think about the poor woman dying up there, closed up in that room, like people were saying, while the Russell man and his boy went half insane. Hell, they'd damn near driven the entire holler crazy at times, the way they went on every morning and every evening for hours. From what he'd heard, it sounded more like they were practicing some sort of voodoo instead of anything Christian. Two of the Lynch boys had come across some dead animals hanging in the trees up there a couple of weeks ago; and then one of their hounds turned up missing. Lord, the world was getting to be an awful place. Just yesterday, he'd read in the newspaper that Henry Dunlap's wife and her black lover had been arrested on suspicion of killing him. The law had yet to find the body, but Hank thought her lying with a Negro was damn near proof that they'd done it. Everybody knew the lawyer; he owned land all over Ross County, used to stop in the store once in a while sniffing around for moonshine to impress some of his big-shot friends. From what Hank had seen of the man, he probably deserved killing, but why didn't the woman just get a divorce and move up to White Heaven with the coloreds? People didn't use their brains anymore. It's a wonder the lawyer didn't have her killed first, that is, if he knew about the boyfriend. Nobody would have blamed him for that, but now he was dead and probably better off. It would have been a hell of a thing to have to live with, everyone knowing your wife ran around with a black man.

The Reds came up to bat, and Hank began thinking about Cincinnati. Sometime soon, he was going to drive down to the River City and see a doubleheader. His plan was to buy a good seat, drink beer, stuff himself with their hot dogs. He'd heard wieners tasted better in a ballpark, and he wanted to find out for himself. Cincinnati was just ninety miles or so on the other side of the Mitchell Flats, a straight shot down Route 50, but he'd never been there, hadn't been any farther west than Hillsboro his entire twenty-two years. Hank had the feeling that his life would really begin once he made that trip. He didn't have the details all figured out yet, but he also wanted to buy a whore after the games were over, some pretty girl who would treat him nice. He'd pay her extra to undress him, pull off his pants and shoes. He was going to buy a new shirt for the occasion, stop in at Bainbridge on his way down and get a decent haircut. He'd remove her clothes slowly, take his time with each little button or whatever it was that whores fastened their clothes with. He'd spill some whiskey on her titties and lick it off, like he heard some of the men talk about when they came in the store after having a few up at the Bull Pen. When he finally got inside her, she'd tell him to take it easy, that she wasn't used to being with a man his size. She wouldn't be anything like that loudmouth Mildred McDonald, the only woman he'd ever been with so far.

"One little pop," Mildred had told everyone at the Bull Pen, "and then nothing but smoke." That had been over three years ago, and people still razzed him about it. The whore in Cincinnati would insist that he keep his money after he finished with her, ask him for his phone number, maybe even beg him to take her away. He figured he'd probably come back home a different person, just like Slim Gleason had when he returned from the Korean War. Before he left Knockemstiff for good, Hank thought he might even stop in at the Bull Pen and buy some of the boys a farewell beer, just to show there weren't any hard feelings about all the jokes. In a way, he supposed, Mildred had done him a favor; he'd put away a lot of money since he'd quit going up there.

He was half listening to the game and thinking about the dirty way Mildred had done him when he noticed someone with a flashlight walking up through Clarence's pasture. He saw the small figure bend down and slip through the barbwire fence and head toward him. It was nearly dark now, but as the person got closer, Hank realized it was the Russell boy. He'd never seen the boy off the hill by himself before, heard his father wouldn't allow it. But they'd buried his mother just this afternoon, and maybe that had changed things, softened the Russell man's heart a little. The boy was wearing a white shirt and a pair of new overalls. "Hey there," Hank said as Arvin got closer. The boy's face was gaunt and sweaty and pale. He didn't look good, not good at all. It looked like he had blood or something smeared on his face and clothes.

Arvin stopped a few feet from the storekeeper and turned off the flashlight. "The store's closed," Hank said, "but if you need something, I can open back up."

"How would a person go about getting hold of the law?"

"Well, either cause some trouble or call them on the telephone, I reckon," Hank said.

"Could you call 'em for me? I ain't never used a telephone before."

Hank reached in his pocket and turned the radio off. The Reds were getting clobbered anyway. "What do you want with the sheriff, son?"

"He's dead," the boy said.

"Who is?"

"My dad," Arvin said.

"You mean your mom, don't you?"

A confused look came over the boy's face for a moment, then he shook his head. "No, my mom's been dead three days. I'm talking about my dad."

Hank stood up and reached in his pants for the keys to the back door of the store. He wondered if maybe the boy had gone simple with grief. Hank remembered the rough time he'd gone through when his own mother passed. It was something a person never really got over, he knew that. He still thought about her every day. "Come on inside. You look thirsty."

"I ain't got no money," Arvin said.

"That's all right," Hank said. "You can owe me."

They went inside and the storekeeper slid the top of the metal pop cooler open. "What kind you like?"

The boy shrugged.

"Here's a root beer," Hank said. "That's the kind I used to drink." He handed the boy the bottle of pop and scratched at his day-old beard. "Now your name's Arvin, ain't it?"

"Yes, sir," the boy said. He set his flashlight down on the counter and took a long drink and then another.

"Okay, so what makes you think there's something wrong with your daddy?"

"His neck," Arvin said. "He cut himself."

"That ain't blood you got on you, is it?"

Arvin looked down at his shirt and his hands. "No," he said. "It's pie."

"Where is your dad?"

"A little ways from the house," the boy said. "In the woods."

Hank reached under the counter for the phone book. "Now look," he said, "I don't mind calling the law for you, but don't be fooling with me, okay? They don't take kindly to wild-goose chases." Just a couple of days ago, Marlene Williams had him call and report another window peeper. It was the fifth time in just two months. The dispatcher had hung up on him.

"Why would I do that?"

"No," Hank said. "I guess you wouldn't."

After he made the call, he and Arvin went out the back door and Hank picked up his beers. They walked around and sat down on the bench in front of the store. A cloud of moths fluttered around the security light that stood over the gas pumps. Hank thought about the beating the boy's daddy had given Lucas Hayburn last year. Not that he probably didn't deserve it, but Lucas hadn't been right since. Just yesterday, he had sat on this bench all morning bent over with a gob of spit hanging from his mouth. Hank opened another beer and lit a smoke. He hesitated a second, then offered the boy one from his pack.

Arvin shook his head and took another drink of the pop. "They ain't pitching horseshoes tonight," he said after a couple of minutes.

Hank looked up the holler, saw the lights on at the Bull Pen. Four or five cars were parked in the yard. "Must be taking a break," the storekeeper said, leaning back against the wall of the store and stretching his legs out. He and Mildred had gone to the hog barn over at Platter's Pasture. She said she liked the rich smell of the pig manure, liked to imagine things a little different than most girls.

"What is it you like to imagine?" Hank had asked her, a little worry in his voice. For years, he had listened to boys and men talk about getting laid, but not once had any of them said anything about hog shit.

"That ain't none of your business what's in my head," she told him. Her chin was sharp as a hatchet, her eyes like lusterless gray marbles. Her only redeeming feature was the thing between her legs, which some had said reminded them of a snapping turtle.

"Okay," Hank said.

"Let's see what you got," Mildred said, tugging at his zipper and pulling him down in the dirty straw.

After his miserable performance, she shoved him off and said, "Jesus Christ, I should have just played with myself."

"I'm sorry," he said. "You just had me worked up. It'll be better next time."

"Ha! I doubt very much they'll be a next time, Bub," she said.

"Well, don't you at least want a ride home?" he'd asked as he was leaving. It was nearly midnight. The two-room shack she lived in with her parents over in Nipgen was a couple of hours away if she walked it.

"No, I'm gonna hang around here awhile," she said. "Maybe someone worth a shit will show up."

Hank flipped his cigarette into the gravel lot and took another drink of beer. He liked to tell himself that things had turned out for the best in the end. Although he wasn't a spiteful person, not at all, he had to admit that he got some satisfaction out of knowing that Mildred was now hooked up with a big-bellied boy named Jimmy Jack who rode an old Harley and kept her penned up on his back porch in a plywood doghouse when he wasn't selling her ass out behind one of the bars in town. People said she'd do anything you could think of for fifty cents. Hank had seen her in Meade this past Fourth of July, standing by the door outside Dusty's Bar with a black eye, holding the biker's leather helmet. The best years of Mildred's life were behind her now, and his own were just getting ready to begin. The woman he was going to pick up in Cincinnati would be a hundred times finer than any old Mildred McDonald. A year or two after he moved away from here, he probably wouldn't even be able to recall her name. He rubbed a hand over his face and looked over, saw the Russell boy watching him. "Damn, was I talking to myself?" he asked the boy.

"Not really," Arvin said.

"Hard to tell when that deputy will show up," Hank said. "They don't much like to come out here."

"Who's Mildred?" Arvin asked.

9

LEE BODECKER'S SHIFT WAS NEARLY OVER when the call came through on the radio. Another twenty minutes and he would have been picking up his girlfriend and heading out Bridge Street to Johnny's Drive-in. He was starving. Every night, after he got off, he and Florence drove to either Johnny's or the White Cow or the Sugar Shack. He liked to go all day without eating, then wolf down cheeseburgers and fries and milk shakes; and finish things off with a couple of ice-cold beers down along the River Road, leaned back in his seat while Florence jacked him off into her empty Pepsi cup. She had a grip like an Amish milk maiden. The entire summer had been a succession of almost perfect nights. She was saving the good stuff for the honeymoon, which suited Bodecker just fine. At twenty-one years old, he was just six months out of the peacetime army, and in no hurry to be tied down with a family. Although he had been a deputy only four months, he could already see a lot of advantages to being the law in a place as backward as Ross County, Ohio. There was money to be made if a man was careful and not get the big head, like his boss had done. Nowadays, Sheriff Hen Matthews had a picture of his round, stupid puss on the front page of the *Meade Gazette* three or four times a week, often for no conceivable reason. Citizens were starting to joke about it. Bodecker was already planning his campaign strategy. All he had to do was get some dirt on Matthews before the next election, and he could move Florence into one of the new houses they were building on Brewer Heights when they finally tied the knot. He had heard that every single one of them had two bathrooms.

He turned the cruiser around on Paint Street near the paper mill and headed out Huntington Pike toward Knockemstiff. Three miles out of town, he passed by the little house in Brownsville where he lived with his sister and mother. A light was on in the living room. He shook his head and reached in his shirt pocket for a cigarette. He was paying most of the bills right now, but he had made it clear to them when he came back from the service that they couldn't depend on him much longer. His father had left them years ago, just went off to the shoe factory one morning and never returned. Recently, they had heard a rumor that he was living in Kansas City, working in a pool room, which made sense if you had ever known Johnny Bodecker. The only time the man ever smiled was when he was busting a rack of balls or running a table. The news had been a big disappointment to his son; nothing would have made Bodecker happier than discovering that the fucker was still earning his keep somewhere stitching soles onto loafers in a dingy red-brick building lined with high, dirty windows. Occasionally, when he was driving around on patrol and things were quiet, Bodecker imagined his father returning to Meade for a visit. In his fantasy, he followed the old man out into the country away from any witnesses and arrested him on a phony charge. Then he beat the shit out of him with a nightstick or the butt of his revolver before taking him to Schott's Bridge and pushing him over the rail. It was always a day or so after a heavy rain and Paint Creek would be up, the water swift and deep on its way east to the Scioto River. Sometimes he let him drown; other times he allowed him to swim to the muddy bank. It was a good way to pass the time.

He took a drag off the cigarette as his thoughts drifted from his father to his sister, Sandy. Though she had just turned sixteen, Bodecker had already found her a job waiting tables in the evening at the Wooden Spoon. He had pulled over the owner of the diner a few weeks ago for driving drunk, the man's third time in a year, and one thing had led to another. Before he knew it, he was a hundred dollars richer and Sandy had work. She was as bashful and anxious around people as a possum caught out in daylight, always had been, and Bodecker didn't doubt that learning to deal with customers those first couple of weeks had been torture for her, but the owner had told him yesterday morning that she seemed to be getting the hang of it now. On nights when he couldn't pick her up after work, the cook, a thickset man with sleepy blue eyes who liked to draw risqué pictures of cartoon characters on his white paper chef's hat, had been giving her a ride home, and that worried him a little, mostly because Sandy was inclined to go along with whatever anyone asked her to do. Not once had Bodecker ever heard her speak up for herself, and like a lot of things, he blamed their father for that. But still, he told himself, it was time she began learning how to make her own way in the world. She couldn't hide in her room and daydream the rest of her life; and the sooner she started bringing in some money, the sooner he could get out. A few days ago, he had gone so far as to suggest to his mother that she let Sandy quit school and work full-time, but the old lady wouldn't hear of it. "Why not?" he asked. "Once someone finds out how easy she is, she's bound to get knocked up anyway, so what does it matter if she knows algebra or not?" She didn't offer a reason, but now that he had planted the seed, he knew he just had to wait a day or two before bringing it up again. It might take a while, but Lee Bodecker always got what he wanted.

Lee made a right onto Black Run Road and drove to Maude's grocery. The storekeeper was sitting on the bench out front drinking a beer and talking to some young boy. Bodecker got out of the cruiser with his flashlight. The storekeeper was a sad, worn-out-looking fucker, even though the deputy figured they were roughly the same age. Some people were born just so they could be buried; his mother was like that, and he'd always figured that's why the old man had left, though he hadn't been any great prize himself. "Well, what we got this time?" Bodecker asked. "I hope it ain't another one of those goddamn window peepers you keep calling about."

Hank leaned over and spit on the ground. "I wish it was," he said, "but no, it's about this boy's daddy."

Bodecker trained the flashlight on the skinny, dark-haired boy. "Well, what is it, son?" he said.

"He's dead," Arvin said, putting a hand up to block the light shining in his face.

"And they just buried his poor mother today," Hank said. "It's a damn shame, it is."

"So your daddy's dead, is he?"

"Yes, sir."

"Is that blood you got on your face?"

"No," Arvin said. "Somebody gave us a pie."

"This ain't some joke, is it? You know I'll take you to jail if it is."

"Why you all think I'm lying?" Arvin said.

Bodecker looked at the storekeeper. Hank shrugged and turned his beer up and drained it. "They live at the top of Baum Hill," he said. "Arvin here, he can show you." Then he stood up and belched and headed around the side of the store.

"I might have some questions for you later on," Bodecker called out.

"It's a goddamn shame, that's all I can tell you," he heard Hank say.

Bodecker put Arvin in the front seat of the cruiser and drove up Baum Hill. At the top, he turned down a narrow dirt lane lined with trees that the boy pointed out. He slowed the car down to a crawl. "I never been back this way before," the deputy said. He reached down and quietly unsnapped his holster.

"Ain't nobody new been back here in a long time," Arvin said. Looking out the side window into the dark woods, he realized that he'd left his light in the store. He hoped the storekeeper didn't sell it before he got back down there. He glanced over at the brightly lit instrument panel. "You gonna turn the siren on?"

"No sense in scaring someone."

"There's nobody left to scare," Arvin said.

"So this where you live?" Bodecker asked as they pulled up to the small, square house. There were no lights on, no sign that anyone lived here at all except for a rocking chair on the porch. The grass was at least a foot high in the yard. Off to the left was an old barn. Bodecker parked behind a rusted-out pickup. Just your typical hillbilly trash, he thought. Hard to tell what kind of mess he was getting into. His empty stomach gurgled like a broken commode.

Arvin got out without answering and stood in front of the cruiser waiting for the deputy. "This way," he said. He turned and started around the corner of the house.

"How far is it?" Bodecker asked.

"Not too far. Maybe ten minutes."

Bodecker flipped on his flashlight and followed behind the boy along the edge of an overgrown field. They entered the woods and went several hundred feet down a well-worn path. The boy suddenly stopped and pointed ahead into the darkness. "He's right there," Arvin said.

The deputy trained his light on a man, dressed in a white shirt and dress pants, crumpled loosely over a log. He took a few steps closer, could make out a gash in the man's neck. The front of his shirt was soaked in blood. He sniffed the air and gagged. "My God, how long he been laying here like this?"

Arvin shrugged. "Not long. I fell asleep for a little while and there he was."

Bodecker pinched his nostrils together, tried to breathe through his mouth. "What the hell is that smell then?"

"That's them up there," Arvin said, pointing into the trees.

Bodecker lifted his flashlight. Animals in various states of decay hung all around them, some in the branches and others from tall wooden crosses. A dead dog with a leather collar around its neck was nailed up high to one of the crosses like some kind of hideous Christ-like figure. The head of a deer lay at the foot of another. Bodecker fumbled with his gun. "Goddamn it, boy, what the hell is this?" he said, turning the light back on Arvin just as a white, squirming maggot dropped onto the boy's shoulder. He brushed it off as casually as someone would a leaf or a seed. Bodecker waved his revolver around as he started to back away.

"It's a prayer log," Arvin said, his voice barely a whisper now.

"What? A prayer log?"

Arvin nodded, staring at his father's body. "But it don't work," he said.

PART TWO

On the Hunt

10

THE COUPLE HAD BEEN ROAMING the Midwest for several weeks
during the summer of 1965, always on the hunt, two nobodies in a
black Ford station wagon purchased for one hundred dollars at a
used-car lot in Meade, Ohio, called Brother Whitey's. It was the third
vehicle they had gotten off the minister in as many years. The man
on the passenger's side was turning to fat and believed in signs and
had a habit of picking his decayed teeth with a Buck pocketknife. The
woman always drove and wore tight shorts and flimsy blouses that
showed off her pale, bony body in a way they both thought enticing.
She chain-smoked any kind of menthol cigarettes she could get her
hands on while he chewed on cheap black cigars that he called dog
dicks. The Ford burned oil and leaked brake fluid and threatened to
spill its metal guts all over the highway anytime they pushed it past
fifty miles an hour. The man liked to think that it looked like a hearse,
but the woman preferred limousine. Their names were Carl and
Sandy Henderson, but sometimes they had other names, too.

Over the past four years, Carl had come to believe that hitchhikers were the best, and there were plenty of them on the road in those
days. He called Sandy the *bait*, and she called him the *shooter*, and
they both called the hitchhikers the *models*. That very evening, just
north of Hannibal, Missouri, they had tricked and tortured and killed
a young enlisted man in a wooded area thick with humidity and mosquitoes. As soon as they picked him up, the boy had kindly offered
them sticks of Juicy Fruit, said he'd drive for a while if the lady needed
a break. "That'll be the goddamn day," Carl said; and Sandy rolled her
eyes at the snide tone her husband sometimes used, as if he thought
he was a better class of trash than the stuff they found along the roads.
Whenever he got like that, she just wanted to stop the car and tell the

poor fool in the backseat to get out while he still had a chance. One of these days, she promised herself that was exactly what she was going to do, hit the brakes and knock Mister Big Shot down a notch or two.

But not tonight. The boy in the backseat was blessed with a face smooth as butter and tiny brown freckles and strawberry-colored hair, and Sandy could never resist the ones who looked like angels. "What's your name, honey?" she asked him, after they'd gone a mile or two down the highway. She made her voice nice and easy; and when the boy looked up and their eyes met in the rearview mirror, she winked and gave him the smile that Carl had taught her, the one he'd made her practice night after night at the kitchen table until her face was ready to fall off and stick to the floor like a pie crust, a smile that hinted at every dirty possibility a young man could ever imagine.

"Private Gary Matthew Bryson," the boy said. It sounded odd to her, him saying his full name like that, like he was up for inspection or some such shit, but she ignored it and went right on talking. She hoped he wasn't going to be the serious type. Those kinds always made her part of the job that much harder.

"Now that's a nice name," Sandy said. In the mirror, she watched as a shy grin spread over his face, saw him stick a fresh piece of gum in his mouth. "Which of them you go by?" she asked.

"Gary," he said, flipping the silver gum wrapper out the window. "That was my daddy's name."

"That other one, Matthew, that one's from the Bible, ain't it, Carl?" Sandy said.

"Hell, everything's from the Bible," her husband said, staring out the windshield. "Ol' Matt, he was one of the apostles."

"Carl used to teach Sunday school, didn't you, baby?"

With a sigh, Carl twisted his big body around in the seat, more to take another look at the boy than anything else. "That's right," he said with a tight-lipped smile. "I used to teach Sunday school." Sandy patted his knee, and he turned back around without another word and pulled a road map from the glove box.

"You probably already knew that, though, didn't you, Gary?" Sandy said. "That your middle name is right out of the Good Book?"

The boy quit chomping his gum for a moment. "We never went to church much when I was a kid," he said.

A worried look swept across Sandy's face, and she reached for her cigarettes on the dash. "But you been baptized, right?" she asked.

"Well, sure, we ain't complete heathens," the boy said. "I just don't know any of that Bible stuff."

"That's good," Sandy said, a hint of relief in her voice. "No sense takin' chances, not with something like that. Lord, who knows where a person might end up if he wasn't saved?"

The soldier was going home to see his mother before the army shipped him off to Germany or that new place called Vietnam, Carl couldn't recall which now. He didn't give a damn if he was named after some crazy sonofabitch in the New Testament, or that his girlfriend had made him promise to wear her class ring around his neck until he returned from overseas. Knowing stuff like that only complicated things later on; and so Carl found it easier to ignore the small talk, let Sandy handle all the dumb questions, the pitter-patter bullshit. She was good at it, flirting and flapping her jaws, putting them at ease. They had both come a long way since they'd first met, her, a lonely, scrawny stick of a girl waiting tables at the Wooden Spoon in Meade, eighteen years old and taking shit off customers in hopes of a quarter tip. And him? Not much better, a flabby-faced mama's boy who had just lost his mother, with no future or friends except for what a camera might bring. He'd had no idea, as he walked into the Wooden Spoon that first night away from home, of what that meant or what to do next. The only thing he had known for sure, as he sat in the booth watching the skinny waitress finish wiping the tables off before turning out the lights, was that he needed, more than anything else in the world, to take her picture. They had been together ever since.

Of course, there were also things that Carl needed to say to the hitchhikers, but that could usually wait until after they parked the car. "Take a look at this," he'd begin, when he pulled the camera out of the glove box, a Leica M3 35mm, and held it up for the man to see. "Cost four hundred new, but I got it for damn near nothing." And though the sexy smile never left Sandy's lips, she couldn't help but feel a little bitter every time he bragged about it. She didn't know why she had followed Carl into this life, wouldn't even try to put such a thing into mere words, but she did know that that damn camera had never been a bargain, that it was going to cost them plenty in the end. Then she'd hear him ask the next model, in a voice that sounded almost like he was joking, "So, how would you like to have your picture took with a good-looking woman?" Even after all this time, it still amazed her that grown-up men could be so easy.

After they carried and dragged the army boy's naked body a few yards into the woods and rolled it under some bushes heavy with purple berries, they went through his clothes and duffel bag and found nearly three hundred dollars tucked away in a pair of clean white socks. That was more money than Sandy made in a month. "The lying little weasel," Carl said. "Remember me asking him for some gas money?" He swiped at a cloud of insects gathered around his sweaty, red face, stuck the wad of bills in his pants pocket. A pistol with a long pitted barrel lay beside him on the ground next to the camera. "Like my old mother used to say," he went on, "you can't trust any of them."

"Who?" Sandy said.

"Them goddamn redheads," he said. "Hell, they'll spit out a lie even when the truth fits better. They just can't help it. It's something got fucked up in their evolution."

Up on the main road a car with a burned-out muffler went by slowly, and Carl cocked his head and listened to the *pop-pop* sound until it faded away. Then he looked over at Sandy kneeling beside him, studied her face for a moment in the gray dusk. "Here, clean yourself off," he said, handing her the boy's T-shirt, still damp with his sweat. He pointed at her chin. "You got some splatter right there. That skinny bastard was full as a tick."

After wiping the shirt over her face, Sandy tossed it on top of the green duffel and stood up. She buttoned her blouse with shaky hands, brushed the dirt and bits of dead leaf off her legs. Walking to the car, she bent down and examined herself in the side mirror, then reached through the window and grabbed her cigarettes off the dash. She leaned against the front bumper and lit a smoke, dug a tiny piece of gravel out of one skinned knee with a pink fingernail. "Jesus, I hate it when they cry like that," she said. "That's the worst."

Carl shook his head as he flipped through the boy's wallet one more time. "Girl, you got to get over that shit," he said. "Them tears he shed is the kind of thing makes for a good picture. Those last couple minutes was the only time in his whole miserable life when he wasn't faking it."

As Sandy watched him stuff everything that belonged to the boy back into the duffel, she was tempted to ask if she could keep the girlfriend's class ring, but decided it wasn't worth the hassle. Carl had everything figured out, and he could turn into a raging maniac if she tried to flaunt even one little rule. Personal items had to be disposed of properly. That was Rule #4. Or maybe it was #5. Sandy could never keep the order of the rules straight, no matter how many times he tried to drill them into her head, but she would always remember that Gary Matthew Bryson loved Hank Williams and hated the army's powdered eggs. Then her stomach growled and she wondered, just for a second, if those berries hanging over his head back there in the woods were fit to eat or not.

AN HOUR LATER, they pulled into a deserted gravel pit they had passed by earlier when Sandy and Private Bryson were still cracking jokes and making fuck-eyes at each other. She parked behind a small utility shed cobbled together out of scrap lumber and rusty sheets of tin and shut off the engine. Carl climbed out of the car with the duffel bag and a can of gasoline they always carried. A few yards past the shed, he set the bag down and sprinkled some gas on it. After he had it burning good, he went back to the car and searched the backseat with a flashlight, found a wad of gum stuck under one of the armrests. "Worse than some kid," he said. "You'd think the military would teach them better than that. With soldiers like that one, we'll be fucked if those Russians ever decide to invade." He peeled the gum off carefully with his thumbnail and then returned to the fire.

Sandy sat in the car and watched him poke the flames with a stick. Orange and blue sparks hopped and fluttered and disappeared into the darkness. She scratched at some jigger bites around her ankles and worried about the burning sensation between her legs. Though she hadn't mentioned it to Carl yet, she was pretty sure that another boy, one they had picked up in Iowa a couple of days ago, had given her some kind of infection. The doctor had already warned her that another dose or two would ruin her chances of ever having a baby, but Carl didn't like the look of rubbers in his pictures.

When the fire died out, Carl kicked the ashes around in the gravel, then took a dirty bandanna from his back pocket and picked up the hot belt buckle and the smoking remains of the army boots. He flung them out into the middle of the gravel pit and heard a faint splash. As he stood at the edge of the deep hole, Carl thought about the way that Sandy had wrapped her arms around the army boy when she saw him set the camera down and pull the pistol out, like that was going to save him. She always tried that shit with the pretty ones, and though he couldn't really blame her for wanting it to last a while longer, this wasn't just some damn fuck party. To his way of thinking, it was the one true religion, the thing he'd been searching for all his life. Only in the presence of death could he feel the presence of something like God. He looked up, saw dark clouds beginning to gather in the sky. He wiped some sweat out of his eyes and started back to the car. If they were lucky, maybe it would rain tonight and wash some of the scum out of the air, cool things off a bit.

"What the hell were you doing over there?" Sandy asked.

Carl pulled a new cigar from his shirt pocket and started peeling off the wrapper. "You get in a hurry, that's when you make a mistake."

She held her hand out. "Just give me the fucking flashlight."

"What you doing?"

"I got to pee, Carl," she said. "Jesus, I'm about ready to bust, and you're over there daydreaming."

Carl chewed on the cigar and watched her make her way around the back of the shed. A couple of weeks on the road and she was down to nothing again, her legs like goddamn toothpicks, her ass flat as a washboard. It would take three or four months to put some meat back on those bones. Slipping the roll of film he'd shot of her and the army boy into a small metal canister, he stuck it in the glove box with the others. By the time Sandy returned, he had loaded a new roll into the camera. She handed him the light and he stuck it under the seat. "Can we get a motel tonight?" she asked in a tired voice as she started the car.

Carl pulled the cigar out of his mouth and picked at a shred of tobacco caught between his teeth. "We need to do some driving first," he said.

Heading south on 79, they crossed the Mississippi into Illinois on Route 50, a road they'd become mighty familiar with over the last couple of years. Sandy kept trying to hurry things, and he had to remind her several times to slow down. Wrecking the car and being pinned inside or knocked out was one of his biggest fears. Sometimes he had nightmares about it, saw himself lying handcuffed to a hospital bed trying to explain those rolls of film to the law. Just thinking about it started to fuck with the high he'd gotten off the army boy, and he reached over and twisted the knob on the radio until he found a country music station coming out of Covington. Neither of them spoke, but every once in a while, Sandy hummed along to one of the slower songs. Then she'd yawn and light another cigarette. Carl counted the bugs that splattered against the windshield, stayed ready to grab the wheel in case she nodded off.

After driving through a hundred miles of small, hushed towns and vast, dark cornfields, they came upon a run-down motel built out of pink cement blocks called the Sundowner. It was nearly one o'clock in the morning. Three cars sat in the potholed parking lot. Carl rang the buzzer several times before a light finally popped on inside the office and an elderly lady with metal curlers in her hair opened the door a crack and peered out. "That your wife in the car?" she asked, squinting past Carl at the station wagon. He looked around, could just barely make out the glow of Sandy's cigarette in the shadows.

"You got good eyes," he said, managing a brief smile. "Yeah, that's her."

"Where you all from?" the woman asked.

Carl started to say Maryland, one of the few states he hadn't been to yet, but then remembered the tag on the front of the car. He figured the nosy old bag had already checked it out. "Up around Cleveland," he told her.

The woman shook her head, pulled her housecoat tighter around her. "You couldn't pay me to live in a place like that, all that robbing and killing going on."

"You got that right," Carl said. "I worry all the time. Too many spooks for one thing. Heck, my wife won't hardly leave the house anymore." Then he pulled the army boy's money out of his pocket. "So how much for a room?" he asked.

"Six dollars," the woman said. He wet his thumb and counted off some singles and handed them to her. She left for a moment and came back with a key on a worn and wrinkled cardboard tag. "Number seven," she said. "Down on the end."

The room was hot and stuffy and smelled like Black Flag. Sandy headed straight for the bathroom and Carl flipped the portable TV set on, though there wasn't anything on the air but snow and static that time of night, not out here in the sticks anyway. Kicking off his shoes, he started to pull down the thin plaid bedspread. Six dead flies lay scattered on top of the flat pillows. He stared at them for a minute, then sat down on the edge of the bed and reached inside Sandy's purse for one of her cigarettes. He counted the flies again, but the number didn't change.

Looking across the room, he rested his eyes on a cheap framed picture hanging on the wall, a flowers-and-fruit piece of shit that nobody would ever remember, not one person who ever slept in this stinking room. It served no purpose that he could think of, other than to remind a person that the world was a sorry-ass place to be stuck living in. He leaned forward and set his elbows on his knees, tried to imagine one of his pictures in its place. Maybe the beatnik from Wisconsin with the little cellophane of reefer, or that big blond bastard from last year, the one who put up such a fight. Of course, some were better than others, even Carl would admit that; but one thing that he knew for certain: whoever looked at one of his photos, even one of the lousy ones from three or four years ago, they would never forget it. He'd bet the army boy's wad of greenbacks on that.

He mashed the cigarette out in the ashtray and looked back down at the pillow. Six was the number of models they had worked with this trip; and six was what the old bitch had charged him for the room; and now here were six poisoned flies lying in his bed. The lingering stench of the bug spray began to burn his eyes and he dabbed at them with the end of the bedspread. "And what do these three sixes mean, Carl?" he asked himself out loud. Pulling out his knife, he fiddled with a hole in one of his molars while searching his mind for a suitable answer, one that avoided the most obvious implication of those three numbers, the biblical sign that his crazy old mother would have gleefully pointed out to him if she were still alive. "It means, Carl," he finally said, snapping his penknife shut, "that it's time to head home." And with a sweep of his hand, he brushed the tiny winged corpses off onto the dirty carpet and flipped the pillows over.

II

EARLIER THAT SAME DAY, BACK IN MEADE, OHIO, Sheriff Lee
Bodecker sat at his desk in an oak swivel chair eating a chocolate
bar and looking through some paperwork. He hadn't had a drink of
alcohol, not even a lousy beer, in two months, and his wife's doctor
had told her that sweets would take the edge off. Florence had spread
candy all over the house, even stuck hardtack under his pillow. Sometimes he woke himself up at night crunching on it, his throat sticky as
flypaper. If it weren't for the red sleeping capsules, he never would get
any rest. The worry in her voice, the way she babied him now, it made
him sick to think of how he'd let himself go. Although county elec-
tions were still over a year away, Hen Matthews was proving himself
to be a sore loser. His former boss was already playing dirty, spreading
shit about lawmen who can't catch crooks any better than they can
hold their liquor. But every candy bar Bodecker ate made him want
ten more, and his belly was starting to hang over his belt like a peck
sack of dead bullfrogs. If he kept it up, by the time he had to start
campaigning again he'd be as sloppy fat as his pig-faced brother-in-
law, Carl.

The telephone rang, and before he had a chance to say hello, an
old woman's reedy voice on the other end asked, "You the sheriff?"

"That's me," Bodecker said.

"You got a sister works at the Tecumseh?"

"Maybe," Bodecker said. "I ain't talked to her lately." From the
tone of the woman's voice, he could tell that this wasn't a friendly call.
He set the rest of the candy bar down on top of the paperwork. These
days, talk of his sister made Lee nervous. Back in 1958, when he had
come home from the army, he would have busted a gut laughing if
someone had suggested that shy, skinny Sandy was going to turn out

wild, but that was before she met up with Carl. Now he hardly recognized her. Several years back, Carl had talked her into quitting her job at the Wooden Spoon and moving to California. Though they were gone only a couple of weeks, when she returned something about her was different. She took a job tending bar at the Tecumseh, the roughest joint in town. Now she walked around in short skirts that barely covered her ass, her face painted up like one of the whores he had run off Water Street when he first got elected. "Been too busy chasing bad guys," he joked, trying to lighten the caller's mood a little. He glanced down and noticed a scuff mark on the toe of one of his new brown boots. He spit on his thumb and leaned over and tried to wipe it out.

"Oh, I bet you have," the woman said.

"You got some kind of problem?" Bodecker said.

"I sure do," the woman said viciously. "That sister of yours, she's been peddling her ass right out the back door of that filthy place for over a year now, but as far as I can see, Sheriff, you ain't never lifted a hand to stop it. Hard to tell how many good marriages she's broke up. Like I told Mr. Matthews just this morning, it makes a person wonder how you ever got elected, you havin' family like that."

"Who the hell is this?" Bodecker said, leaning forward in his chair.

"Ha!" the woman said. "I ain't falling for that. I know how the law operates in Ross County."

"We operate just fine," Bodecker said.

"That ain't what Mr. Matthews says." And with that, she hung up.

Slamming the receiver down, Bodecker pushed back his chair and stood up. He glanced at his watch and grabbed his keys off the top of the file cabinet. Just as he got to the door, he stopped and turned back to the desk. He rummaged around in the top drawer, found an open bag of butterscotch balls. He stuck a handful of them in his pocket.

As Bodecker passed by the front desk on his way out, the dispatcher, a young man with bulging green eyes and a flattop haircut, looked up from a dirty magazine he was reading. "Everything all right, Lee?" he asked.

His big face red with aggravation, the sheriff continued on without a word, then paused at the door and looked back. The dispatcher was holding the magazine up to the overhead light now, studying some naked female form tightly bound in leather straps and nylon rope, a balled-up pair of panties stuck in her mouth. "Willis," Bodecker said, "don't you let somebody walk in here and catch you looking at that damn cock book, you hear? I got enough people on my ass as it is."

"Sure, Lee," the dispatcher said. "I'll be careful." He started to turn another page.

"Jesus Christ, man, can't you take a hint?" Bodecker yelled. "Put that goddamn thing away."

As he drove over to the Tecumseh, he sucked on one of the butterscotch balls and thought about what the woman on the phone had said about Sandy whoring. Though he suspected that Matthews had put her up to the call just to fuck with him, he had to admit that he wouldn't be that surprised to find out it was true. A couple of banged-up beaters sat in the parking lot, along with an Indian motorcycle crusted over with dried mud. He took off his hat and badge and locked them in the trunk. The last time he'd been here, at the beginning of the summer, he had puked Jack Daniel's all over the pool table. Sandy had run everyone out early and closed the place up. He had lain on the sticky floor among the cigarette butts and hockers and spilled beer while she soaked up his mess off the green felt with towels. She then set a small fan down on the dry end of the table and turned it on. "Leroy's gonna shit when he sees this," she said, her hands on her skinny hips.

"Fuck that sumbitch," Bodecker mumbled.

"Yeah, that's easy for you to say," Sandy said, as she helped him get up off the floor and into a chair. "You don't have to work for the prick."

"I'll shut the goddamn place down," Bodecker said, flailing his arms wildly at the air. "I swear I will."

"Just settle down, big brother," she said. She wiped his face off with a soft, wet rag and fixed him a cup of instant coffee. Just as Bodecker started to take a sip, he dropped the cup. It shattered on the floor. "Jesus, I should have known better," Sandy said. "Come on, I better get you home."

"What kind of goddamn junker you drivin' now?" he slurred as she helped him into the front seat of her car.

"Honey, this ain't no junker," she said.

He looked around inside the station wagon, tried to focus his eyes. "What the fuck is it then?" he said.

"It's a limousine," Sandy said.

12

IN THE MOTEL BATHROOM, Sandy ran the tub full of water and peeled the wrapper off one of the candy bars she kept in her makeup bag for those days when Carl refused to stop and eat. He could go days without food when they were traveling, never thinking about anything but finding the next model. He could suck on those damn cigars and run that dirty knife through his fangs all he wanted, but she wasn't about to go to bed hungry.

The hot water relieved the itching between her legs, and she leaned back and closed her eyes as she nibbled on the Milky Way. The day they came across the Iowa boy, she had gotten off the main highway looking for a place to pull over and take a nap when he jumped up out of a soybean field looking like a scarecrow. As soon as the boy stuck his thumb out, Carl slapped his hands together and said, "Here we go." The hitchhiker was covered with mud and shit and bits of straw like he'd slept in a barnyard. Even with all the windows down, the rotten smell of him filled the car. Sandy knew it was hard to stay clean out on the road, but the scarecrow was the worst they'd ever picked up. Setting the candy bar on the edge of the tub, she took a deep breath and dunked her head under the water, listened to the faraway sound of her heart beating, tried to imagine it stopping forever.

They hadn't driven very far when the boy started chanting in a high-pitched voice, "California, here I come, California, here I come"; and she knew that Carl was going to be extra mean to this one because they just wanted to forget all about that goddamn place. At a gas station outside of Ames, she'd filled the car with gas and bought two bottles of orange screwdriver, thinking that might quiet the boy down some; but once he got a couple of sips in him, he started singing along to the radio, and that made things even worse. After the scarecrow squawked his sorry way through five or six songs, Carl leaned over to her and said, "By God, this bastard's gonna pay."

"I think he might be retarded or something," she said in a low voice, hoping Carl might let him go because he was superstitious that way.

Carl glanced back at the boy, then turned around and shook his head. "He's just stupid is all. Or a goddamn nutcase. There's a difference, you know."

"Well, at least turn the radio off," she suggested. "No sense egging him on."

"Fuck it, let him have his fun," Carl said. "I'll take the songbird out of him directly."

She dropped the candy wrapper on the floor and ran some more hot water. She hadn't argued at the time, but she wished to God now she hadn't touched the boy. She lathered up the washcloth and pushed the end of it inside her, squeezed her legs together. Out in the other room, Carl was talking to himself, but that usually didn't mean anything, especially right after they had finished with another model. Then he got a little louder, and she reached up and made sure the door was locked, just in case.

With the Iowa boy, they had parked at the edge of a garbage dump, and Carl had taken the camera out and started his spiel while he and the boy finished off the second bottle of screwdriver. "My wife loves to play around, but I'm just too damn old to get it up anymore," he told the boy that afternoon. "You know what I mean?"

Sandy had puffed on her cigarette, watched the scarecrow in the rearview mirror. He rocked back and forth, grinning wildly and nodding his head to everything that Carl said, his eyes blank as pebbles. For a moment, she thought she was going to vomit. It was more nerves than anything else, and the sick feeling passed quickly, like it always did. Then Carl suggested that they get out of the car, and while he spread a blanket on the ground, she reluctantly began taking off her clothes. The boy started up his damn singing again, but she put her finger to her lips and told him to be quiet for a little while.

"Let's have some fun now," she said, forcing a smile and patting a spot next to her on the blanket.

It took the Iowa boy longer than most to realize what was happening, but even then he didn't struggle too much. Carl took his time and managed at least twenty photos of junk sticking out of various places: lightbulbs and clothes hangers and soup cans. The light was starting to fade by the time he set the camera down and finished things off. He wiped his hands and knife on the boy's shirt, then walked around until he found a discarded Westinghouse refrigerator half buried in the trash. With the shovel from the car, he cleared the top off and pried the door open while Sandy went through the boy's pants. "That's it?" Carl said when she handed him a plastic whistle and an Indian head penny.

"What did you expect?" she said. "He don't even have a billfold." She glanced inside the icebox. The walls were covered with a thin coat of green mold, and a mason jar of gooey, gray jam lay smashed in one corner. "Jesus, you going to put him in there?"

"I'd say he's slept in worse places," Carl said.

They folded the boy double and crammed him inside the refrigerator, then Carl insisted on one last photo, one of Sandy in her red panties and bra getting ready to close the door. He squatted down and aimed the camera. "That's a good one," he said, after he clicked the shutter. "Real sweet." Then he stood up and stuck the boy's whistle in his mouth. "Go ahead and shut the goddamn thing. He can dream about California all he wants now." With the shovel, he began spreading trash over the top of the metal tomb.

The water grew cold, and she stepped out of the tub. She brushed her teeth and smeared some cold cream on her face and ran a comb through her wet hair. The army boy had been the best she'd had in a long time, and she planned to go to sleep tonight thinking about him. Anything to chase that damn scarecrow out of her head. When she came out of the bathroom in her yellow nightgown, Carl was lying on the bed, staring at the ceiling. It had been a week, she figured, since he'd bathed. She lit a cigarette and told him that he wasn't sleeping with her unless he washed the smell of those boys off.

"They're called models, not boys," he said. He rose up and swung his heavy legs off the bed. "How many times I got to tell you that?"

"I don't care what they're called," Sandy said. "That's a clean bed."

Carl glanced down at the flies on the rug. "Yeah, that's what you think," he said, heading for the bathroom. He peeled off his grimy clothes and sniffed himself. He happened to like the way he smelled, but maybe he should be more careful. Lately, he was beginning to worry that he was turning into some kind of fairy, and he suspected that Sandy thought the same thing. He tested the shower water with his hand, then stepped into the tub. He rubbed the bar of soap over his hairy, bloated body. Beating off to the photos wasn't a good sign, he knew that, but sometimes he couldn't help it. It was hard for him when they were back home, sitting alone in that crummy apartment night after night while Sandy was pouring drinks in the bar.

As he dried himself off, he tried to recall the last time they had made love. Last spring maybe, though he couldn't be sure. He tried to imagine Sandy young and fresh again, before all their shit started. Of course, he had soon found out about the cook who had taken her cherry and the one-nighters with the pimple-faced punks, but still, there was an air of innocence about her back then. Perhaps, he some-times thought, that was because he didn't have that much experience himself when he first met her. Sure, he'd slept with a few whores—the neighborhood had been full of them—but he'd only been in his mid-twenties when his mother had the stroke that left her paralyzed and practically speechless. By then, there hadn't been any boyfriends bang-ing on her door for several years, and so Carl was stuck with looking after her. For the first several months, he considered pressing a pillow over her twisted face and freeing them both, but she was his mother after all. Instead, he began applying himself to recording her long downward slide on film, a new photo of her shriveled-up body twice a week for the next thirteen years. Eventually, she got used to it. Then one morning he found her dead. He sat on the edge of the bed and tried to eat the egg he'd mashed up for her breakfast, but he couldn't get it down. Three days later, he tossed the first shovelful of dirt on her coffin.

Besides his camera, he had $217 left after paying for her funeral and a rickety Ford that would run only in dry weather. The odds of the car ever making it across the United States were slim to none, but he had dreamed of a new life almost as long as he had been alive, and now his best and last excuse was finally at peace in St. Margaret's Cemetery. And so, on the day before the rent ran out, he boxed up the curling stacks of sickbed photos and set them by the curb for the garbage truck. Then he drove west from Parson's Avenue to High Street and headed out of Columbus. His destination was Hollywood, but he had no sense of direction in those days, and somehow that evening he ended up in Meade, Ohio, and the Wooden Spoon. Looking back on it, Carl was convinced that fate had steered him there, but sometimes, when he remembered the soft, sweet Sandy of five years ago, he almost wished he had never stopped.

Shaking himself from his reverie, he squeezed some toothpaste into his mouth with one hand while fondling himself with the other. It took a few minutes, but finally he was ready. He walked out of the bathroom naked and a bit apprehensive, the purple tip of his hard-on pressing against his sagging, stretch-marked belly.

But Sandy was already asleep; and when he reached out and touched her shoulder, she opened her eyes and groaned. "I don't feel good," she said, turning over and curling up on the other side of the bed. Carl stood over her for a couple of minutes, breathing through his mouth, feeling the blood leave him. Then he turned the light off and went back into the bathroom. Fuck it, she didn't give a damn that he was asking for something important tonight. He sat down on the commode, and his hand fell between his legs. He saw the army boy's smooth, white body, and he picked up the wet washcloth off the floor and bit down on it. The sharp end of the leafy branch had initially been too big to fit in the bullet hole, but Carl had worked it back and forth until it stayed erect, looking like a young tree sprouting from Private Bryson's muscled chest. After he finished, he stood up and spit the washcloth into the sink. As he stared at his panting reflection in the mirror, Carl realized that there was a good chance he and Sandy would never make love again, that they were worse off than he had ever imagined.

Later that night, he awoke in a panic, his fat heart quivering in its ribbed cage like a trapped and frightened animal. According to the clock on the nightstand, he had been asleep less than an hour. He started to roll over, but then lurched out of bed and stumbled to the window, jerked the curtain open. Thank God, the station wagon was still sitting in the parking lot. "You dumb bastard," he said to himself. Pulling on his pants, he walked across the gravel to the car in his bare feet and unlocked the door. A mass of thick clouds hovered over him. He took the six rolls of film from the dash and carried them back to the room, stuffed them inside his shoes. He'd completely forgotten about them, a clear violation of his Rule #7. Sandy muttered something in her sleep about scarecrows or some such shit. Going back to the open doorway, Carl lit another of her cigarettes and stood looking out into the night. As he cursed himself for being so careless, the clouds shifted, revealing a small patch of stars off to the east. He squinted through the cigarette smoke and started to count them, but then he stopped and closed the door. One more number, one more sign, that wouldn't change a goddamn thing tonight.

13

THREE MEN WERE SITTING AT A TABLE drinking beer when Bodecker entered the Tecumseh Lounge. The dark room lit up with sunlight for a brief moment, casting the sheriff's long shadow across the floor. Then the door swung shut behind him and everything settled into gloom again. A Patsy Cline song came to a sad, quavering end on the jukebox. None of the men said a word as the sheriff walked past them toward the bar. One was a car thief and another a wife beater. They'd both spent time in his jail, waxed his cruiser on several occasions. Though he didn't know the third man, he figured it was just a matter of time.

Bodecker sat down on a stool and waited for Juanita to finish frying a hamburger on the greasy grill. He recalled that she had served him his first whiskey in this bar not so many years ago. He'd chased after the feeling he'd gotten that night for the next seven years, but never found it again. He reached in his pocket for one of the candies, then decided to hold off. She laid the sandwich on a paper plate along with a few potato chips she scooped out of a metal lard bucket and a long pale pickle she forked from a dirty glass jar. Carrying the plate to the table, she set it down in front of the car thief. Bodecker heard one of the men say something about covering up the pool table before somebody got sick. Another one laughed and he felt his face begin to burn. "You quit that," Juanita said in a low voice.

She went to the register and made the car thief's change and took it back to him. "These tater chips are stale," he told her.

"Then don't eat 'em," she said.

"Now, darling," the wife beater said, "that ain't no way to be."

Ignoring him, Juanita lit a cigarette and walked down to the end of the bar where Bodecker sat. "Hey, stranger," she said, "what can I get—"

"—and by God if her ass didn't drop open like a lunch bucket," one of the men said loudly just then, and the table erupted into laughter.

Juanita shook her head. "Can I borrow your gun?" she said to Bodecker. "Those bastards been in here since I opened up this morning."

He watched them in the long mirror that ran behind the bar. The car thief was giggling like a schoolgirl while the wife beater mashed the potato chips on the table with his fist. The third man was leaned back in his chair with a bored expression on his face, cleaning his fingernails with a matchstick. "I could run 'em out if you want," Bodecker said.

"Nah, that's okay," she said. "They'd just come back later wanting to give me some more grief." She blew smoke out of the side of her mouth and half smiled. She hoped her boy wasn't in trouble again. The last time, she'd had to borrow two weeks' pay to get him out of jail, all over five record albums he'd stuck down his pants at the Woolworth's. Merle Haggard or Porter Wagoner, that would have been bad enough, but Gerry and the Pacemakers? Herman's Hermits? The Zombies? Thank God his father was dead, that's all she could say. "So what can I do you for?"

Bodecker gazed for a moment at the bottles lined up behind the bar. "You got any coffee?"

"Just instant," she said. "Don't get many coffee drinkers in here."

He made a face. "That stuff hurts my stomach," he said. "How about a Seven-Up?"

After Juanita set the bottle of pop down in front of him, Bodecker lit a cigarette and said, "So Sandy ain't come in yet, huh?"

"Ha," Juanita said. "I wish. She's been gone over two weeks now."

"What? She quit?"

"No, nothing like that," the barmaid said. "She's on vacation."

"Again?"

"I don't know how they do it," Juanita said, lightening up, relieved that his visit didn't seem to have anything to do with her son. "I don't reckon they stay any place fancy, but I barely make enough here to pay the rent on that ol' trailer I live in. And you know damn well Carl ain't paying for none of it."

Bodecker took a sip of the pop and thought again about the phone call. So it probably was true, but if Sandy's been tricking for over a year, like the bitch said, why in the hell hadn't he heard about it before now? Maybe it was a good thing he had taken the pledge. The whiskey had evidently started turning his brain to mush. Then he glanced over at the pool table and considered other things he might have been careless about the past few months. A sudden cold chill swept over him. He had to swallow several times to keep the 7-Up from coming back up. "When she coming back?" he asked.

"She told Leroy she'd be home by the end of this week. I sure hope so. The tight ass won't hire no extra help."

"You got any idea where they were going?"

"It's hard to tell about that girl," Juanita said with a shrug. "She was talking about Virginia Beach, but I just can't picture Carl sunning himself by some ocean for two weeks, can you?"

Bodecker shook his head. "To tell you the truth, I can't picture that sonofabitch doing anything." Then he stood up and laid a dollar on the bar. "Look," he said, "when she gets back, tell her I need to talk to her, okay?"

"Sure, Lee, I'll do that," the barmaid said.

After he walked out the door, one of the men yelled, "Hey, Juanita, have you heard what Hen Matthews been saying about that big-headed bastard?"

14

A CAR DOOR SLAMMED in the parking lot. Carl opened his eyes, looked across the room at the flowers and fruit on the wall. The clock said it was still early morning, but he was already covered in sweat. He got out of bed and went to the bathroom, emptied his bladder. He didn't comb his hair or brush his teeth or wash his face. He dressed in the same clothes he'd worn for the past week, his purple shirt, a baggy pair of shiny, gray suit pants. Sticking the film canisters in his pockets, he sat on the edge of a chair and put his shoes on. He thought about waking Sandy up so they could get a move on, but then decided to let her rest. They'd slept in the car the past three nights. He figured he owed her that, and besides, they were going home anyway. No reason to hurry now.

While he waited for her to wake up, Carl chewed on a cigar and took the army boy's wad of money out of his pocket. As he counted it again, he remembered a time the year before when they were cutting across the lower end of Minnesota. They were clinging to their last three dollars when the radiator on this '49 Chevy coupe they were traveling in that summer blew a hole. He managed to temporarily seal the leak with a can of black pepper he carried for just such an emergency, a trick he'd heard about at a truck stop one time. They found a hick gas station a mile or so off the highway before it busted open again, ended up spending the bigger part of a day waiting around while some grease monkey with a pack of Red Man hanging out of his back pocket kept promising to fix it as soon as he finished a tune-up his boss wanted done yesterday. "Won't be long now, mister," he told Carl every fifteen fucking minutes. Sandy didn't help matters any. She parked her ass on a bench right outside the garage door and filed her nails and teased the poor bastard with glimpses of her pink underwear until he didn't know whether to shit or go blind, she had him so tore up.

Carl finally threw up his hands in disgust and got the rolls of film out of the glove box and locked himself in the restroom behind the station. He sat for several hours in that stinking sweatbox thumbing through a pile of ragged detective magazines stacked on the damp floor next to the filthy, crusted commode. Every once in a while, he heard the little bell ring around front, announcing another gas customer. A brown cockroach crawled sluggishly up the wall. He lit one of his dog dicks, thinking that might help move his bowels, but his insides were like cement. The best he could do was dribble a little blood now and then. His fat thighs grew numb. At one point, someone pounded on the door, but he wasn't about to give up his seat just so some no-good sonofabitch could wash his dainty hands.

He was about to wipe his bloody ass when he came across the article in a soggy copy of *True Crime*. He settled back down on the commode, flicked the ash off his cigar. The detective being interviewed in the story said that two male bodies had been found, one stuffed in a culvert near Red Cloud, Nebraska, and the other nailed to the floor of a shed on an abandoned farm outside Seneca, Kansas. "We're talking within a hundred miles of each other," the detective pointed out. Carl looked at the date on the cover of the magazine: November 1964. Hell, the story was already nine months old. He read the three pages over carefully five times. Though he refused to offer any specifics, the detective suggested there was a good chance the two murders were connected because of the *nature* of the crimes. So, judging from the condition of the remains, we're looking at the summer of 1963, thereabouts anyway, he said. "Well, at least you got the year right," Carl muttered to himself. That was their third time out, when they got those two. One was a runaway husband hoping to find a new beginning in Alaska and the other a tramp they'd seen scrounging for something to eat in a trash can behind a veterinarian's office. Those spikes had made for a damn good picture. There'd been a coffee can full of them right inside the door of the shed, like the Devil had set them there knowing that Carl was going to show up some day.

He cleaned himself off and wiped his sweaty hands on his pants. He tore the story out of the magazine and folded it, stuck the pages in his wallet. Whistling a little tune, he wet his comb in the sink and slicked back his thin, graying hair, squeezed a couple of whore bumps on his face. He found the grease monkey talking to Sandy in a low voice inside the garage. He had one skinny leg pressed up against hers. "Jesus Christ, it's about time," she said, when she looked up and saw him.

Ignoring her, Carl asked the mechanic, "Did you get it fixed?"

The man stepped away from Sandy, nervously stuck his greasy hands in the pockets of his coveralls. "I think so," he said. "I filled her up with water, and she's holdin' so far."

"What else did you fill up?" Carl said, eyeing him suspiciously.

"Nothing, not a thing, mister."

"Did you let it run awhile?"

"We ran it for ten minutes," Sandy said. "While you was back there in the can doing whatever you was doing."

"All right," Carl said. "What we owe you?"

The mechanic scratched his head, pulled out his pack of chew. "Oh, I don't know. Does five bucks sound all right?"

"Five bucks?" Carl said. "Hell, man, the way you been playing around with my ol' lady? She's gonna be sore for a week. I'll be damn lucky if you didn't knock her up."

"Four?" the mechanic said.

"Listen to this shit," Carl said. "You like to take advantage, don't you?" He glanced over at Sandy and she winked. "Okay, you throw in a couple of bottles of cold pop, I'll give you two dollars, but that's my final offer. My wife ain't just some cheap whore."

It was late in the evening by the time they drove out of there, and they slept in the car that night along a quiet country road. They shared a can of potted meat, using Carl's penknife for a spoon; and then Sandy climbed over the backseat and said good night. A short while later, just as he was starting to nod off in the front, a sharp spasm shot through Carl's guts and he fumbled for the door handle. Bolting from the car, he climbed over a drainage ditch that ran alongside the road. He jerked his pants down just in time, emptied a week's worth of nerves and junk into the weeds while holding on to the trunk of a pawpaw tree. After he cleaned himself off with some dead leaves, he stood outside the car in the moonlight and read the magazine story one more time. Then he took his lighter out and set it aflame. He decided not to mention it to Sandy. Sometimes she had a big mouth, and he didn't like to worry about what he might have to do to it on down the road.

15

THE DAY AFTER TALKING TO THE BARMAID at the Tecumseh, Bodecker drove over to the apartment where his sister and her husband lived on the east side of town. For the most part, he didn't give a damn how Sandy carried on her sorry life, but she wasn't going to peddle her snatch in Ross County, not as long as he was sheriff. Fucking around on Carl was one thing—hell, he couldn't blame her for that—but working it for money was something else entirely. Although Hen Matthews would try to shame him with dirt like that come election time, Bodecker was worried about it for other reasons. People are like dogs: once they start digging, they don't want to stop. First, it would just be that the sheriff had a whore for a sister, but eventually someone would find out about his dealings with Tater Brown; and after that, all the bribes and other shit that had piled up since he had first pinned on a badge. Looking back on it, he should have busted that thieving, pimp sonofabitch when he had a chance. A big arrest like that might have nearly wiped his slate clean. But he'd let his greed get the best of him, and now he was stuck in it for the long haul.

Parked in front of the shabby duplex, he watched a flatbed truck bulging with cattle turn into the stockyards across the street. The tangy smell of manure hung heavy in the hot August air. The old beater Sandy had hauled him home in that last night before he took the pledge was nowhere to be seen, but he got out of the cruiser anyway. He was pretty certain it had been a station wagon. He walked around the side of the house and climbed the rickety stairs that led to their door on the second floor. At the top was a little landing that Sandy called the patio. A sack of garbage lay overturned in one corner, green flies crawling over egg shells and coffee grounds and wadded-up hamburger wrappers. Next to the wooden railing sat a padded kitchen

chair and underneath it a coffee can half full of cigar butts. Carl and
Sandy were worse than the coloreds up on White Heaven and the
holler trash out in Knockemstiff, he thought, the way the two of them
lived. God, how he hated slobs. The prisoners in the county jail took
turns washing his cruiser every morning; the creases in his khaki pants
were as sharp as knives. He kicked an empty Dinty Moore can out of
the way and knocked on the door, but nobody answered.

As he started to leave, he heard a sliver of music coming from
somewhere close by. Looking over the railing, he saw a chubby
woman in a flowered swimsuit lying on a yellow blanket in the yard
next door. The rusted frames and parts of old motorcycles were scattered around her in the tall grass. Her brown hair was pinned on top
of her head, and she held a tiny transistor radio in her hand. She was
slathered with baby oil, shiny as a new penny in the bright sun. He
watched as she twisted the dial around searching for another station,
heard the faint twang of some hillbilly song about heartbreak. Then
she set the radio on the edge of the blanket and closed her eyes. Her
slick belly rose and fell. She turned over, then raised her head and
glanced around. Satisfied that no one was watching, she undid the top
of the bathing suit. After a moment's hesitation, she reached down
and tugged the lower half up to reveal three or four inches of the
white cheeks of her ass.

Bodecker lit a cigarette and started back down the stairs. He
imagined his brother-in-law sitting out here in the sun sweating
buckets and trying to get his eyes full. It was easy enough to do,
the way the woman lay spread out there for anybody to see. Taking
pictures seemed to be the only thing that Carl thought about, and
Bodecker wondered if he ever took any of the neighbor without her
knowing it. Though he wasn't sure, he figured there was a law against
shit like that. And if there wasn't, there sure as hell ought to be.

16

BY THE TIME THEY LEFT THE SUNDOWNER, it was noon. Sandy had woken up at eleven, then spent an hour in the bathroom getting ready. She was only twenty-five, but her brown hair was already beginning to show traces of gray. Carl worried about her teeth, which had always been her best feature. They were stained an ugly yellow from all the cigarettes. He'd noticed, too, that her breath was bad all the time now, regardless of how many mints she consumed. Something was starting to rot inside her mouth, he was sure of it. Once they got back home, he needed to get her to a dentist. He hated to think of the expense, but a nice smile was an important part of his photographs, providing a needed contrast to all the pain and suffering. Though he'd tried time and time again, Carl had yet to get one of the models to fake even a little smirk once he took the gun out and started on them. "Girl, I know sometimes it's hard, but I need you to look happy if these are gonna turn out good," he told Sandy, whenever he'd done something to one of the men that upset her. "Just think of that Mona Lisa picture. Pretend you're her hanging up on the wall in that museum."

They hadn't driven but a few miles when Sandy braked suddenly and pulled into a little diner called the Tiptop. It was shaped somewhat like a wigwam and painted different shades of red and green. The parking lot was nearly full. "What the hell are you doing?" Carl said.

Sandy shut off the engine, stepped out of the car, went around to the passenger's side. "I ain't drivin' another mile until I get some real food," she said. "I been eating nothing but candy for three days. Shit, my teeth are getting loose."

"Jesus Christ, we just got on the road," Carl said, as she turned and started walking toward the diner door. "Hold up," he yelled. "I'm coming."

After locking the car, he followed her inside and they found a booth near a window. The waitress brought two cups of coffee and a ragged menu spattered with ketchup. Sandy ordered French toast and Carl asked for a side of crisp bacon. She put her sunglasses on, watched a man in a stained apron try to install a new roll of paper in the cash register. The place reminded her of the Wooden Spoon. Carl looked around the crowded room, farmers and old people mostly, a couple of haggard salesmen studying a list of prospects. Then he noticed a young man, early twenties maybe, sitting at the counter eating a piece of lemon meringue pie. Sturdy build, thick, wavy hair. A backpack with a small American flag sewn on it leaned against the stool beside him.

"So?" Carl said, after the waitress brought the food. "You feeling any better today?" As he talked, he kept one bloodshot eye on the man at the counter, the other on their car.

Sandy swallowed and shook her head. She poured some more syrup on the French toast. "That's something we need to talk about," she said.

"What is it?" he asked, pulling the burnt rind off a slice of the bacon and sticking it in his mouth. Then he took a cigarette from her pack and rolled it between his fingers. He shoved what remained on his plate over to her.

She took a sip of her coffee, glanced at the table of people next to them. "It can wait," she said.

The man at the counter stood up and handed the waitress some money. Then he slung the backpack over his shoulder with a weary groan and went out the door with a toothpick stuck in his mouth. Carl watched him go to the edge of the road and try to thumb a passing car. The car went on without stopping, and the man started walking west at a lazy pace. Carl turned to Sandy, nodded toward the window. "Yeah, I seen him," she said. "Big deal. They're all over the place. They're like cockroaches."

Carl watched the road for traffic while Sandy finished eating. He thought about his decision to head home today. The signs were so clear to him last night, but now he wasn't so sure. One more model would jinx the three sixes, but they could drive for a week and not find another who looked like that boy. He knew better than to fuck with the signs, but then he recalled that *seven* was the number of their room last night. And not a single car had passed by since the boy left. He was out there right now, looking for a ride in the hot sun.

"Okay," Sandy said, wiping her mouth with a paper napkin, "I can drive now." She got up and reached for her purse. "Better not keep the fucker waiting."

PART THREE

Orphans and Ghosts

17

ARVIN WAS SENT TO LIVE WITH HIS GRANDMOTHER right after his father's suicide, and though Emma made sure that he went to church with Lenora and her every Sunday, she never asked him to pray or sing or kneel at the altar. The welfare people from Ohio had told the old woman about the terrible summer the boy had endured while his mother was dying, and she decided not to push anything other than regular attendance on him. Knowing that Reverend Sykes was prone to be a little too zealous at times in his attempts at bringing hesitant newcomers into the fold, Emma had gone to him a couple of days after Arvin's arrival and explained that her grandson would come into the faith his own way when he was ready. Hanging roadkill from crosses and pouring blood on logs had secretly impressed the old preacher—after all, weren't all the famous Christians fanatical in their beliefs?—but he went ahead and agreed with Emma that maybe that wasn't the best way to introduce a young person to the Lord. "I see what you're getting at," Sykes said. "No sense turning him into one of them Topperville nut jobs." He was sitting on the church steps peeling a bruised yellow apple with a pocketknife. It was a sunny September morning. He wore his good suit coat over a pair of faded bib overalls and a white shirt starting to unravel around the collar. Lately, his chest had been hurting him, and Clifford Odell was supposed to give him a ride to a new doctor over in Lewisburg, but he hadn't shown up yet. Sykes had overheard someone at Banner's store say that the sawbones had gone to college for six years, and he was looking forward to meeting him. He figured a man with that much education could cure anything.

"What's that supposed to mean, Albert?" Emma asked.

Sykes glanced up from the apple and saw the hard look the

woman was giving him. It took him a moment to realize what he had said, and his wrinkled face flushed red with embarrassment. "I'm sorry, Emma," he sputtered. "I wasn't talking about Willard, no way. He was a good man. One of the best. Shoot, I still remember the day he got saved."

"That's all right," she said. "No sense buttering up the dead, Albert. I know what my son was like. Just don't go pestering his boy, that's all I ask."

LENORA, ON THE OTHER HAND, couldn't seem to get enough of her religion. She carried a Bible with her everywhere she went, even to the outhouse, just like Helen had; and each morning, she got up before everyone else and prayed for an hour on her knees on the splintered wooden floor beside her and Emma's bed. Although she had no memory of either of her parents, the girl directed most of the prayers that she let Emma hear on her murdered mother's soul and most of her silent ones on some news of her missing father. The old woman had told her time and time again that it would be best to forget about Roy Laferty, but Lenora couldn't help wondering about him. Nearly every night, she fell asleep with an image of him stepping up on the porch in a new black suit and making everything all right. It gave her a small comfort, and she allowed herself to hope that, with the Lord's help, her father really would return someday if he was still alive. Several times a week, no matter what the weather, she visited the cemetery and read the Bible out loud, especially the Psalms, while seated on the ground next to her mother's grave. Emma had once told her that the book of Songs was Helen's favorite part of the Scriptures, and by the time she finished the sixth grade, Lenora knew them all by heart.

THE SHERIFF HAD LONG SINCE GIVEN UP on finding Roy and Theodore. It was as if they had turned into ghosts. Nobody was able to find a photograph or record of any kind on either of them. "Hell, even the retards up in Hungry Holler got birth certificates," he offered as an excuse, whenever one of his constituents brought up the two's disappearance. He didn't mention to Emma the rumor that he'd heard right after they disappeared, that the cripple was in love with Roy, that there might have been some queer homo thing going on between them before the preacher married Helen. During the initial investigation, several people testified that Theodore had complained bitterly that the woman had taken the edge off Roy's spiritual message. "It's ruined many a good man, that ol' nasty hair pie," the cripple was heard to say after he'd had a few drinks. "Preacher, shit," he'd go on, "all he thinks about now is getting his dick wet." It irked the sheriff to no end that those two sodomite fools might have committed murder in his county and gotten away with it; and so he kept repeating the same old story, that in all likelihood the same maniac that butchered the Millersburg family had also killed Helen and hacked Roy and Theodore to pieces or dumped their bodies in the Greenbrier River. He told it so much that he half believed it himself at times.

THOUGH ARVIN NEVER CAUSED HER any serious trouble, Emma could easily see Willard in him, especially when it came to the fighting. By the time he was fourteen, he had been kicked out of school several times for using his fists. Pick your own time, he remembered his father telling him, and Arvin learned that lesson well, catching whoever his enemy happened to be at the moment alone and unaware in the restroom or stairwell or under the bleachers in the gymnasium. For the most part, however, he was known throughout Coal Creek for his easygoing ways, and to his credit, most of the scraps he got caught up in were because of Lenora, defending her from bullies who made fun of her pious manner and pinched face and that damn bonnet she insisted on wearing. Though just a few months younger than Arvin, she already seemed dried up, a pale winter spud left too long in the furrow. He loved her like his own sister, but it could be embarrassing, walking into the schoolhouse in the morning with her following meekly on his heels. "She ain't never gonna make cheerleader, that's for sure," he told Uncle Earskell. He wished to hell his grandmother had never given her the black-and-white photograph of Helen standing under the apple tree behind the church in a long, shapeless dress with a ruffled hat covering her head. As far as he was concerned, Lenora certainly didn't need any new ideas on how to make herself look more like the shade of her pitiful mother.

WHENEVER EMMA ASKED HIM about the fighting, Arvin always thought of his father and that damp fall day long ago when he had defended Charlotte's honor in the Bull Pen parking lot. Though it was the best day he ever remembered spending with Willard, he never told anybody about it, or, for that matter, mentioned any of the bad days that soon followed. Instead, he would simply say to her, his father's voice echoing faintly in his head, "Grandma, there's a lot of no-good sonsofbitches out there."

"My Lord, Arvin, why do you keep saying that?"

"Because it's true."

"Well, maybe you should try praying for them then," she'd suggest. "That wouldn't hurt none, would it?" It was times like this when she regretted ever telling Reverend Sykes to leave the boy to find the path to God on his own terms. As far as she could tell, Arvin was always on the verge of heading the other direction.

He rolled his eyes; that was her advice for everything. "Maybe not," he said, "but Lenora already does enough of that for the both of us, and I don't see where it's doing her much good."

18

THEY SHARED A TENT DOWN AT THE END of the midway with
the Flamingo Lady, a rail-thin woman with the longest nose Roy had
ever seen on a human being. "She ain't really a bird, is she?" Theodore asked him after the first time they met her, his usual brash voice
turned timid and shaky. Her strange appearance had frightened him.
They had worked with freaks before, but nothing that looked quite
like this one.

"No," Roy assured him. "She's just putting on a show."

"I didn't think so," the cripple said, relieved to find out that she
wasn't real. He looked over and noticed Roy checking out her ass
as she walked toward her trailer. "Hard to tell what kind of diseases
something like that's got," he added, his cockiness quickly returning
once he was satisfied she was out of hearing range. "Women like that,
they'll fuck a dog or a donkey or anything else for a buck or two."

The Flamingo Lady's wild, bushy hair was dyed pink, and she
wore a bikini that had ragged pigeon feathers glued to the flesh-
colored material. Her act consisted mostly of standing on one leg in
a little rubber swimming pool filled with dirty water while preening
herself with her pointy beak. A record player sat on a table behind her
playing slow, sad violin music that sometimes made her cry if she had
accidentally taken too many of her nerve pills that day. Just as he had
feared, Theodore figured out after a couple of months that Roy was
tapping it, though try as he might, he could never actually catch them
in the filthy act. "That ugly bitch is gonna hatch an egg one of these
days," he railed at Roy, "and I'd bet a dollar to a doughnut the goddamn chick will look just like you." Sometimes he cared; sometimes
he didn't. It depended on how he and Flapjack the Clown were getting along at the moment. Flapjack had come to Theodore wanting to

learn a few chords on the guitar, but then he'd showed the cripple how to play the skin flute instead. Roy once made the mistake of pointing out to his cousin that what he and the clown were doing was an abomination in the eyes of God. Theodore had set his guitar down on the sawdust floor and spit some brown juice in a paper cup. He'd recently taken to chewing tobacco. It made him a little sick to his stomach, but Flapjack liked the way it made his breath smell. "Damn, Roy, if you ain't a good one to talk, you crazy bastard," he said.

"What the hell does that mean? I ain't no peter puffer."

"Maybe not, but you sure as hell murdered your old lady with that screwdriver, didn't you? You ain't forgot about that, have you?"

"I ain't forgot," Roy said.

"Well then, you figure the Lord thinks any worse of me than He does of you?"

Roy hesitated for a minute before answering. According to what he had read in a pamphlet that he had found under a pillow in a Salvation Army shelter one time, a man laying with another man was probably equal to killing your wife, but Roy wasn't sure if it was any worse or not. The manner in which the weight of certain sins was calculated sometimes confused him. "No, I don't reckon," he finally said.

"Then I suggest you stick to your pink-haired crow or pelican or whatever the hell she is and leave me and Flapjack the fuck alone," Theodore said, digging the wet wad of chew out of his mouth and slinging it toward the Flamingo Lady's wading pool. They both heard a tiny splash. "We ain't hurting nobody."

The banner outside the tent read THE PROPHET AND THE PICKER. Roy delivered his grisly version of the End Times while Theodore provided the background music. It cost a quarter to get inside the tent, and convincing people that religion could be entertaining was tough when just a few yards away were a number of other more exciting and less serious distractions, so Roy came up with the idea of eating insects during his sermon, a slightly different take on his old spider act. Every couple of minutes, he'd stop preaching and pull a squirming worm or crunchy roach or slimy slug out of an old bait bucket and chew on it like a piece of candy. Business picked up after that.

Depending on the crowd, they did four, sometimes five shows every evening, alternating with the Flamingo Lady every forty-five minutes. At the end of each show, Roy would quickly step out behind the tent to regurgitate the bugs and Theodore would follow in his wheelchair. While waiting to go on again, they smoked and sipped from a bottle, half listened to the drunks inside whoop and holler and try to coax the fake bird into stripping off her plumes.

By 1963, they had been with this particular carnival, Billy Bradford Family Amusements, for almost four years, traveling from one end of the hot, humid South to the other from early spring until late fall in a retired school bus packed with moldering canvas and folding chairs and metal poles, always setting up in dusty, pig-shit towns where the locals thought a couple of creaky whirly rides and some toothless, flea-bitten jungle cats along with a tattered freak show was high-class entertainment. On a good night, Roy and Theodore could make twenty or thirty bucks. The Flamingo Lady and Flapjack the Clown got most of what they didn't spend on booze or bugs or at the hot dog stand. West Virginia seemed like a million miles away, and the two fugitives couldn't imagine the arm of the law in Coal Creek ever stretching that far. It had been nearly fourteen years since they had buried Helen and fled south. They didn't even bother to change their names anymore.

19

ON ARVIN'S FIFTEENTH BIRTHDAY, Uncle Earskell handed him a pistol wrapped in a soft cloth along with a dusty box of shells. "This was your daddy's," the old man told him. "It's a German Luger. Brought it back from the war. I figure he'd want you to have it." The old man had never had any use for handguns, and so he'd hid it away under a floorboard in the smokehouse right after Willard left for Ohio. The only time he'd touched it since was to clean it occasionally. Seeing the elated look on the boy's face, he was glad now he'd never broken down and sold it. They had just finished supper, and there was one piece of fried rabbit left on the platter in the middle of the table. Earskell debated whether or not to save the haunch for his breakfast, then picked it up and started gnawing on it.

Arvin unwrapped the cloth carefully. The only gun his father had kept at home was a .22 rifle, and Willard never allowed him to touch it, let alone shoot it. Earskell, on the other hand, had handed the boy a 16-gauge Remington and took him to the woods just three or four weeks after he came to live with them. "In this house, you better know how to handle a gun unless you want to starve to death," the old man had told him.

"But I don't want to shoot anything," Arvin said that day, when Earskell stopped and pointed out two gray squirrels jumping back and forth on some branches high in a hickory tree.

"Didn't I see you eatin' a pork chop this morning?"

"Yeah."

The old man shrugged his shoulders. "Somebody had to kill that hog and butcher it, didn't they?"

"I guess so."

Earskell lifted his own shotgun then and fired. One of the squirrels fell to the ground, and the old man started toward it. "Just try not to tear 'em up too bad," he said over his shoulder. "You want to have something left to put in the pan."

The coat of oil made the Luger shine like new in the wavering light cast from the kerosene lamps hanging at both ends of the room. "I never did hear him talk about it," Arvin said, lifting the gun up by the grip and pointing it toward the window. "About being in the service, I mean." There had been quite a few things his mother had warned him about when it came to his father, and asking questions about what he had seen in the war was high on the list.

"Yeah, I know," Earskell said. "I remember when he got back, I wanted him to tell me about the Japs, but anytime I brought it up, he'd start in about your mother again." He finished the rabbit and laid the bone on his plate. "Hell, I don't think he even knew her name at the time. Just saw her waiting tables in some eatin' place when he was coming home."

"The Wooden Spoon," Arvin said. "He took me there once after she got sick."

"I think he saw some rough things over on them islands," the old man said. He looked around for a rag, then wiped his hands on the front of his overalls. "I never did find out if they ate their dead or not."

Arvin bit his lip and swallowed hard. "This is the best present I ever got."

Just then, Emma entered the kitchen carrying a plain yellow cake in a small pan. A single candle was planted in the middle of it. Lenora followed behind dressed in the long blue dress and bonnet that she usually wore only to church. She held a box of matches in one hand and her cracked leather Bible in the other. "What's that?" Emma said when she saw Arvin holding the Luger.

"That's Willard's gun he give me," Earskell said. "I figured it was time to pass it on to the boy."

"Oh, my," Emma said. She set the cake down on the table and grabbed up the hem of her checkered apron to wipe back a tear. Seeing the gun reminded her once again of her son and the promise she'd failed to keep all those years ago. Sometimes she couldn't help but wonder if they would all still be alive today if she had only convinced Willard to stay here and marry Helen.

Everyone was silent for a moment, almost as if they knew what the old woman was thinking. Then Lenora struck a match and said in a singsong voice, "Happy birthday, Arvin." She lit the candle, the same one they had used to celebrate her fourteenth birthday a few months ago.

"It ain't much use for anything," Earskell went on, ignoring the cake and nodding at the gun. "You got to be right up on something to hit it."

"Go ahead, Arvin," Lenora said.

"Might as well throw a rock," the old man joked.

"Arvin?"

"The shotgun will do you more good."

"Make your wish before the candle burns out," Emma said.

"Them's nine-millimeter shells," Earskell pointed out. "Banner don't carry them at the store, but he can order them special."

"Better hurry!" Lenora yelled.

"Okay, okay," the boy said, setting the gun down on the cloth. He bent down and blew out the tiny flame.

"So what did you wish for?" Lenora asked. She hoped it had something to do with the Lord, but the way Arvin was, she wasn't going to hold her breath. Every night, she prayed that he would wake up with a love for Jesus Christ glowing in his heart. She hated to think that he was going to end up in hell like that Elvis Presley and all those other sinners he listened to on the radio.

"Now you know better than to ask that," Emma said.

"That's all right, Grandma," Arvin said. "I wished that I could take you all back to Ohio and show you where we lived. It was nice, up there on the hill. At least it was before Mom took sick."

"Did I ever tell you about the time I lived in Cincinnati?" Earskell said.

Arvin looked at the two women and winked. "No," he said, "I don't recall it."

"Lord, not again," Emma muttered, while Lenora, smiling to herself, lifted the stub of the candle off the cake and put it in the matchbox.

"Yep, followed me a girl up there," the old man said. "She was from over on Fox Knob, was raised right next to the Riley place. Her house ain't there no more. Wanted to go to secretary school. I wasn't much older than you are now."

"Who wanted to go to secretary school," Arvin asked, "you or the girl?"

"Ha! Her did," Earskell said. He took a long breath, then slowly let it out. "Her name was Alice Louise Berry. You remember her, don't you, Emma?"

"Yes, I do, Earskell."

"So why didn't you stay?" Arvin said, without thinking. Though he had heard parts of the story a hundred times, he'd never before asked the old man why he had ended up back in Coal Creek. From living with his father, Arvin had learned that you didn't pry too much into other people's affairs. Everyone had things they didn't want to talk about, including himself. In the five years since his parents had passed, he had never once mentioned the hard feelings he held against Willard for leaving him. Now he felt like an ass for opening his mouth and putting the old man on the spot. He began wrapping the pistol back up in the cloth.

Earskell peered across the room with dim, cloudy eyes as if he was searching for the answer in the flowered wallpaper, though he knew the reason well enough. Alice Louise Berry had died in the influenza epidemic of 1918, along with 3 million or so other poor souls, just a few weeks after starting her classes at the Gilmore Sanderson Secretarial School. If only they had stayed in the hills, Earskell often thought, she might still be alive. But Alice always had big dreams, which was one of the things he had loved about her, and he was glad that he hadn't tried to talk her out of it. He was certain those days they spent in Cincinnati among the tall buildings and crowded streets before she took the fever were the happiest ones of her life. His, too, for that matter. After a minute or so, he blinked away the memories and said, "That sure looks like a dandy cake."

Emma took up her knife and cut it into four pieces, one for each of them.

20

ONE DAY ARVIN WENT LOOKING FOR LENORA after school let out
and found her backed up against the trash incinerator next to the bus
garage, surrounded by three boys. As he walked up behind them, he
heard Gene Dinwoodie tell her, "Hell, you're so damn ugly I'd have
to put a sack over your head before I could get a hard-on." The other
two, Orville Buckman and Tommy Matson, laughed and squeezed
in closer to her. They were seniors who had been held back a year or
two, and all of them were bigger than Arvin. They spent most of their
time at school sitting in the shop building trading dirty jokes with
the worthless industrial arts teacher and smoking Bugler. Lenora had
shut her eyes tight and begun praying. Tears were running down her
pink face. Arvin got only a couple of licks in on Dinwoodie before
the others tackled him to the ground and took turns punching him.
While he was lying in the gravel, he thought, as he often did when in
the middle of a fight, of the hunter that his father had beaten so badly
that day in the outhouse mud. But unlike that man, Arvin never gave
up. They might have killed him if the janitor hadn't come along with
a cart of cardboard boxes to burn. His head ached for a week, and he
had trouble reading the blackboard for several more.

Though it took him almost two months, Arvin managed to
catch each of them alone. One evening right before dark, he followed
Orville Buckman to Banner's store. He stood behind a tree a hundred
yards down the road and watched the boy come back out swigging a
pop and eating the last of a Little Debbie. Just as Orville started past
him with the bottle tipped up to take another drink, Arvin stepped
out into the road. He smacked the bottom of the Pepsi bottle with the
palm of his hand and sent the glass neck halfway down the big boy's
throat, breaking two of his rotten front teeth off. By the time Orville

realized what had hit him, the fight was pretty much finished except for the blow that put his lights out. An hour later, he woke up lying in the ditch along the road choking on blood and a paper sack over his head.

A couple of weeks later, Arvin drove Earskell's old Ford over to the Coal Creek High School basketball game. They were playing the team from Millersburg, which always brought a big turnout. He sat in the car smoking Camel cigarettes and watching the front door for Tommy Matson to show his face. It was drizzling rain, a chilly, dark Friday night in early November. Matson liked to think of himself as the school cock-hound, was always bragging about the pussy he picked up at the games while their stupid boyfriends scrambled up and down the gym floor chasing a rubber ball. Right before halftime, just as Arvin flipped another butt out the window, he saw his next target walk outside with his arm around a freshman girl named Susie Cox and head to the row of school buses parked in the back of the lot. Arvin got out of the Ford carrying a tire iron and followed them. He watched Matson open the rear door of one of the yellow buses and help Susie up inside. After waiting a few minutes, Arvin twisted the handle on the door and let it swing open with a raspy squeak. "What was that?" he heard the girl say.

"Nothing," Matson told her. "I must not got it shut all the way. Now come on, girl, let's get them bloomers off."

"Not until you close that door," she said.

"Goddamn it," Matson grumbled, raising up off her. "You better be worth it." He walked down the narrow aisle holding his pants up with one hand.

When he leaned out to grab the latch and pull the door back, Arvin swung the tire iron and hit Matson across the kneecaps, toppling him out of the bus. "Jesus!" he yelled when he hit the gravel, landing hard on his right shoulder. Swinging the tire iron again, Arvin cracked two of his ribs, then kicked him until he stopped trying to get up. He took a paper bag out of his jacket and knelt down beside the moaning boy. Grabbing hold of Matson's curly hair, he pulled his head up. The girl inside the bus didn't make a peep.

The next Monday at school, Gene Dinwoodie walked up to Arvin in the cafeteria and said, "I'd like to see you try and put a sack over my head, you sonofabitch."

Arvin was sitting at a table with Mary Jane Turner, a new girl at the school. Her father had grown up in Coal Creek, then spent fifteen years in the merchant marine before returning home to claim his inheritance, a run-down farm on the side of a hill that his grandfather had left him. The redheaded girl could curse like a sailor when the opportunity presented itself, and though Arvin wasn't sure why, he liked that a lot, especially when they were making out. "Leave us alone, you dumb prick," she said, glaring scornfully at the tall boy standing over them. Arvin smiled.

Ignoring her, Gene said, "Russell, after I get done with you, I might just take your little girlfriend out for a nice long ride. She ain't no beauty queen, but I gotta say, she's not nearly as bad as that rat-faced sister of yours." He stood over the table with his fists clenched, waiting for Arvin to leap up and start swinging, then watched dumbfounded as the boy closed his eyes and put his hands together. "You got to be shittin' me." Gene looked around the crowded lunchroom. The gym teacher, a burly man with a red beard who wrestled for extra money in Huntington and Charleston on the weekends, was scowling at him. The rumor around the school was that he'd never been pinned, and that he won all his matches because he hated everybody and everything in West Virginia. Even Gene was afraid of him. Leaning over, he said to Arvin in a low voice, "Don't think praying's gonna get you out of this, motherfucker."

After Gene walked away, Arvin opened his eyes and took a drink from a carton of chocolate milk. "Are you all right?" Mary said.

"Sure," he said. "Why you ask that?"

"Were you really praying?"

"I was," he said, nodding his head. "Praying for the right time."

He finally caught Dinwoodie a week later in his old man's garage changing a spark plug in his '56 Chevy. By then, Arvin had collected a dozen paper bags. Gene's head was tightly encased in them when his younger brother found him several hours later. The doctor said he was lucky that he hadn't suffocated. "Arvin Russell," Gene told the sheriff after he came to his senses. He'd spent the last twelve hours in the hospital believing that he was running dead last in a race at the Indy 500. It had been the longest night of his life; every time he stomped the accelerator, the car slowed down to a crawl. The roar of the engines passing him by was still ringing in his ears.

"Arvin Russell?" the sheriff, a hint of doubt in his voice. "I know that boy likes to scrap, but hell, son, you twice as big as he is."

"He caught me off guard."

"So you seen him before he put that knot on your head?" the sheriff asked.

"No," Gene said, "but he's the one."

"And how exactly do you know this?"

Gene's father was leaning against the wall watching his son with sullen, bloodshot eyes. The boy could smell the Wild Irish Rose wafting off his old man clear across the room. Carl Dinwoodie wasn't too bad if he stuck to beer, but when he got on the wine, he could be downright dangerous. This might come back to bite me in the ass if I'm not careful, Gene thought. His mother went to the same church as the Russell bunch. His father would kick the shit out of him all over again if he heard he'd been harassing that little Lenora bitch. "I could be wrong," Gene said.

"Why did you say the Russell boy did it then?" the sheriff said.

"I don't know. Maybe I dreamed it."

Over in the corner, Gene's father made a sound like a dog retching, then said, "Nineteen years old and still in school. What you think about that, Sheriff? Worthless as tits on a boar hog, ain't he?"

"Who we talking about?" the sheriff said, a puzzled look on his face.

"That no-account thing laying right there in that bed, that's who," Carl said, then turned and staggered out the door.

The sheriff looked back to the boy. "Well, any idea why whoever did do it put them sacks over your head like that?"

"No," Gene said. "Not a clue."

21

"WHAT YOU GOT THERE?" Earskell said, as Arvin stepped up onto
the porch. "I heard you over in there shooting that pop gun." His cat-
aracts were getting worse every week, like dirty curtains being slowly
pulled shut in an already dim room. A couple more months and he
was afraid he wouldn't be able to drive anymore. Getting old was next
to the worst goddamn thing that had ever happened to him. Lately,
he'd been thinking about Alice Louise Berry more and more. They
had both missed out on a lot, her dying so young.

Arvin held up three red squirrels. He had his father's pistol stuck
in the waistband of his pants. "We'll eat good tonight," he said.
Emma had served nothing but beans and fried potatoes for four days
now. Things always got lean toward the end of the month, before her
pension check came. Both he and the old man were starving for some
meat.

Earskell leaned forward in his chair. "You surely didn't get those
with that German piece of shit, did you?" Secretly, he was proud of
the way the boy could handle the Luger, but he still didn't think much
of handguns. He'd rather have a pepper gun or a rifle any day.

"It ain't a bad gun," Arvin said. "You just got to know how to
shoot it." It was the first time the old man had ridiculed the pistol in
quite a while.

Earskell laid down the implement catalog he'd been peering
through all morning and pulled his penknife out of his pocket. "Well,
go fetch us something to put 'em in, and I'll help you clean 'em."

Arvin pulled the skins off the squirrels while the old man held
them by their front legs. They gutted the carcasses on a sheet of newspaper and cut the heads and feet off and laid the bloody meat in a pan
of salted water. After they finished, Arvin folded up the mess in the
paper and carried it out to the edge of the yard. Earskell waited until

he came back up on the porch, then pulled a pint out of his pocket and took a drink. Emma had asked him to talk to the boy. She was at her wit's end after hearing about the latest incident. He wiped his mouth and said, "Played cards over at Elder Stubb's garage last night."

"So did you win?"

"No, not really," Earskell said. He stretched his legs out, looked down at his battered shoes. He was going to have to try mending them again. "Saw Carl Dinwoodie there."

"Yeah?"

"He wasn't none too happy."

Arvin sat down on the other side of his great-uncle in a creaky cast-off kitchen chair held together with baling wire. He studied the gray woods across the road and chewed at the inside of his mouth for a minute. "He pissed off about Gene?" he asked. It had been over a week since he'd bagged the sonofabitch.

"A little maybe, but I think he's more ticked off about the hospital bill he's gonna have to pay." Earskell looked down at the squirrels floating in the pan. "So what happened?"

Though Arvin didn't ever see the point of offering up any details to his grandmother for beating the shit out of someone, mostly because he didn't want to upset her, he knew the old man wouldn't be satisfied with anything other than the facts. "He's been teasing Lenora, him and a couple of his candy-ass buddies," he said. "Calling her names, shit like that. So I fixed his wagon for him."

"What about the others?"

"Them, too."

Earskell heaved a long sigh, scratched at the whiskers on his neck. "You think maybe you should have held back just a little bit? Boy, I understand what you're saying, but still, you can't go sending people to the hospital over some name-calling. Puttin' a couple knots on his head is one thing, but from what I hear, you hurt him pretty bad."

"I don't like bullies."

"Jesus Christ, Arvin, you going to meet lots of people you might not take a liking to."

"Maybe so, but I bet he won't pick on Lenora anymore."

"Look, I want you to do me a favor."

"What's that?"

"Stick that Luger away in a drawer and forget about it for now."

"Why?"

"Handguns ain't made for hunting. They're for killin' people."

"But I didn't shoot the bastard," Arvin said. "I beat him up."

"Yeah, I know. This time anyway."

"What about them squirrels? I hit every one of them in the head. You can't do that with no shotgun."

"Just put it up for a while, okay? Use the rifle if you want to go after some game."

The boy studied the floor of the porch for a moment, then looked up at the old man with narrowed, suspicious eyes. "He get mouthy with you?"

"You mean Carl?" Earskell asked. "No, he knows better than that." He didn't see any sense in telling Arvin that he had drawn a royal flush on the last and biggest pot of the night, or that he had folded so that Carl could take the money home with two pissy pair. Though he knew it had been the right thing to do, it still made him half sick thinking about it. There must have been two hundred dollars in that kitty. He just hoped the boy's doctor got a chunk of it.

22

ARVIN WAS LEANING AGAINST THE ROUGH RAIL of the porch late on a clear Saturday night in March looking at the stars hanging over the hills in all their distant mystery and solemn brilliance. He and Hobart Finley and Daryl Kuhn, his two closest friends, had bought a jug earlier that evening from Slot Machine, a one-armed bootlegger who operated over on Hungry Holler, and he was still sipping on it. The wind had a bite to it, but the whiskey kept him warm enough. He heard Earskell inside the house moan and mutter something in his sleep. In the good weather, the old man slept in a drafty lean-to he had nailed on the back of his sister's house when he moved in a few years ago, but once it turned cold out, he lay on the floor next to the wood stove on a pallet made up of scratchy, homespun blankets that smelled like kerosene and mothballs. Down the hill, parked in the pull-off behind Earskell's Ford was Arvin's prized possession, a blue 1954 Chevy Bel Air with a loose transmission. It had taken him four years doing whatever kind of work he could get—chopping firewood, building fence, picking apples, slopping hogs—to save enough money to buy it.

Earlier that day, Arvin had driven Lenora to the cemetery to visit her mother's grave. Though he would never admit it, the only reason he went to the graveyard with her now was because he hoped she might recall some buried memory about her daddy or the cripple he ran with. He had become fascinated with the riddle of their disappearance. Although Emma and many others in Greenbrier County seemed convinced that the two were alive and well, Arvin found it hard to believe that two bastards as nutty as Roy and Theodore were purported to be could have vanished into thin air and never be heard from again. If it was that easy, he figured a lot more people would do it. He'd wished many times that his father had taken that route.

"Don't you think it's funny how we both ended up orphans and living in the same house like we do?" Lenora had said after they entered the cemetery. She set her Bible down on a nearby tombstone and loosened her bonnet a bit and pulled it back. "It's almost like everything happened so we'd meet each other." She was standing next to her mother's place looking down at the square marker lying flat to the ground: HELEN HATTON LAFERTY 1926–1948. A small winged but faceless angel was carved into each top corner. Arvin had pushed spit between his teeth and glanced around at the dead remains of last year's flowers on the other graves, the clumps of grass and rusty wire fence that surrounded the cemetery. It made him uneasy when Lenora talked like that, and she had been doing it a lot more since she'd turned sixteen. They might not have been blood relation, but it made him squeamish to think of her any other way than as his sister. Though he realized the odds weren't good, he kept hoping she might find a boyfriend before she said something really stupid.

He weaved a little as he moved from the edge of the porch over to Earskell's rocking chair and sat down. He started thinking about his parents, and his throat got tight and dry all of the sudden. He loved whiskey, but sometimes it brought on a deep sadness that only sleep would erase. He felt like crying, but lifted the bottle and took another drink instead. A dog barked somewhere over the next knob, and his thoughts wandered to Jack, the poor harmless mutt that his father had killed just for some more lousy blood. That had been one of the worst days of that summer, the way he remembered it, almost as bad as the night his mother died. Soon, Arvin promised himself, he was going to go back to the prayer log and see if the dog's bones were still there. He wanted to bury them proper, do what he could to make up for some of what his crazy father had done. If he lived to be a hundred, he vowed, he would never forget Jack.

Sometimes he wondered if perhaps he was just envious that Lenora's father might still be alive while his was dead. He had read all the faded newspaper accounts, had even gone out combing the woods where Helen's corpse had been found, hoping to discover some piece of evidence that would prove everybody wrong: a shallow pit with two skeletons slowly rising side by side up through the earth, or a rusty wheelchair pocked with bullet holes hidden deep in an overlooked gully. But the only things he'd ever come across were two spent shotgun shells and a Spearmint gum wrapper. As Lenora ignored his questions that morning about her father and kept on blabbing about fate and star-crossed lovers and all that other romance shit she read about in books checked out from the school library, he'd realized that he should have stayed home and worked on the Bel Air. It hadn't run right since the day he bought it.

"Damn it, Lenora, stop talking that nonsense," Arvin had told her. "Besides, you might not even be an orphan. As far as everyone around here's concerned, you daddy's still alive and kicking. Hell, he might pop over the hill any day now dancing a jig."

"I hope so," she'd said. "I pray every day that he will."

"Even if it meant he killed your mother?"

"I don't care," she said. "I've already forgiven him. We could start all over."

"That's crazy."

"No, it's not. What about your father?"

"What about him?"

"Well, if he could come back—"

"Girl, just shut up about it." Arvin started toward the cemetery gate. "We both know that ain't gonna happen."

"I'm sorry," she said, her voice breaking into a sob.

Taking a deep breath, Arvin stopped and turned around. Sometimes it seemed as if she spent half of her life crying. He held his car keys in his hand. "Look, if you want a ride, come on."

When he got home, he cleaned the Bel Air's carburetor with a wire brush dipped in gasoline, then left again right after supper to pick up Hobart and Daryl. He had been down all week, thinking about Mary Jane Turner, and he felt the need to get good and sloshed. Her father hadn't taken long to decide that life in the merchant marine was a hell of a lot easier than plowing rocks and worrying about whether it rained enough or not, and so he had packed his family up and headed for Baltimore and a new ship the previous Sunday morning. Though Arvin had kept after her from their first date, he was glad now that Mary hadn't let him in her pants. Saying goodbye had been hard enough as it was. "Please," he'd asked as they stood at her front door the night before she left; and she had smiled and stood on her tiptoes and one last time whispered dirty words in his ear. He and Hobart and Daryl had pooled their money together for the bottle and a twelve-pack and a couple of packs of Pall Malls and a tank of gas. Then they drove up and down the dull streets of Lewisburg until midnight listening to the radio fade in and out and blowing off about what they were going to do after high school, until their voices turned as rough as gravel from all the smoke and whiskey and grandiose plans for the future.

Leaning back in the rocker, Arvin wondered who was living in his old house now, wondered if the storekeeper still stayed by himself in that little camper and if Janey Wagner was knocked up by now. "Stink finger," he muttered to himself. He thought again about the way the deputy named Bodecker had locked him in the back of the patrol car after he had led him to the prayer log, like the lawman was afraid of him, a ten-year-old kid with blueberry pie on his face. They had put him in an empty cell that night, not knowing what else to do with him, and the welfare lady had showed up the next afternoon with some of his clothes and his grandmother's address. Holding the bottle up, he saw that there was maybe two inches left in the bottom. He stuck it under the chair for Earskell in the morning.

23

REVEREND SYKES COUGHED A LITTLE, and the congregation of the Coal Creek Church of the Holy Ghost Sanctified watched a trickle of bright blood run down his chin and drip onto his shirt. He kept preaching, though, gave the people a decent sermon about helping your neighbor; but then at the end he announced that he was stepping down. "Temporary," he said. "Just till I get to feeling better." He said that his wife had a nephew down in Tennessee who had just graduated from one of those Bible colleges. "He claims he wants to work with poor people," Sykes went on. "I figure he must be a Democrat." He grinned, hoping for a laugh to lighten the mood a little, but the only sound he heard was a couple of women in the back near the door crying with his wife. He realized now that he should have made her stay home today.

Taking a careful breath, he cleared his throat. "I ain't seen him since he was a boy, but his mother says he's all right. Him and his wife should be here in two weeks, and like I said, he's just gonna help out for a while. I know he ain't from around here, but try to make him feel welcome anyway." Sykes started to weave a bit and grabbed hold of the pulpit to steady himself. He pulled the empty Five Brothers pack from his pocket and held it up. "Just in case any of you need it, I'm gonna hand this over to him." A hacking fit came over him then, bent him double, but this time he managed to cover his mouth with his handkerchief and hide the blood. When he got his breath back, he rose up and looked around, his face red and sweaty with the strain of it all. He was too embarrassed to tell them that he was dying. The black lung that he'd been fighting for years had finally gotten the better of him. Within the next few weeks or months, according to the doctor, he'd be meeting his Maker. Sykes couldn't honestly say that he was actually looking forward to it, but he knew that he'd had a better life than most men. After all, hadn't he lived forty-two years longer than those poor wretches who had died in the mine cave-in that had pointed him toward his calling? Yes, he'd been a lucky man. He wiped a tear from his eye and shoved the bloody rag in his pants pocket. "Well," he said, "no sense keeping you folks any longer. That's all I got."

24

ROY LIFTED THEODORE OUT OF THE WHEELCHAIR and carried
him across the dirty sand. They were at the north end of a public
beach in St. Petersburg, a little south of Tampa. The cripple's use-
less legs swung back and forth like a rag doll's. He was rank with the
smell of piss, and Roy had noticed that he wasn't using his milk bottle
anymore, just soaking his rotten dungarees whenever he needed to go.
He had to set Theodore down several times and rest, but he finally
got him to the edge of the water. Two stout women wearing wide-
brimmed hats rose up and looked over at them, then hurriedly gathered up their towels and lotions and headed for the parking lot. Roy
went back to the chair and got their supper, two fifths of White Port
and a package of boiled ham. They had lifted it from a grocery store
a couple of blocks away right after a truck driver hauling oranges let
them out. "Didn't we spend some time locked up here once?" Theodore asked.

Roy swallowed the last slice of meat and nodded. "Three days, I
think." The cops had picked them up for vagrancy just before dark.
They had been preaching on a street corner. America was getting as bad as Russia, a thin, balding man yelled at them as they
were escorted past his cell to their own that night. Why could the
police throw a man in jail just because he didn't have any money or
an address? What if the man didn't want any goddamn money or a
fuckin' address? Where was all this freedom they bragged about? The
cops took the protestor out of the block every morning and made
him carry a stack of telephone books up and down the stairs all day.
According to some of the other prisoners, the man had been arrested
for vagrancy twenty-two times just in the past year, and they were sick
of feeding the Communist bastard. If nothing else, they were going to
make him sweat for his bologna and grits.

"I can't remember," Theodore said. "What was the jail like?"

"Not bad," Roy said. "I believe they gave out coffee for dessert." The second night they were there, the cops brought in a big, hulking brute with a carved-up face called the Zit-Eater. Right before bedtime, they stuck him in the cell down at the end of the hall with the Communist. Everyone in the jail had heard about the Zit-Eater except for Roy and Theodore. He was famous up and down the Gulf Coast. "Why do they call him that?" Roy had asked the paper hanger with the handlebar mustache in the cell next to theirs.

"Because the fucker gets you down and pops your pimples if you got any," the man said. He twisted the waxed ends of his black mustache. "Lucky for me I've always had a nice complexion."

"What the hell does he do that for?"

"He likes to eat 'em," another man said, from a cell across the way. "Some claim he's a cannibal, got leftovers buried all over Florida, but I don't buy it. He just likes to get attention, that's what I think."

"Jesus, someone oughta kill a sonofabitch like that," Theodore said. He glanced at the acne scars on Roy's face.

The mustache shook his head. "He'd be a hard one to kill," he said. "You ever see one of them retards that can carry a car on his back? They had one of 'em at this alligator farm where I worked one summer down by Naples. You couldn't have stopped that bastard with a machine gun once he got started. The Zit-Eater, he's like that." Then they heard some commotion down at the end of the hall. Evidently, the Communist wasn't going to give up easy, and that cheered Roy and Theodore a little, but after a couple of minutes all they could hear was his crying.

The next morning, three broad-chested men in white coats came in with billy clubs and hauled the Zit-Eater away in a straitjacket to a nuthouse on the other side of town. The Communist quit bitching about the law after that, didn't complain once about the fresh squeeze marks on his face or the blisters on his feet, just carried his phone books up and down the stairs like he was thankful they'd given him some meaningful work to do.

Theodore sighed, looked out over the blue gulf, the water smooth as a pane of glass that day. "That sounds nice, coffee for dessert. Maybe we could let them take us in, get a little break."

"Shit, Theodore, I don't want to spend the night in jail." Roy kept one eye on the new wheelchair. He'd slipped into an old folks' home a couple of days ago and borrowed it after the wheels on the last one gave out. He wondered how many miles he had pushed Theodore since they had left West Virginia. Though he wasn't good with numbers, he estimated it had to be up around a million by now.

"I'm tired, Roy."

Theodore hadn't been acting right since he cost them the job with the carnival the summer before. A young boy, maybe five or six years old, eating a cardboard scoop of cotton candy, had wandered into the back of the tent while Roy was out front trying to drum up some customers. Theodore swore that the boy asked for help in zipping his pants up, but not even Roy could buy that one. Within minutes, Billy Bradford had loaded them up in his Cadillac and dumped them a few miles out in the country. They didn't even get a chance to say their goodbyes to Flapjack or the Flamingo Lady; and though they had tried to get on with several other outfits since then, word of the crippled pedophile and his bug-eating buddy had spread fast among the carny owners. "Want me to go get your guitar?" Roy asked.

"Nah," Theodore said. "I ain't got no music in me today."

"You sick?"

"I don't know," the crippled boy said. "It's like there's never no letup."

"Want one of them oranges the trucker gave us?"

"Hell no. I've et enough of them damn things to last me till the Judgment Day. They still give me the shits."

"I could drop you off at the hospital," Roy said. "Come back for you in a day or two."

"Hospitals, they worse than jails."

"Want me to pray over you?"

Theodore laughed. "Ha. That's a good one, Roy."

"Maybe that's what's wrong with you. You don't believe no more."

"Don't start in on that shit again," Theodore said. "I've served the Lord in various capacities. And I got the legs to prove it."

"You just need some rest," Roy said. "We'll find us a good tree to sleep under before dark."

"It still sounds mighty nice. Them passing out coffee for dessert."

"Jesus, you want a cup of coffee, I'll go get you one. We still got some change left."

"I wish we was still with the carnival," Theodore sighed. "That was the best we ever had it."

"Yeah, well, you should have kept your hands off that kid if that's the way you feel."

Theodore picked up a pebble and threw it in the water. "It makes you wonder, don't it?"

"What's that?" Roy asked.

"I don't know," the cripple said with a shrug. "Just makes you wonder, that's all."

PART FOUR

Winter

25

IT WAS A COLD FEBRUARY MORNING in the early part of 1966, Carl and Sandy's fifth year together. The apartment was like an ice-box, but Carl was afraid if he kept knocking on the landlady's door downstairs about turning up the thermostat, he might snap and strangle her with her own filthy hairnet. He had never killed anyone in Ohio, didn't believe in shitting in his own nest. That was Rule #2. So Mrs. Burchwell, although she deserved it more than anything, was off-limits. Sandy woke up a little before noon and headed for the living room with a blanket draped over her narrow shoulders, dragging the ends of it through the dust and dirt on the floor. She curled up on the couch in a shivering ball and waited for Carl to bring her a cup of coffee and turn the TV on. For the next several hours she smoked cigarettes and watched her soap operas and coughed. At three o'clock, Carl yelled from the kitchen that it was time to get ready for work. Sandy tended bar six nights a week, and though she was supposed to let Juanita off at four, she was always running late.

With a groan, she sat up and stabbed out her cigarette in the ashtray and flung the blanket off her shoulders. She turned off the TV, then shivered her way to the bathroom. Bending over the sink, she splashed some water around in the bowl. She dried off her face, studied herself in the mirror, tried vainly to brush the yellow stains off her teeth. With a tube of red lipstick, she made up her mouth, fixed her eyes, pulled her brown hair back in a limp ponytail. She was sore and bruised. Last night, after she closed up the bar, she let a paper mill worker who had recently lost a hand in a rewinder bend her over the pool table for twenty bucks. Her brother was watching her closely these days, ever since that goddamn phone call, but twenty bucks was twenty bucks, no matter how you looked at it. She and Carl could drive halfway across a state on that much money, or pay the electric bill for the month. It still irked her, all the crooked shit that Lee was into, and then him worried about her costing him votes. The man told her he would fork over another ten if she'd let him stick the metal hook up inside her, but Sandy told him that sounded like something he should save for his wife.

"My wife ain't no whore," the man said.

"Yeah, right," Sandy shot back as she pulled down her panties. "She married you, didn't she?" She'd held on to the twenty the whole time he pounded her. It was the hardest she'd been fucked in a long time; the old bastard was definitely going for his money's worth. He sounded like he was going to have a heart attack, the way he was grunting and gasping for air, the cold metal hook pressed against her right hip. By the time he finished, the money was wadded up into a little ball in her hand, soaked with sweat. After he backed away, she smoothed it out on the green felt and stuck it inside her sweater. "Besides," she said, as she walked over to unlock the door and let him out, "that thing ain't got no more feeling than a beer can." Sometimes, after a night like that, she wished she was back working the morning shift at the Wooden Spoon. At least Henry, the old grill cook, had been gentle. He'd been her first, right after she turned sixteen. They had lain together on the floor of the stockroom a long time that night, covered with flour from a fifty-pound bag they had knocked over. He still stopped by the bar once in a while to shoot the shit and tease her about rolling out some more pie dough.

When she came into the kitchen, Carl was sitting in front of the stove reading the newspaper for the second time that day. His fingers were gray with ink. All the burners on the stove were lit and the oven door was open. Blue flames danced behind him like miniature camp-fires. His pistol lay on the kitchen table, the barrel pointed toward the door. The whites of his eyes were laced with red veins, and his fat, pale, unshaven face looked like some cold and distant star in the reflection from the bare lightbulb hanging over the table. He'd spent most of the night bent over in the tiny closet in the hallway that he used as a darkroom, coaxing life into the last of the film he had saved back from the previous summer. He hated to see it end. He'd nearly cried when he developed that last photo. Next August was a long ways off.

"Those people are so screwed up," Sandy said as she searched inside her purse for the keys to the car.

"Which people?" Carl asked, turning another page of the paper.

"Them ones on TV. They don't know what they want."

"Damn it, Sandy, you pay too much attention to those fuckers," he said, glancing at the clock impatiently. "Hell, you think they give a shit about you?" She should have been at work five minutes ago. He had been waiting all day for her to leave.

"Well, if it wasn't for the doctor, I wouldn't watch it anymore," she said. She was always going on about the M.D. on one of the shows, a tall, handsome man whom Carl was convinced must be the luckiest bastard on the planet. The man could fall down a rat hole and climb out with a suitcase stuffed with money and the keys to a new El Dorado. Over the years that Sandy had been watching him, he'd probably performed more miracles than Jesus. Carl couldn't stand him, that fake movie star nose, those sixty-dollar suits.

"So whose dick did he suck today?" Carl said.

"Ha! You're one to talk," Sandy said, as she pulled on her coat. She was sick of always having to defend her soaps.

"What the hell does that mean?"

"It means whatever you think it means," Sandy said. "You were in that closet all night again."

"I'll tell you what, I'd like to meet up with that sonofabitch."

"I bet you would," Sandy said.

"I'd make him squeal like a goddamn pig, I swear to God!" Carl yelled as she slammed the door behind her.

A few minutes after she left, Carl quit cursing the actor and turned the stove off. He laid his head in his arms at the table and dozed off for a while. The room was dark when he woke up. He was hungry, but all he could find in the refrigerator were two moldy heels of bread and a dab of crusty pimento cheese in a plastic container. Opening the kitchen window, he tossed the bread into the front yard.

A few flakes of snow drifted through the ray of light coming from the landlady's porch. From over in the stockyards across the street, he heard somebody laugh, the metal clang of a gate being slammed shut. He realized that he hadn't been outside in over a week.

He closed the window and walked into the living room and paced back and forth singing old religious songs and waving his arms in the air like he was leading a choir. "Bringing in the Sheaves" was one of his favorites, and he sang it several times in a row. When he was a boy, his mother used to sing it while doing the wash. She had a certain song for every chore, every heartache, every goddamn thing that happened to them after the old man died. She did laundry for rich people, got cheated half the time by the no-good bastards. Sometimes he would skip school and hide under the rotting porch with the slugs and spiders and the little that remained of the neighbor's cat, and listen to her all day. Her voice never seemed to tire. He would ration the butter sandwich she'd packed for his lunch, sip dirty water from a rusty soup can he kept stored in the cat's rib cage. He'd pretend it was vegetable beef or chicken noodle, but no matter how hard he tried, it always tasted like mud. He wished to hell he had bought some soup the last time he went to the store. The memory of that old can made him hungry again.

He sang for several hours, his loud voice booming through the rooms, his face red and sweaty with the effort. Then, just before nine o'clock, the landlady began pounding furiously with the end of a broom handle on her ceiling below. He was in the middle of a rousing version of "Onward Christian Soldiers." Any other time he would have ignored her, but tonight he sputtered to a stop; he was in the mood to move on to other things. But if she didn't turn the fucking heat up soon, he'd start keeping her up until midnight. He could stand the cold easy enough, but Sandy's constant shivering and complaining were getting on his nerves.

Going back to the kitchen, he got a flashlight from the spoon drawer and made sure the door was locked. Then he went around closing all the curtains, ended up in the bedroom. He got down on his knees and reached under the bed for a shoe box. He carried the box into the living room and turned off all the lights and settled down on the couch in the darkness. Cold air blew in around the loose windows, and he drew Sandy's blanket over his shoulders.

With the box on his lap, he closed his eyes and reached a hand under the cardboard lid. There were over two hundred photos inside, but he pulled just one out. He rubbed his thumb slowly over the slick paper, tried to divine which image it might be, a little thing he did to make it all last longer. After making his guess, he opened his eyes and flipped the flashlight on just for a second. *Click, click.* A tiny taste and he set that photo to the side, closed his eyes again, and took out another. *Click, click.* Bare backs and bloody holes and Sandy with her legs spread. Sometimes he went through the entire box without guessing a single one of them correctly.

Once he thought he heard a noise, a car door slam, footsteps on the back stairs. He got up and tiptoed from room to room with the pistol, peeking out the windows. Then he checked the door and returned to the couch. Time seemed to shift, speed up, slow down, move back and forth like a crazy dream he kept having over and over. One second he was standing in a muddy soybean field outside of Jasper, Indiana; and the next click of the flashlight took him to the bottom of a rocky ravine north of Sugar City, Colorado. Old voices crawled through his head like worms, some bitter with curses, others still pleading for mercy. By midnight, he'd traveled through a large portion of the Midwest, relived the last moments of twenty-four strange men. He remembered everything. It was as if he resurrected them every time he brought out the box, stirred them awake and allowed them to do their own kind of singing. One last click and he decided to call it a night.

After he returned the box to its hiding place under the bed, he switched the lights back on and wiped off the blanket as best he could with her washcloth. For the next couple of hours, he sat at the kitchen table cleaning the pistol and studying his road maps and waiting on Sandy to get off work. He always felt the need for her company after a bout with the box. She had told him about the paper mill man, and he thought about that for a while, what he'd do with the hook if they ever picked up a hitchhiker like that.

He'd forgotten how hungry he was until she walked in with two cold hamburgers slathered with mustard, three bottles of beer, and the evening newspaper. While he ate, she sat opposite him and carefully added up her tips, stacking the nickels, dimes, and quarters into small, neat piles, and he recalled the way he'd acted earlier about her stupid TV show. "You did pretty good tonight," he said, when she finally finished counting.

"Not bad for a Wednesday, I guess," she said with a tired smile. "So what did you do today?"

He shrugged. "Oh, cleaned out the fridge, sang a few songs."

"You didn't piss the old lady off again, did you?"

"Just kidding," he said. "I got some new pictures to show you."

"Which one is it?" she asked.

"The one had that bandanna tied around his head. They turned out pretty good."

"Not tonight," she said. "I'd never get to sleep." Then she pushed half the change over to him. He scooped it up and dumped it in a coffee can he kept under the sink. They were always saving for the next junker, the next roll of film, the next trip. Opening the last beer, he poured her a glass. Then he got down on his knees in front of her and pulled her shoes off, began rubbing the work out of her feet. "I shouldn't have said anything about your damn doctor today," he said. "You watch whatever you want."

"It's just something to do, baby," Sandy said. "Takes my mind off things, you know?" He nodded, gently worked his fingers into the soft soles of her feet. "That's the spot," she said, stretching out her legs. Then, after she finished the beer and a last cigarette, he scooped her skinny body up and carried her giggling down the hallway and into the bedroom. He hadn't heard her laugh in weeks. He would keep her warm tonight, that was the least he could do. It was nearly four in the morning, and somehow, with lots of luck and little regret, they had made it through another long winter day.

26

A FEW DAYS LATER, CARL DROVE SANDY TO WORK, told her he needed to get out of the apartment for a while. It had snowed several inches the night before, and that morning the sun finally managed to break through the thick, gray bank of clouds that had hovered over Ohio like some dismal, unrelenting curse for the past several weeks. Everything in Meade, even the paper mill smokestack, was sparkling and white. "Want to come in for a minute?" she asked when he pulled up in front of the Tecumseh. "I'll buy you a beer."

Carl looked around at the cars in the slushy parking lot. He was surprised it was so crowded in the middle of the day. He'd kept himself shut up in the apartment for so long that he didn't think he could tolerate that many people his first time back out in the real world since before Christmas. "Ah, I think I'll pass," he said. "I figured I'd just ride around for a while, try to get home before dark."

"Suit yourself," she said, opening her car door. "Just don't forget to pick me up tonight."

As soon as she went inside, Carl headed straight back to the apartment on Watt Street. He sat staring out the kitchen window until the sun went down, then walked out to the car. He stuck his camera in the dash and the pistol under the seat. There was half a tank of gas in the station wagon and five dollars in his wallet that he'd taken from their travel money jar. He promised himself he wasn't going to do anything, just drive around town a little and pretend. Sometimes, though, he wished he hadn't ever made up those goddamn rules. Hell, around here, he could probably kill a hick every night if he wanted to. "But that's why you got the rules in the first goddamn place, Carl," he told himself as he started down the street. "So you don't fuck everything up."

As he passed by the White Cow Diner on High Street, he saw his brother-in-law standing beside his cruiser at the edge of the parking lot talking to someone sitting behind the wheel of a shiny black Lincoln. They appeared to be arguing, the way Bodecker was slinging his arms around. Carl slowed down and watched them in his rearview as long as he could. He thought about something that Sandy had said one night a couple of weeks ago, that her brother was going to end up in prison if he didn't stop hanging around guys like Tater Brown and Bobo McDaniels. "Who the hell are they?" he had asked. He was sitting at the kitchen table unwrapping one of the cheeseburgers she had brought him from work. Someone had taken a bite out of one corner of it. He scraped the diced onion off with his penknife.

"They run everything from Circleville clear down to Portsmouth," she told him. "Everything that's illegal anyway."

"Right," Carl said. "And how do you happen to know this?" She was always coming home with another bullshit story some drunk had fed her. Last week she had talked to someone who was in on the Kennedy assassination. Sometimes it irritated the shit out of Carl that she could be so gullible, but then again, he knew that was probably one of the main reasons she had stuck with him all this time.

"Well, because this guy stopped in the bar today right after Juanita left and handed me an envelope to give to Lee." She lit a cigarette and blew some smoke toward the stained ceiling. "It was plumb full of money, and it wasn't all singles, either. There must have been four or five hundred dollars in there, maybe more."

"Jesus Christ, did you take any of it?"

"You gotta be kidding me, right? These ain't the kind of people you steal from." She picked up one of the french fries from the greasy cardboard container sitting in front of Carl, dabbed it into a glob of ketchup. All evening, she had thought about hopping in the car and taking off with the envelope.

"But he's your brother, goddamn it. He ain't gonna do nothing to you."

"Shit, Carl, the way Lee is now, I doubt if he would think twice about getting rid of us. At least not you anyway."

"Well, what did you do with it then? You still got it on you?"

"Hell no. When he came in I just gave it to him and played dumb." She looked at the french fry in her hand, dropped it in the ashtray. "He still didn't seem none too happy, though," she said.

Still thinking about his brother-in-law, Carl turned onto Vine Street. Every time he ran into Lee, which, thank God, wasn't that often, the sonofabitch asked him, "So where you working, Carl?" He'd give anything to see his ass caught in a jam he couldn't get out of by flashing that big fucking badge around. Up ahead, he saw two boys, maybe fifteen or sixteen years old, moving slowly along the sidewalk. He pulled over and shut off the engine, rolled down the window and took several gulps of the cold air. He watched them split up at the end of the block, one going east, the other west. He rolled down the passenger's-side window and started the car, drove to the stop sign and made a right.

"Hey," Carl said, when he pulled up beside the skinny boy wearing a dark blue jacket with Meade High School stitched on the back of it in white. "You need a ride?"

The boy stopped and looked at the driver behind the wheel of the dumpy station wagon. The man's sweaty face was shiny in the glare from the streetlight. A brown stubble covered his fat jowls and neck. His eyes were beady and cruel, like a rodent's. "What'd you say?" the boy asked.

"I'm just riding around," Carl said. "Maybe we could go get some beer." He swallowed and caught himself before he started begging.

The boy smirked. "You got the wrong guy, mister," he said. "I ain't built that way." Then he started walking again, faster this time.

"Fuck you then," Carl said under his breath. He sat in the car and watched the boy disappear into a house a few doors down. Though a little disappointed, he was mostly relieved. He knew he wouldn't have been able to stop himself if he got the punk in the car. He could almost picture it, the little bastard lying in the snow turned inside out. Someday, he thought, he was going to have to do a winter scene.

He drove back to the White Cow Diner, saw that Bodecker was

gone now. He parked the car and went inside, sat at the counter and ordered a cup of coffee. His hands were still shaking. "Damn, it's cold out," he said to the waitress, a tall, skinny girl with a red nose.

"That's Ohio for you," she said.

"I'm not used to it," Carl said.

"Oh, so you ain't from around here?"

"No," Carl said, taking a sip of the coffee and pulling out one of his dog dicks. "I'm passing through from California." Then he frowned and looked down at the cigar. He wasn't sure why he said that, unless maybe he wanted to impress the girl. The mere mention of the state usually made him sick. He and Sandy had moved out there just a few weeks after they got married. Carl had thought he would find success there, taking photographs of movie stars and beautiful people, getting Sandy some work as a model, but instead they ended up broke and hungry, and he finally sold her to two men he met outside a fly-by-night talent agency who wanted to make a dirty movie. She had refused at first, but that night, after he plied her with vodka and promises, they drove their old beater up into the foggy Hollywood Hills, came to a small, dark cottage with newspapers taped over the windows. "This might be our big break," Carl said as he led her to the door. "Make some connections."

Besides the two men he'd made the deal with, there were seven or eight others standing along the lemon yellow walls of the living room, bare except for a movie camera on a tripod and a double bed covered with wrinkled sheets. A man handed Carl a drink and another asked Sandy to take her clothes off in a gentle voice. A couple of them took photographs as she stripped. Nobody said a word. Then somebody clapped his hands and the bathroom door swung open. A midget with a shaved head that was way too big for his body led a tall, dazed-looking man out into the room. The midget wore nice slacks rolled up several inches above his pointy Italian shoes and a Hawaiian shirt, but the big man was buck naked, a long, blue-veined penis as big around as a coffee cup dangling between his tanned, muscular legs. When she saw the grinning midget unhook the leash from the dog collar around the man's neck, Sandy rolled off the bed and started grabbing frantically for her clothes. Carl stood up and said, "Sorry, boys, the lady's changed her mind."

"Get that cocksucker out of here," the one behind the movie camera growled. Before Carl knew what was happening, three men had dragged him out the door and put him in his car. "Now you wait here or she's going to get hurt real bad," one of them told him. He chewed on his cigar and watched shadows move back and forth behind the covered windows, tried to convince himself that everything was going to be all right. After all, it was the movie business, couldn't be anything too serious go wrong. Two hours later, the front door opened and the same three men carried Sandy out to the car, tossed her in the backseat. One of them came around to the driver's side and handed Carl twenty dollars. "This ain't right," Carl said. "The agreement was for two hundred."

"Two hundred? Shit, she wasn't worth ten. Once that big sonofabitch got it in her ass, she passed out and laid there like a dead fish."

Carl turned and looked at Sandy lying on the seat. She was starting to come to a little. They had put her blouse on backward. "Bullshit," he said. "I want to talk to them guys I made the deal with."

"You mean Jerry and Ted? Hell, they left an hour ago," the man said.

"I'll call the law, that's what I'll do," Carl said.

"No, you won't," the man said, shaking his head. Then he reached through the window and grabbed Carl by the throat and squeezed. "In fact, if you don't quit your bitching and get the hell out of here, I'm going to take you back inside and turn ol' Frankie loose on your chubby ass. Let him and Tojo make another hundred." As the man walked back toward the house, Carl heard him say over his shoulder, "And don't try bringing her back. She ain't got what it takes for this business."

The next morning, Carl went out and bought an ancient-looking Smith & Wesson .38 at a pawnshop with the twenty dollars the porno man had given him. "How do I know this thing even works?" he asked the pawnbroker.

"Follow me," the man said. He took Carl into a back room and fired two bullets into a barrel filled with sawdust and old magazines. "They quit making this model in 1940 or thereabouts, but it's still a damn good gun."

He went back to the Blue Star Motel, where Sandy was soaking in a tub of hot water and Epsom salts. Showing her the gun, he swore that he was going to plug the two bastards who had set them up; but then he went down the street and sat on a bench in a park the rest of the day thinking about killing himself instead. Something broke in him that day. For the first time, he could see that his whole life added up to absolutely nothing. The only thing he knew how to do was work a camera, but who needed another fat guy with thin hair taking boring pictures of whiny, red-faced babies and sluts in their prom dresses and grim-faced married couples celebrating twenty-five years of misery? When he returned to their room that night, she was already asleep.

They headed back to Ohio the next afternoon. He drove and she sat on the pillows they had stolen from the motel room. He found that he had a hard time looking her in the eye, and they barely said two words to each other all the way across the desert and into Colorado. As they started up into the Rockies, the bleeding finally stopped and she told him that she would rather drive than sit there thinking about being raped by that midget's doped-up slave while all those men cracked jokes about her. When she got behind the wheel, she lit a cigarette and turned the radio on. They were down to their last four dollars. A couple of hours later, they picked up a man smelling of gin thumbing his way back to his mother's house in Omaha. He told them that he had lost everything, including his car, in a whorehouse— just a house trailer, really, with three broads working shifts, an aunt and her two nieces—out in the sand north of Reno. "Pussy," the man said. "It's always been a problem for me."

"So it's like some kind of sickness gets hold of you?" Carl said.

"Buddy, you sound like that head doctor I had to talk to one time." They rode along in silence for a few minutes, then the man leaned forward and laid his arms casually on the top of the front seat. He offered them a drink from a flask, but neither of them were in the mood for a party. Carl opened up the dash to take the camera out. He was thinking that he might as well take some nature shots. Good chance he would never see these mountains again. "This your wife?" the man asked, after he scooted back again in his seat.

"Yeah," Carl said.

"I'll tell you what, friend. I don't know what your situation is, but I'll give you twenty bucks for a quickie with her. To tell you the truth, I don't think I can last to Omaha."

"That's it," Sandy said. She hit the brakes and flipped the turn signal on. "I've had my fill of motherfuckers like you."

Carl glanced down at the pistol in the glove box half hid under a map. "Wait a minute," he said to Sandy in a low voice. He turned and looked at the man, nice clothes, black hair, olive complexion, high cheekbones. A hint of cologne mixed with the smell of the gin. "I thought you lost all your money."

"Well, I did, all I had anyway, but I called Mom when I got to Vegas. She wouldn't buy me another set of wheels this time, but she did send me a few dollars to get home on. She's good about stuff like that."

"How about fifty?" Carl said. "You got that much?"

"Carl!" Sandy screeched. She was on the verge of telling him that he could get his fucking ass out, too, when she saw him slip the gun out of the dash. She turned her eyes back to the road and brought the car back up to cruising speed.

"Boy, I don't know," the man said, scratching his chin. "Sure, I got it, but fifty bucks oughta buy some fireworks, you know what I mean? You care to throw in some extras?"

"Sure, anything you want," Carl said, his mouth turning dry as his heart started beating faster. "We'll just have to find somewhere private to pull over." He sucked in his gut and slid the gun down in his pants.

A week later, when he finally got up the nerve to develop the photographs he'd taken that day, Carl knew with the first glimpse, with a certainty that he had never felt before, that the beginning of his life's work was staring back at him in that shallow pan of fixer. Though it hurt him to see Sandy once again with her arms wrapped around the whore hound's neck in the throes of her first real orgasm, he knew he would never be able to stop. And the humiliation he had felt in California? He vowed that would never happen again. The next summer they went out on their first hunt.

The waitress waited until Carl lit the cigar, then asked, "So what do you do out there?"

"I'm a photographer. Movie stars mostly."

"Really? You ever took any pictures of Tab Hunter?"

"No, can't say that I have," Carl said, "but I bet he'd be a nice one to work with."

27

WITHIN A FEW DAYS, Carl was a regular at the White Cow. It felt good to be out among people again after spending so much of the winter holed up in the apartment. When the waitress asked him when he was heading back to California, he told her that he had decided to stay put for a while, take a break from all the Hollywood crap. One evening he was sitting at the counter when a couple of men who looked to be in their sixties pulled up in a long black El Dorado. They parked just a few feet from the front door and strutted inside. One was dressed in a Western outfit trimmed in sparkling sequins. His potbelly pushed against a belt buckle designed to look like a Winchester rifle, and he walked bowlegged, as if, Carl thought, he had either just gotten off a mighty wide horse or was hiding a cucumber up his ass. The other wore a dark blue suit, decorated across the front with various badges and patriotic ribbons, and a square VFW cap at a jaunty angle. Both of their faces were flushed red with strong drink and arrogance. Carl recognized the cowboy from the newspaper, a Republican loudmouth on the city council, always complaining at the monthly meetings about the degenerate, wide-open sex scene in the Meade city park. Though Carl had driven through there a hundred times at night, the hottest thing he'd ever encountered was a couple of gawky teenagers attempting a kiss in front of the little World War II memorial.

The two men sat down in a booth and ordered coffee. After the waitress served them, they began talking about a man with long hair they had seen walking down the sidewalk on their way over from the American Legion. "Never thought I'd see anything like that around here," the suit said.

"You just wait," the cowboy said. "If something ain't done, they'll be thick as fleas on a monkey's ass within a year or two." He took a sip of his coffee. "I got a niece lives in New York City, and that boy of hers looks just like a girl, hair clear down over his ears. I keep telling her, you send him to me, I'll straighten his ass out, but she won't do it. Says I'd be too rough on him."

They lowered their voices a bit, but Carl could still hear them talking about the way they used to hang niggers, how someone needed to start lynching again, even if it was goddamn hard work, but with the longhairs this time. "Stretch a few of their dirty necks," the cowboy said. "That will wake 'em up, by God. At least keep 'em out of these parts."

Carl could smell their aftershave clear across the diner. He stared at the sugar bowl in front of him on the counter and tried to imagine their lives, the irrevocable steps they had taken to get to where they were on this cold, dark night in Meade, Ohio. It was electric, the sensation that went through him just then, the awareness he had of his own short time on this earth and what he had done with it, and these two old fucks and their connection to it all. It was the same sort of feeling he got with the models. They had chosen one ride or one direction over another, and they had ended up in his and Sandy's car. Could he explain it? No, he couldn't explain it, but he sure as hell could feel it. *The mystery*, that's all Carl could ever say. Tomorrow, he knew, it wouldn't mean anything. The feeling would be gone until the next time. Then he heard water running in the sink back in the kitchen, and the clear image of a soggy grave he'd once dug on a starry night rose to the surface of his memory—he'd dug in a wet spot, and a half-moon, high in the sky and as white as new snow, had bobbed and settled on top of the water seeping into the bottom of the hole and he had never seen anything so beautiful—and he tried to hold on to the image because he hadn't thought about it for a while, but the old men's voices broke in again and disturbed his peace.

His head began to ache a little and he asked the young waitress for one of the aspirins he knew she kept in her purse. She liked to smoke them, she had confessed to him one night, crush them and put the powder in a cigarette. Small-town dope, Carl had thought, and he had to restrain himself from laughing at her, this poor stupid girl. She handed him two tablets with a wink, Jesus, like she was passing him a shot of morphine or something. He smiled at her and thought again about taking her out for a trial run, watch a hitcher get his jollies with her while he took some pictures and assured her that this was the way all models got their start. No doubt she'd believe him. He'd told her some pretty wild stories, and she didn't act embarrassed anymore. Then he swallowed the aspirins and turned a bit on his stool so he could hear the two old men better.

"The Democrats gonna be the ruination of this country," the cowboy said. "What we need to do, Bus, is start our own little army. Kill a few of them and the rest will get the idea."

"You mean the Democrats or the longhairs, J.R.?"

"Well, we'd start with the sissies first," the cowboy said. "Remember that crazy sonofabitch had that chicken stuck to him out on the highway that time? Bus, I guarantee you these longhairs is going to be ten times worse than that."

Carl took a sip of his coffee and listened while the two men fantasized about a private militia. It would be their final contribution to the country before they died. They would gladly sacrifice themselves if need be. It was their duty as citizens. Then Carl heard one of them say loudly, "What the hell you looking at?"

They were both staring at him. "Nothing," Carl said. "Just drinking my coffee."

The cowboy winked at the suit and asked, "What you think, boy? You like them longhairs?"

"I don't know," Carl said.

"Shit, J.R., he's probably got one at home waiting on him," the suit joked.

"Yeah, he don't have the grit for what we need," the cowboy said, turning back to his coffee. "Shit, probably never even served in the military. Soft as a doughnut, that boy." He shook his head. "Whole damn country's gettin' like that."

Carl didn't say anything, but he wondered what it would be like to kill a couple of dried-up fuckers like them. For a moment, he thought about following them when they left, have them screw each other just for starters. He bet he could have that cowboy shitting in the suit's little hat by the time he got serious. Those two pricks could look at Carl Henderson and regard him as a nothing all they wanted, he didn't care. They could blow off from now until doomsday about the killing they would like to do, but neither of them had the guts for it. In fifteen minutes he could have them both begging for a seat in hell. There were things he could do that would make them eat each other's fingers for just two minutes of relief. All he had to do was make the decision. He took another sip of his coffee, looked out the window at the Cadillac, the foggy street. Sure, just an old fat boy, boss. Soft as a fucking doughnut.

The cowboy lit another cigarette and coughed up some brown gunk that he spit in the ashtray. "Turn one of them goddamn things into a pet, that's what I'd like to do," he said, wiping his mouth on a paper napkin the other handed him.

"Would you want it to be a man or a woman, J.R.?"

"Hell, they look the same, don't they?"

The suit grinned. "What would you feed it?"

"You know damn well what I'd feed it, Bus," the cowboy said, and they both laughed.

Carl turned back around. He had never thought of that before. A pet. Keeping such a thing wasn't possible right now, but maybe someday. See, he thought to himself, there was always something new and exciting to look forward to, even in this life. Except for the weeks they were out on the hunt, he always had a hard time staying upbeat, but then something would happen that would remind him that it wasn't all shit. Of course, to even consider turning a model into some sort of pet, they would have to move out of town, get a place out in the sticks. You'd need a basement or, at the very least, some sort of outbuilding close to the house, a toolshed or a barn. Maybe he could eventually train it to do his bidding, though he doubted, even at the same time he was considering it, that he'd have the patience. Just trying to keep Sandy in line was hard enough.

28

BODECKER WALKED INTO THE TECUMSEH one afternoon near the end of February, right after Sandy started her shift, and ordered a Coke. Nobody else was in the bar. She poured it for him without saying a word, then turned back to the sink behind the bar where she was cleaning dirty beer mugs and shot glasses left over from last night. He noticed the dark circles around her eyes and the gray streaks in her hair. She didn't look like she weighed ninety pounds, the loose way her jeans hung on her. He blamed Carl for the way she'd gone downhill. Bodecker hated the thought of that fat sonofabitch living off her like he did. Though he and Sandy hadn't been what you'd call close in years, she was still his sister. She had just turned twenty-four her last birthday, five years younger than himself. The way she looked today she'd have a hard time passing for forty.

Lee moved to a stool down at the end of the bar so he could watch the door. Ever since that night he'd had to come in the bar and pick up that bag of money—the dumbest fucking thing that Tater Brown had pulled on him so far, and the bastard had heard about it, too—Sandy had hardly spoken to him. It bothered him, at least a little when he took the time to consider it, that she would think badly of him. He figured she was still pissed off because of all the hell he'd raised about her selling her ass out of the back of this dump. He turned to look at her. The place was dead, the only sound that of glasses clinking together in the water as she picked one up to wash it. Fuck it, he thought. He began talking, mentioned that Carl sure was spending a lot of time talking to a young waitress at the White Cow while she was stuck here serving drinks to pay the bills.

Sandy set the glass in the plastic drainer and dried off her hands while she thought of something to say. Carl had been driving her to work an awful lot lately, but that was none of Lee's business. What would he do with some girl anyway? The only time Carl got hard anymore was when he looked at his photographs. "So what?" she finally said. "He gets lonely."

"Yeah, he lies a lot, too," Bodecker said. Just the other evening, he had seen Sandy's black station wagon sitting at the White Cow. He parked across the street and watched his brother-in-law flap his jaws with the skinny waitress. They looked like they were having a good time together, and he'd gotten curious. After Carl left, he went in and sat down at the counter, asked for a cup of coffee. "That guy that just left," he said. "You happen to know his name?"

"You mean Bill?"

"Bill, huh?" Bodecker said, trying not to smile. "He a friend of yours?"

"I don't know," she said. "We get along all right."

Bodecker pulled a little notebook and a pencil out of his shirt pocket, pretended to write something down. "Quit the horse shit and tell me what you know about him."

"Am I in some kind of trouble?" she asked. She stuck a strand of hair in her mouth, started shuffling nervously back and forth.

"Not if you talk, you ain't."

After listening to the girl repeat a few of Carl's stories, Bodecker glanced at his watch and stood up. "That's enough for now," he said, putting the notebook back in his pocket. "It don't sound like he's the one we're looking for." He thought for a moment, looked at the girl. She was still nibbling on her hair. "How old are you?" he said.

"Sixteen."

"This Bill ever ask you to pose for any pictures?"

The girl's face turned red. "No," she said.

"The first time he starts talkin' that kind of stuff, you call me, okay?" If Carl hadn't been the one trying to fuck the girl, he wouldn't have even bothered. But the sonofabitch had ruined his sister, and Bodecker couldn't forget about it, no matter how often he told himself it wasn't any of his business. It just kept eating at him, like a cancer. The best he could do right now was let Sandy know about this little waitress. But someday he still wanted to make Carl pay big-time. It wouldn't be that hard, he thought, not much different from castrating a hog.

He had left the diner after questioning the girl and drove out to the state park by the prison and waited for Tater Brown to bring him some money. The dispatcher squawked something on the radio about a hit-and-run on the Huntington Pike, and Bodecker reached over and turned the volume down. A few days ago, he had done another job for Tater, used his badge to flush a man named Coonrod from an old shack where he was hiding out along the Paint Creek bottoms. Handcuffed in the backseat, he thought the sheriff was taking him to town for questioning until the cruiser stopped along the gravel road at the top of Reub Hill. Bodecker didn't say a word, just yanked him out of the car by the metal bracelets and half dragged him into the woods a hundred yards or so. Just as Coonrod switched from yelling about his rights to pleading for mercy, Bodecker stepped behind him and shot him in the back of the head. Now Tater owed him five thousand dollars, a thousand more than the sheriff had charged him the first time. The sadist had beat up one of the better whores who worked upstairs in Tater's strip club, tried to extract her womb with a toilet plunger. It had cost the gangster another three hundred at the hospital to have everything pushed back inside her. The only one who ended up making out on the deal was Bodecker.

Sandy sighed and said, "Okay, Lee, what the fuck are you talking about?"

Bodecker tipped his glass up, started chewing on some ice. "Well, according to this girl, your hubby's name is Bill and he's a big-shot photographer from California. Told her he's good buddies with a bunch of movie stars."

Sandy turned back to the sink, dipped a couple more dirty glasses in the lukewarm water. "He was probably just messing with her. Sometimes Carl likes to bullshit people for fun, just to see how they'll react."

"Well, from what I've seen, he's getting a pretty good reaction. I gotta say, I never thought the fat bastard had it in him."

Sandy threw down her drying rag and turned around. "What the hell you doing? Spying on him?"

"Hey, I wasn't trying to tick you off," Bodecker said. "I figured you'd want to know."

"You never did like Carl," she said.

"Jesus Christ, Sandy, he had you whorin' for him."

She rolled her eyes. "Like you don't do nothing wrong."

Bodecker put his sunglasses on and forced a smile, showed Sandy his big white teeth. "But I'm the law around here, girl. You gonna find out that makes all the difference." He threw a five-dollar bill on the bar and walked out the door and got into his cruiser. He sat there for a few minutes, staring through the windshield at the run-down trailers in Paradise Acres, the mobile-home court that sat next to the bar. Then he laid his head back against the seat. It had been a week and so far nobody had reported the plunger bastard missing. He thought maybe he'd buy Charlotte a new car with part of the money. He wanted so much to close his eyes for a few minutes, but falling asleep out in the open wasn't a good idea these days. The shit was starting to get deep. He wondered how long it would be before he had to kill Tater or, for that matter, before some sonofabitch decided to kill him.

29

ON A SUNDAY MORNING, Carl fixed some pancakes for Sandy, her
favorite food. She'd come home drunk the night before in one of her
sad-ass moods. Whenever she got tangled up in all those worthless
feelings again, there was little he could say or do to make things better. She just had to work it out herself. A couple of nights of drinking
and whining about it and she'd come back around. Carl knew Sandy
better than she knew herself. Tomorrow night, or maybe the next,
she would fuck one of her patrons after the bar closed, some crew-cut
country boy with a wife and three or four snot-nosed kids at home.
He'd tell Sandy that he wished he had met her before he ever married
the old sow, that she was the sweetest piece he'd ever had, and then
everything would be fine and dandy until the next time she got the
blues.

Beside her plate he had laid a .22 pistol. He had bought it a few
days ago for ten dollars from an elderly man he'd met at the White
Cow. The poor sonofabitch was afraid that he would shoot himself
if he kept the gun around. His wife had passed away last fall. He had
treated her badly, he admitted, even when she was lying on her deathbed; but now he was so lonely, he couldn't stand it. He told all this to
Carl and the teenage waitress while icy snow pinged against the plate-
glass windows of the diner and the wind shook the metal sign out by
the street. The old man wore a long overcoat that smelled of wood
smoke and Vicks VapoRub and a blue watch cap speckled with lint
pulled down tight on his head. While he was confessing, it occurred
to Carl that it might be good for Sandy to have her own weapon
when they went out hunting, just as a backup in case something
ever went haywire. He wondered why he hadn't thought of it before.
Though he was always careful, even the best fucked up sometimes. He

had felt good about buying the gun, thought maybe it meant that he was getting wiser.

You'd have to shoot someone in the eye or stick it directly in their ear to ever kill anyone with a .22, but it would still be better than nothing. He'd done that once with a college boy, stuck a gun in his ear, some curly-haired Purdue prick who had snickered when Sandy told him that she'd once dreamed of going to beauty college, but then she ended up tending bar and everything had turned out just the way it was supposed to. Carl had found a book in the boy's coat pocket after he tied him up, *The Poems of John Keats*. He tried asking the fucker nice what his favorite rhyme was, but by then the smart-aleck bastard had shit his pants and had a hard time concentrating. He opened the book to a poem and started reading it while the boy cried for his life, Carl's voice getting louder and louder to drown out the other's pleading until he came to the last line, which he has forgotten now, some bullshit about love and fame that he had to admit made the hair stand up on his arms at the time. Then he pulled the trigger and a wad of wet, gray brains shot out the other side of the college boy's head. After he fell over, blood pooled in the sockets of his eyeballs like little lakes of fire, which made a hell of a picture, but that was with the .38, not some goddamn peashooter .22. Carl was sure that if he could show the smelly geezer the picture of the boy, the sad sack would think twice about ever doing himself in, at least not with a gun. The waitress had thought Carl was pretty slick the way he got the pistol away from the old man before he hurt himself. He could have fucked her that night in the backseat of the station wagon if he'd wanted to, the way she kept going on about how wonderful he was. There was a time a few years ago when he would have been all over that little bitch, but something like that just didn't hold much appeal these days.

"What's this?" Sandy said when she saw the pistol beside her plate.

"It's just in case something ever goes wrong."

She shook her head, pushed the gun across to his side of the table. "That's your job, making sure that never happens."

"I'm just saying—"

"Look, if you ain't got the balls for it anymore, just say so. Jesus Christ, at least let me know before you get us both killed," Sandy said.

"I told you before, I don't like that kind of mouth," he said. He looked at the stack of pancakes getting cold. She hadn't touched them. "And you're going to eat those goddamn griddle cakes, too, you hear me?"

"Fuck you," she said. "I'll eat what I want." She stood up and he watched her take her coffee into the living room, heard the TV come on. He picked up the .22 and aimed it at the wall that divided the kitchen from the couch that she had no doubt plopped her skinny ass down on. He stood there for a couple of minutes, wondering if he could make the shot, then put the gun in a drawer. They spent the rest of the cold morning silently watching a Tarzan movie marathon on Channel 10, and then Carl went to the Big Bear and bought a gallon of vanilla ice cream and an apple pie. She'd always liked the sweets. If he had to, he'd force it down her, he thought as he paid the clerk.

Many years ago, he'd heard one of his mother's boyfriends say that, back in the old days, a man could sell his wife if he got hard up or sick of her, drag her ass to the town market with a horse collar clamped tight around her lousy neck. Making Sandy choke on a little ice cream wouldn't be that big a deal. Sometimes they didn't know what was best for them. His mother sure didn't. A man named Lyndon Langford, the smartest of the long line of bastards she had gotten messed up with during her time on earth, a factory worker in the GM plant in Columbus who sometimes read real books when he was trying to stay off the sauce, had given little Carl his first lessons in photography. Just remember, Lyndon had once told him, most people love to have their picture taken. They'll do damn near anything you want if you point a camera at them. He would never forget the first time he saw his mother's naked body, in one of Lyndon's pictures, tied to her bed with extension cords, a cardboard box over her head with two holes cut in it for her eyes. Still, he was a halfway decent man when he wasn't drinking. Then Carl fucked everything up by eating a slice of the deli ham that Lyndon kept in their icebox for the nights when he stayed over. His mother never forgave him for it, either.

30

WHEN OHIO STARTED TO TURN WARM and green again, Carl began seriously planning the next trip. He was considering the South this time, give the Midwest a break. He spent evenings studying his road atlas: Georgia, Tennessee, Virginia, the Carolinas. Fifteen hundred miles a week, that's what he always planned for. Though they usually traded cars around the time the peonies bloomed, he had decided that the station wagon was in good enough shape for one more outing. And Sandy wasn't bringing home the money she used to when she was whoring regular. Lee had taken care of that.

Lying in bed late one Thursday night, Sandy said, "I been thinking about that gun, Carl. Maybe you're right." Though she hadn't mentioned it, she'd also been doing a lot of thinking about the waitress at the White Cow. She'd even stopped in there once, ordered a milk shake, checked the girl out. She wished Lee had never told her. What bothered her most was the way the girl reminded Sandy of herself right before Carl walked into her life: nervous and shy and eager to please. Then, a few nights ago, pouring a drink for a man she had recently fucked for free, she couldn't help but notice that he wouldn't even give her a second glance now. As she watched the man leave a few minutes later with some toothy bimbo in a fake fur jacket, it occurred to her that maybe Carl was looking for her replacement. It hurt to think he'd turn on her like that, but then why should he be any different from any of the other bastards she had known? She hoped she was wrong, but having her own gun might not be such a bad idea.

Carl didn't say anything. He had been staring miserably at the ceiling, wishing the landlady was dead. It surprised him, Sandy mentioning the gun after all this time, but maybe she had just come to her senses. Who in the hell wouldn't want to carry a gun doing the shit they did? He rolled over, tossed his share of the bedsheet off his fat legs. It was sixty fucking degrees outside at three in the morning, and the old bitch still had the thermostat cranked up. He was certain that she did it on purpose. They'd had words again the other day about his singing at night. He got up and opened the window, stood there letting the slight breeze cool him off. "What made you change your mind?" he finally asked.

"Oh, I don't know," she said. "Like you said, you never know what might happen, right?"

He stared out into the darkness, rubbed the stubble on his face. He dreaded getting back in the bed. His side was soaked with sweat. Maybe he'd sleep on the floor tonight by the window, he thought. He leaned down near the ripped screen and took several deep breaths. Damn, he felt like he was suffocating. "She's just doing it for spite, goddamn it."

"What?"

"Leaving the fuckin' heat on," he said.

Sandy rose up on her elbows and looked at his dark form crouched by the window, like some brooding, mythical beast about to spread its wings and take off in flight. "But you'll show me how to shoot it, won't you?"

"Sure," Carl said. "That's no big deal." He heard her strike a match behind him, take a drag off a cigarette. He turned back toward the bed. "We'll take it out somewhere on your day off, let you fire a few rounds."

On Sunday they left the apartment around noon and drove to the top of Reub Hill and down the other side. He made a left into a muddy lane and stopped when they got to the trash dump at the end. "How do you know about this place?" Sandy asked. Before Carl came along, she had spent more than a few nights getting screwed back here by boys she didn't care to remember now. Always, she had hoped that if she put out for this next one, he'd treat her like his girlfriend, maybe take her to one of the dances at the Winter Garden or the Armory, but that had never happened. As soon as they got a nut, they were done with her. A couple of them even took her tip money and made her walk home. She looked out her window and saw, lying in the ditch, a used rubber stretched down over the top of a Boone's Farm bottle. Boys used to call the place Train Lane; from the looks of things, she figured they still did. Now that she thought about it, she had never been to a dance in her life.

"Just saw it when I was out driving around one day," he said. "Reminded me of that place in Iowa."

"You mean with the Scarecrow?"

"Yeah," Carl said. "Ol' California, here I come, that cocksucker." He reached across her and opened the glove compartment, grabbed the .22 and a box of shells. "Come on, let's see what you got."

He loaded the gun and set up a few rusty tin cans on top of a soggy, stained mattress. Then he walked back to the front of the car and fired off six shots at thirty feet or so. He knocked four cans over. After he showed her again how to load it, he handed the gun to her. "The fucker goes a little to the left," he said, "but that's okay. Don't try to aim so much as point, like you'd do with your finger. And just take a breath and squeeze the trigger as you let it out."

Sandy held the pistol in both hands and sighted down the barrel. She closed her eyes and pulled the trigger. "Don't shut your eyes," Carl said. She fired off the next five rounds as fast as she could. She put several holes in the mattress. "Well, you're gettin' closer," he said. He handed her the box of shells. "You load this time." He pulled out a cigar and lit it. When she hit the first can, she squealed like a little girl who'd found the prize Easter egg. She missed the next one, then plugged another. "Not bad," he said. "Here, let me see it."

He had just finished loading the gun again when they heard a pickup coming fast down the lane toward them. The truck stopped with a lurch a few yards away, and a middle-aged, gaunt-faced man got out. He wore a pair of blue dress pants and a white shirt, polished black shoes. Probably been stuck in church all morning, sitting in a pew with his fat-ass wife, Carl thought. Getting ready to eat some fried chicken now, take a nap if the old bag would shut her mouth for a few minutes. Then back to work in the morning, hard at it. You had to almost admire someone who had the wherewithal to stick with something like that. "Who gave you permission to shoot out here?" the man said. The rough tone of his voice indicated he was none too happy.

"Nobody." Carl looked around and then shrugged. "Shit, buddy, it's just a dump."

"It's my land is what it is," the man said.

"We're just getting in some target practice, that's all," Carl said. "Trying to teach my wife how to defend herself."

The man shook his head. "I don't allow no shooting on my land. Hell, boy, I got cattle over in there. Besides that, don't you know it's the Lord's Day?"

Carl heaved a sigh and cast a look at the brown fields that surrounded the dump. There wasn't a cow in sight anywhere. The sky was a low canopy of endless, immovable gray. Even this far out of town, he could detect the acrid smell of the paper mill in the air. "Okay, I get the hint." He watched as the farmer headed back to his truck, shaking his gray head. "Hey, mister," Carl suddenly called out.

The farmer stopped and spun around. "What now?"

"I was wondering," Carl said, taking a few steps toward him. "Would you mind if I took your picture?"

"Carl," Sandy said, but he waved his hand for her to keep quiet.

"What the hell you want to do that for?" the man said.

"Well, I'm a photographer," Carl said. "I just think you'd make a good picture. Heck, maybe I could sell it to a magazine or something. I always keep my eyes peeled for fine subjects like yourself."

The man looked past Carl at Sandy standing beside the station wagon. She was lighting a cigarette. He didn't approve of women who smoked. Most of them he'd known were trash, but he figured a man who took pictures for a living probably couldn't get anything decent. Hard to tell where he had picked her up. A few years ago, he'd found a woman named Mildred McDonald in his hog barn, half naked and sucking on a cancer stick. She had told him she was waiting on a man, just as casual as anything, then tried to get him to lie with her in the filth. He glanced at the gun Carl was holding in his hand, noticed that his finger was still on the trigger. "You better go ahead and get out of here," the man said, then started walking fast toward his truck.

"What you gonna do?" Carl said. "Call the law?" He glanced back at Sandy and winked.

The man opened the door and reached inside the cab. "Hell, boy, I don't need a crooked sheriff to take care of you."

Hearing that, Carl began to laugh, but then he looked around and saw the farmer standing behind the door of the truck with a rifle pointed at him through the open window. He had a wide grin on his weathered face. "That's my brother-in-law you're talking about," Carl told him, his voice turning serious.

"Who? Lee Bodecker?" The man turned his head and spit. "I wouldn't go around braggin' about that if I was you."

Carl stood there in the middle of the lane staring at the farmer. He heard the squeak of a door behind him as Sandy got in the car and slammed it shut. For a second, he imagined just raising the pistol up and having it out with the bastard, a regular shootout. His hand began shaking a little, and he took a deep breath to try to calm himself. Then he thought about the future. There was always the next hunt. Just a few more weeks and he and Sandy would be on the road again. Ever since he'd heard the Republicans talking in the White Cow, he'd been thinking about killing one of those longhairs. According to the news he'd seen on the TV lately, the country was heading for turmoil; and he wanted to be around to see it. Nothing would please him more than to watch the whole shithouse go up in flames someday. And Sandy had been eating better lately, was starting to fill out again. She was losing her looks fast—they never had gotten her teeth fixed—but they still had a couple of good years left. No sense throwing that away just because some stupid-ass farmer had a hard-on. As soon as he made his decision, his hand stopped twitching. He turned and started toward the station wagon.

"And don't ever let me catch you back here again, understand?" Carl heard the man yell as he got in the front seat and handed Sandy her pistol. He looked around one more time as he cranked the engine, but he still didn't see any fucking cows.

Preacher

PART FIVE

31

OCCASIONALLY, IF THE LAW GOT TOO ROUGH or the hunger
bad enough, they would head inland, away from the big water that
Theodore loved, so that Roy could find some work. While Roy picked
fruit for a few days or weeks, Theodore sat in a lonely grove of trees
or under some shady bushes waiting for his return every evening. His
body was nothing but a shell now. His skin was gray as slate and his
eyes weak. He passed out for no reason, complained about sharp pains
that numbed his arms, and a heaviness on his chest that sometimes
made him puke up his lunch meat breakfast and the half fifth of warm
wine that Roy left him every morning to keep him company. Still,
every night, he'd try to come alive for a couple of hours, attempt to
play some music, even though his fingers didn't work too well anymore. Roy would walk around their campfire with a jug trying to get
some words started, something from the heart, while Theodore listened and picked at the guitar. They'd practice their big comeback for
a while, and then Roy would collapse on top of his blanket, worn out
from the day's work in the orchard. He'd be snoring within a minute
or two. If he was lucky, he'd dream about Lenora. His little girl. His
angel. He'd been thinking about her more and more lately, but sleeping was as close as he could get to her.

As soon as the fire died down, the mosquitoes would dive in
again, drive Theodore crazy. They didn't bother Roy at all, and the
cripple wished he had blood like that. He woke one night with them
buzzing in his ears, still sitting in his wheelchair, the guitar lying on
the ground in front of him. Roy was curled up like a dog on the other
side of the ashes. They had been camping in the same spot for two
weeks. Little piles of Theodore's stool and vomit were scattered over
the dead grass. "Lord, we may have to think about moving," Roy had

said that evening when he got back from the store down the road. He fanned his hand in front of his face. "Gettin' mighty ripe around here." That had been a few hours ago, in the heat of the day. But now a cool breeze, smelling faintly of the salt water forty miles away, brushed against the leaves of the trees above Theodore's head. He leaned over and picked up the wine jug at his feet. He took a drink and capped the bottle and looked at the stars set against the black sky like the tiny chips of a shattered mirror. They reminded him of the glitter that Flapjack used to brush on his eyelids. Up around Chattahoochee one evening, he and Roy had sneaked back into the carnival just for a few minutes, a year or so after the incident with the little boy. No, the hot dog vendor told them, Flapjack wasn't with them anymore. We were set up right outside this redneck town in Arkansas, and one night he just disappeared. Hell, we were halfway across the state the next day before anyone noticed him missing. The boss said he'd show up eventually, but he never did. You boys know how ol' Bradford is, all business. He said Flapjack was starting to lose his funny anyway.

Theodore was so tired, so sick of it all. "We had some good times though, didn't we, Roy?" he said out loud, but the man on the ground didn't move. He took another drink and set the bottle on his lap. "Good times," he repeated in a low voice. The stars blurred and faded from his sight. He dreamed of Flapjack in his clown suit and bare churches lit with smoky lanterns and loud honky-tonks with sawdust floors, and then a gentle ocean was lapping at his feet. He could feel it, the cool water. He smiled and pushed himself forward and began floating out to sea, farther than he had ever been before. He wasn't afraid; God was calling him home, and soon his legs would work again. But in the morning, he awoke on the hard ground, disappointed that he was still alive. He reached down and felt his pants. He'd pissed himself again. Roy had already taken off for the orchard. He lay with the side of his face pressed against the dirt. He stared at a mound of his fly-covered shit a few feet away and tried to slip back into sleep, back to the water.

32

EMMA AND ARVIN WERE STANDING in front of the meat case in the grocery store in Lewisburg. It was the end of the month, and the old woman didn't have much money, but the new preacher was arriving on Saturday. The congregation was having a potluck supper for him and his wife at the church. "You think chicken livers would be all right?" she asked after some more calculations in her head. The organs were cheapest.

"Why wouldn't they be?" Arvin said. He would have agreed with anything by then; even pig snouts would have been fine with him. The old woman had been staring at the trays of bloody meat for twenty minutes.

"I don't know," she said. "Everyone says they like the way I do 'em, but—"

"All right," Arvin said, "get them all a big steak then."

"Pshaw," she said. "You know I can't afford nothing like that."

"Then chicken livers it is," he said, motioning for the butcher in the white apron. "Grandma, quit worrying about it. He's just a preacher. I'd say he's et a lot worse than that."

That Saturday evening, Emma covered her pan of chicken livers with a clean cloth and Arvin set them carefully on the back floorboard of his car. His grandmother and Lenora were more than a little nervous; they'd been practicing their introductions all day. "Pleased to meet you," they had repeated anytime they passed each other in the small house. He and Earskell had sat on the front porch and chuckled, but after a while, it started getting old. "Jesus Christ, boy, I can't stand it no more," the old man finally said. He got up from his rocker and went around the back of the house and into the woods. It took Arvin several days to get those four words out of his head, that "pleased to meet you" shit.

When they arrived at six o'clock, the gravel lot around the old church was already full of cars. Arvin carried in the pan of livers and placed them on the table near the rest of the meats. The new preacher, tall and portly, was standing in the middle of the room shaking hands and saying, "Pleased to meet you," over and over. His name was Preston Teagardin. His longish blond hair was slicked back over his head with perfumed oil, and a big oval stone glittered on one hairy hand and a thin gold wedding band on the other. He wore shiny powder-blue pants that were too tight and ankle-high boots and a ruffled white shirt that, though it was only the first of April and still cool out, was already soaked through with sweat. Arvin figured him for thirty or so, but his wife appeared to be quite a bit younger, still in her teens perhaps. She was a slim reed of a girl with long auburn hair parted in the middle and a pale, freckled complexion. She stood a couple of feet from her husband, chomping gum and pulling at the lavender and white polka-dot skirt that kept riding up her trim, round ass. The preacher kept introducing her as "my sweet, righteous bride from Hohenwald, Tennessee."

Preacher Teagardin wiped the sweat off his smooth, broad fore-head with an embroidered handkerchief and mentioned a church he had worshipped at for a while down in Nashville that had real air-conditioning. It was clearly evident that he was disappointed with his uncle's setup. Lord, there wasn't even a single fan. By the middle of summer, this old shack would be a torture chamber. His spirits started to flag, and he was beginning to look as sleepy and bored as his wife, but then Arvin noticed him perk up considerably when Mrs. Alma Reaster came through the door with her two teenage daughters, Beth Ann and Pamela Sue, ages fourteen and sixteen. It was as if a couple of angels had fluttered into the room and alighted on the preacher's shoulders. Try as he might, he couldn't keep his eyes off their tanned, tight bodies in matching cream-colored dresses. Suddenly inspired, Teagardin began talking to all those around him about forming a youth group, something he'd seen used to great effect at several churches in Memphis. He was going to do his best, he vowed, to get the young people involved. "They are the lifeblood of any church,"

he said. Then his wife stepped up and whispered something in his
ear while staring at the Reaster girls that must have agitated him
greatly, some of the congregation thought, with the way he puckered
his red lips and pinched the inside of her arm. It was hard for Arvin
to believe that this pussy-sniffing fat boy was any relation to Albert
Sykes.

Arvin slipped outside to smoke just before Emma and Lenora
ventured forward to introduce themselves to the new man. He wondered how they would react when the preacher greeted them with
"Pleased to meet you." He stood under a pear tree with a couple of
farmers dressed in dungarees and shirts buttoned tight around their
necks, watching a few more people hurry inside while listening to
them talk about the going price of veal calves. Finally, someone came
to the door and yelled, "The preacher's ready to eat."

The people insisted that Teagardin and his wife go first, so the
chubby boy grabbed two plates and proceeded around the tables,
sniffing at the food delicately and uncovering dishes and sticking his
finger into this and that for just a taste, putting on a show for the two
Reaster girls, who giggled and whispered to each other. Then all of
the sudden, he stopped and passed his still-empty plates to his wife.
The pinched mark on her arm was already beginning to turn blue.
He looked toward the ceiling with his hand held up high, then
pointed at Emma's pan of chicken livers. "Friends," he began in a
loud voice, "there's no doubt we're all humble people here in this
church this evening and you all have been awful nice to me and my
sweet, young bride, and I thank ye from the bottom of my heart for
the warm welcome. Now, they ain't a one of us got all the money
and fine cars and trinkets and pretty clothes that we would like to
have, but friends, the poor old soul that brung in them chicken livers
in that beat-up pan, well, let's just say I'm inspired to preach on it for
a minute before we set down to eat. Recall, if you can, what Jesus said
to the poor in Nazareth those many centuries ago. Sure, some of us
are better off than others, and I see plenty of white meat and red
meat laid out on this table, and I suspect that the people who carried
them platters in eat mighty good most times. But poor people got to

bring what they can afford, and sometimes they can't afford much at all; and so them organs is a sign to me, telling me that I should, as the new preacher of this church, sacrifice myself so that you all can have a share of the good meat tonight. And that's what I'm going to do, my friends, I'm going to eat those organs, so you all can have a share of the best. Don't worry, it's just the way I am. I model myself on the good Lord Jesus whenever he gives me the chance, and tonight he has blessed me with another opportunity to follow in his footsteps. Amen." Then Preacher Teagardin said something to his red-haired wife in a low voice, and she headed straight for the desserts, wobbling a little in her cardboard high heels, and filled the plates with custard pie and carrot cake and Mrs. Thompson's sugar cookies, while he carried the pan of livers to his place at the head of one of the long plywood tables set up in the front for eating.

"Amen," the congregation repeated. Some looked confused, while others, those who had brought some of the good meat, grinned happily. A few glanced at Emma, who stood near the back of the line with Lenora. When she felt their eyes on her, she started to swoon and the girl grabbed her by the elbow. Arvin rushed forward from where he was standing in the open doorway and helped her outside. He sat her down in a grassy spot under a tree, and Lenora brought her a glass of water. The old woman took a sip and started to cry. Arvin patted her on the shoulder. "Now, now," he said, "don't you worry about that pus-gutted blowhard. He probably don't have two nickels to rub together. You want me to talk to him?"

She dabbed at her eyes with the hem of her good dress. "I never been so embarrassed in my whole life," she said. "I could have crawled under the table."

"You want me to take you home?"

She sniffled some more, then sighed. "I don't know what to do." She looked toward the door of the church. "He sure ain't the preacher I was hoping for."

"Hell, Grandma, that fool ain't no preacher," Arvin said. "He's bad as them they got on the radio begging for money."

"Arvin, you shouldn't talk like that," Lenora said. "Preacher Tea-gardin wouldn't be here if the Lord hadn't sent him."

"Yeah, right." He started to help his grandmother up. "You see the way he was gobbling them livers down," he joked, trying to get her to smile. "Heck, that boy probably ain't had nothing that good to eat in a coon's age. That's why he wanted them all for his own self."

33

PRESTON TEAGARDIN WAS LYING ON THE COUCH reading his old college psychology book in the house the congregation had rented for his wife and him. It was a little square box with four dirty windows and an outhouse surrounded by weeping willows at the end of a dirt path. The leaky gas stove was full of mummified mice, and the cast-off furniture they had provided smelled like dog or cat or some other dirty creature. My God, with the way the people around here lived he wouldn't have been surprised if it wasn't hog. Though he'd been in Coal Creek only two weeks, he already despised the place. He kept trying to look upon his assignment in this outpost in the sticks as some sort of spiritual test coming directly from the Lord, but it was more his mother's doing than anything else. Oh, yes, she had fucked him royally, shoved it right up his ass, the old shrew. Not a penny more allowance until he showed his mettle, she had said after finally finding out—the same week she was getting ready to attend the graduation ceremony—that he had dropped out of Heavenly Reach Bible College at the end of his first semester. And then, just a day or so later, her sister had called and told her that Albert was sick. What perfect timing. She'd volunteered her son without even asking him.

The psychology course he'd taken with Dr. Phillips was the only good thing that came out of his college experience. What the hell did a degree from a place like Heavenly Reach mean in a world of Ohio Universities and Harvard Colleges anyway? Might as well have purchased a diploma through one of those mail-order places advertised in the backs of comic books. He'd wanted to go to a regular university and study law, but no, not with her money. She wanted him to be a humble preacher, like her brother-in-law, Albert. She was afraid she'd spoiled him, she said. She said all kinds of shit, insane shit, but what she really wanted, Preston understood, was to keep him dependent on her, tied to her apron strings, so he'd always have to kiss her ass. He had always been good at figuring people out, their petty wants and desires, especially teenage girls.

Cynthia was one of his first major successes. She was only fifteen years old when he helped one of his teachers at Heavenly Reach dunk her in Flat Fish Creek during a baptism service. That same evening, he fucked her dainty little ass under some rosebushes on the college grounds, and within a year he had married her so that he could work on her without her parents sticking their noses in. In the last three years, he'd taught her all the things he imagined a man might be able to do with a woman. He couldn't begin to add up the hours it had taken him, but she was trained as well as any dog now. All he had to do was snap his fingers and her mouth would start watering for what he liked to refer to as his "staff."

He looked over at her in her underwear, curled up in the greasy easy chair that had come with the dump, her silky-haired gash pressed tight against the thin yellow material. She was squinting at an article about the Dave Clark Five in a *Hit Parader* magazine, trying to sound out the words. Someday, he thought, if he kept her, he would have to teach her how to read. He had discovered lately that he could last twice as long if one of his young conquests read from the Good Book while he nailed her from behind. Preston loved the way they panted holy passages, the way they began to stutter and arch their backs and struggle not to lose their place—for he could become very upset when they got the words wrong—right before his staff exploded. But Cynthia? Shit, a brain-damaged second-grader from the darkest holler in Appalachia could read better. Whenever his mother mentioned that her son, Preston Teagardin, with four years of high school Latin under his belt, had ended up married to an illiterate from Hohenwald, she nearly had another breakdown.

So it was debatable, keeping Cynthia. Sometimes he would glance over at her and, for a second or two, not even be able to recall her name. Gaped open and numb from his many experiments, what had once been fresh and tight was a faded memory now, and so, too, was the excitement she used to arouse in him. His biggest problem with Cynthia, though, was that she no longer believed in Jesus. Preston could abide just about anything but not that. He needed for a woman to believe that she was doing wrong when she lay with him, that she was in imminent danger of going to hell. How could he get turned on by someone who didn't understand the desperate battle raging between good and evil, purity and lust? Every time he fucked some young girl, Preston felt guilty, felt as if he was drowning in it, at least for a long minute or two. To him, such emotion proved that he still had a chance of going to heaven, regardless of how corrupt and cruel he might be, that is, if he repented his wretched, whoring ways before he took his last breath. It all came down to a matter of timing, which, of course, made things all that much more exciting. Cynthia, though, didn't seem to care one way or another. Nowadays, fucking her was like sticking his staff in a greasy, soulless doughnut.

But you take that Laferty girl, Preston thought, turning another page in the psychology book and rubbing his half-hard cock through his pajamas, Lord, that girl was a believer. He'd been watching her closely in church the past two Sundays. True, she wasn't much to look at, but he'd had worse down in Nashville when he volunteered that month at the poor house. He reached over and took a saltine from a pack on the coffee table, crammed it in his mouth. He let it lie on his tongue like a host and melt, turn into a soggy, tasteless glob. Yes, Miss Lenora Laferty would do for now, at least until he could get his hands on one of the Reaster girls. He'd put a smile on that sad, crimped face of hers once he got that faded dress off. According to the church gossips, at one time her father had been a preacher around this county, but then—at least the way they told it—he'd murdered the girl's mother and disappeared. Left poor little Lenora just a babe with the old lady who'd gotten so tore up about those chicken livers. This girl, he predicted, was going to be so easy.

He swallowed the cracker, and a little spark of happiness suddenly swept through his body, ran from the top of his blond head down his legs and into his toes. Thank God, thank God, his mother had decided all those years ago that he was going to be a preacher. All the fresh young meat a man could stand if he played his cards right. The old bag had curled his hair every morning and taught him good hygiene and made him practice his facial expressions in the mirror. She'd studied the Bible with him every night and drove him around to different churches and kept him in nice clothes. Preston had never played baseball, but he could cry on cue; he'd never been in a fist-fight, but he could recite the book of Revelation in his sleep. So, yes, goddamn it, he'd do what she had asked, help out her sick, sad-sack brother-in-law for a while, live in this shit hole of a house, and even pretend to like it. He'd show her his "mettle," by God. And then, when Albert got back on his feet, he'd ask her for the money. He'd probably have to deceive her, feed her some bullshit story, but he'd feel at least a pang of guilt, so that was all right. Anything to get to the West Coast. It was his new obsession. He'd been hearing stuff on the news lately. There was something going on out there that he needed to witness. Free love and runaway girls living in the streets with flowers stuck in their matted hair. Easy pickings for a man blessed with his abilities.

Preston marked his place in the book with his uncle's old tobacco sack and closed the book. Five Brothers? Jesus, what sort of person would put their faith in something like that? He'd nearly laughed in Albert's face when the old man told him it had the power to heal. He looked over at Cynthia, half asleep now, a string of drool hanging from her chin. He snapped his fingers and her eyes popped open. She frowned and tried to shut her eyes again, but it was impossible. She did her best to resist, but then got up from her chair and knelt at the side of the couch. Preston pulled down his pajama bottoms, spread his fat, hairy legs a bit. As she began to swallow him, he said a little prayer to himself: Lord, just give me six months in California, then I'll come home and fly right, settle down with a flock of good people, I swear on my mother's grave. He pushed Cynthia's head down farther, heard her begin to gag and choke. Then her throat muscles relaxed and she quit fighting it. He held her there until her face turned scarlet and then purple from lack of air. He liked it that way, he surely did. Look at her go.

34

ONE DAY ON HER WAY HOME FROM SCHOOL, Lenora stopped at
the Coal Creek Church of the Holy Ghost Sanctified. The front door
was opened wide and Preacher Teagardin's ratty English sports car—
a gift from his mother when he'd first gone off to Heavenly Reach—
was sitting in the shade, same as yesterday and the day before. It
was a warm afternoon in the middle of May. She had ducked Arvin,
watched from inside the schoolhouse until he gave up waiting and
left without her. She stepped inside the church and let her eyes adjust
to the gloom. The new preacher was sitting on one of the benches
halfway down the aisle. It looked as if he was praying. She waited
until she heard him say, "Amen," and then she began moving slowly
forward.

Teagardin felt her presence behind him. He had been waiting
patiently on Lenora for three weeks now. He'd come to the church
nearly every day and opened the door around the time the school let
out. Most days he saw her ride past in that piece-of-shit Bel Air with
that half brother or whatever he was, but once or twice he'd seen her
walking home by herself. He heard her soft steps on the rough wood
floor. He could smell her Juicy Fruit breath as she got closer; he had
the nose of a bloodhound when it came to young women and their
different odors. "Who is it?" he said, raising his head.

"It's Lenora Laferty, Preacher Teagardin."

He crossed himself and turned to her with a smile. "Well, what a
surprise," he said. Then he peered at her more closely. "Girl, you look
like you been crying."

"It's nothing," she said, shaking her head. "Just some kids at
school. They like to tease."

He looked past her for a moment, searching for a suitable

response. "I suspect they just jealous," he said. "Envy tends to bring out the worst in people, especially the young ones."

"I doubt if that's it," she said.

"How old are you, Lenora?"

"Almost seventeen."

"I remember when I was that age," he said. "There I was, full of the Lord, and the other kids making fun of me day and night. It was awful, the horrible notions that ran through my head."

She nodded and sat down on the bench across from him. "What did you do about it?" she asked.

He ignored her question, appeared to be deep in thought. "Yes, that was a rough time," he finally said with a long sigh. "Thank God it's over." Then he smiled again. "You got anywhere you have to be for the next couple hours?"

"No, not really," she said.

Teagardin stood up, took hold of her hand. "Well, then, I think it's about time you and me take a ride."

TWENTY MINUTES LATER, they were parked on an old farm lane that he'd been checking out ever since his arrival in Coal Creek. It had once led to some hay fields a mile or so off the main road, but the land was now overgrown with Johnson grass and thick brush. His tire tracks were the only ones he'd seen on it for the past two weeks. It was a safe spot to bring someone. When he shut the car off, he said a little prayer, then laid his warm, meaty hand on Lenora's knee and told her just what she wanted to hear. Hell, every one of them wanted to hear pretty much the same thing anyway, even the ones full of Jesus. He wished that she had resisted a little bit more, but she was easy, just like he had predicted. Even so, as many times as he'd done this, all the time he was peeling her clothes off, he could hear every bird, every insect, every animal that moved in the woods for what seemed like miles. It was always like that the first time with a new one.

When he finished, Preston reached down and grabbed her gray, dingy panties lying on the floorboard. He wiped the blood off himself and handed them to her. He swatted at a fly buzzing around his crotch, then tugged up his brown slacks and buttoned his white shirt as he watched her struggle back into her long dress. "You ain't gonna tell no one, are you?" he said. Already, he wished he'd stayed home and read his psychology book, maybe even attempted cutting the grass with the push mower Albert had sent over after Cynthia stepped on a black snake curled up in front of the outhouse. Unfortunately, he had never been one of those men adept at physical labor. Just thinking about shoving that mower around and around that rocky yard made him feel a little nauseous.

"No," she said. "I'd never do that. I promise."

"That's good. Some people might not understand. And I sincerely believe that a person's relationship with their preacher should be a private thing."

"Did you mean what you said?" she asked him bashfully.

He struggled to recall which bullshit line he had used on her. "Well, sure I did." His throat was parched. Maybe he'd drive over to Lewisburg and have a cold beer to celebrate busting open another virgin. "By the time we get done," he said, "them boys at your school won't be able to take their eyes off you. It just takes some breaking in for some girls, that's all. But I can tell you one of them that just gets prettier as they get older. You should thank the Lord for that. Yep, you got some sweet years ahead of you, Miss Lenora Laferty."

35

AT THE END OF MAY, ARVIN GRADUATED from Coal Creek
High School, along with nine other seniors. The following Monday, he went to work for a construction crew that was putting a new
coat of blacktop on the Greenbrier County stretch of Route 60. A
neighbor across the knob named Clifford Baker had gotten him on.
He and Arvin's father used to raise hell together before the war, and
Baker figured the boy deserved a break as much as anyone. It was a
good-paying job, nearly union wages, and though he was designated
a laborer, supposedly the worst job on the crew, Earskell had worked
Arvin harder in the garden patch behind the house. The day he got
his first check, he picked up two fifths of good whiskey from Slot
Machine for the old man, ordered Emma a ringer washer from the
Sears catalog, and bought Lenora a new dress for church at Mayfair's,
the priciest store in three counties.

While the girl was trying to find something that fit, Emma said,
"My Lord, I hadn't noticed before, but you sure are starting to fill
out." Lenora turned back to the mirror and smiled. She had always
been straight up and down, no hips, no chest. Last winter, someone
had taped a picture from *Life* magazine of a heap of concentration
camp victims to her locker, wrote in ink, "Lenora Laferty," with an
arrow pointing to the third corpse from the left. If it hadn't been for
Arvin, she wouldn't have even bothered to take the picture down.
But she was finally starting to look like a woman, just like Preacher
Teagardin had promised. She was meeting him three, four, sometimes
five afternoons a week now. She felt bad every time they did it, but
she couldn't tell him no. It was the first time she had ever realized just
how powerful sin could be. No wonder it was so hard for people to
get into heaven. Each time they met, Preston had something new he

wanted to try. Yesterday, he'd brought a tube of his wife's lipstick. "I know it sounds silly, with what we been doing," she said timidly, "but I don't think a woman should paint her face. You ain't mad, are you?"

"Well, heck no, darling, that's all right," he told her. "Shoot, I admire your beliefs. I wish that wife of mine loved Jesus like you do." Then he grinned and pushed her dress up, hooked his thumb over the top of her panties and pulled them down. "Besides, I was thinking about painting something else anyway."

ONE EVENING, AS SHE WASHED THE SUPPER DISHES, Emma looked out the window and saw Lenora coming out of the woods across the road from the house. They had waited on her a few minutes, then went ahead and ate. "That girl sure is spending a lot of time in them woods lately," the old woman said. Arvin was leaned back in his chair drinking the last of the coffee and watching Earskell try to roll a smoke. The old man was bent over the table, a look of intense concentration on his lined face. Arvin watched his fingers tremble, wondered if his great-uncle was beginning to slip a little.

"Knowing her," Arvin said, "she's probably out talkin' to butterflies."

Emma watched the girl scramble up the bank toward the porch. She looked like she had been running, the way her face was flushed. The old woman had noticed a big change in the girl the last few weeks. One day she was happy, the next day filled with despair. A lot of girls went a little crazy for a while when the blood started flowing, Emma reasoned, but Lenora had gone through all that two years ago. She still saw her studying her Bible, though; and she seemed to love going to church more than she ever did, even though Preacher Teagardin couldn't hold a candle to Albert Sykes when it came to giving a good sermon. At times, Emma wondered if the man really cared at all about preaching the Gospel, the way he kept losing his train of thought, like he had other things on his mind. There she was, she realized, getting all stirred up about those chicken livers again. She would have to pray on it again tonight when she went to bed. She turned and looked at Arvin. "You don't figure she might have her a beau, do you?"

"Who? Lenora?" he said, and then rolled his eyes as if it was one of the most ridiculous things he'd ever heard. "I don't think you need to worry about that, Grandma." He glanced over and saw that Earskell had made a mess of his cigarette, was just sitting there with his mouth open, staring at the makings on the table. Reaching over for the little sack of tobacco and the papers, the boy began rolling the old man a new one.

"Looks ain't everything," Emma said harshly.

"That's not what I'm saying," he sputtered, ashamed that he had joked about the girl. There were already too many people doing that. It suddenly dawned on him that he wouldn't be at school anymore to keep them off her back. She was going to have a rough row to hoe next fall. "I just don't think there's any boys around here she'd be interested in, that's all."

The front screen door opened and closed with a squeak, and then they heard Lenora humming a song. Emma listened closely, recognized it as "Poor Pilgrim of Sorrow." Satisfied for now, she dipped her hands in the lukewarm water, began scrubbing on a skillet. Arvin turned his attention back to the cigarette. He licked the paper and gave it another twist, then handed it to Earskell. The old man smiled and fumbled in his shirt pocket for a match. He searched a long time before he found one.

36

BY THE MIDDLE OF AUGUST, Lenora knew she was in trouble. She had missed her period twice and the dress that Arvin had bought her would hardly fit anymore. Teagardin had broken it off a couple of weeks before. He told her that he was afraid if he kept meeting her, his wife was going to find out, perhaps even the congregation. "Ain't neither one of us wants that to happen, right?" he said. She walked by the church several days before she found him there, the door propped open and his little car sitting under the shade tree. He was sitting in the shadows near the front, his head bowed when she stepped inside, just like that day when she first came to him, three months ago, only this time he didn't smile when he turned around and saw who it was. "You ain't supposed to be here," Teagardin said, though he wasn't totally surprised. Some of them just can't quit it all at once.

He couldn't help but notice the way the girl's tits pressed against the top of her dress now. He had seen it time after time, the way their young bodies filled out once they started getting it regular. Glancing at his watch, he saw that he had a few extra minutes. Maybe he should give her one last good fuck, he was thinking, when Lenora blurted out, her voice cracking and hysterical, that she was carrying his baby. He jumped up with a start, then hurried to the front door and closed it. He looked down at his hands, thick but soft as a woman's. He wondered, in the time it took him to draw a deep breath, if he could strangle her with them, but he knew damn well he didn't have the guts for that sort of business. Besides, if he were to accidentally get caught, prison, especially some loathsome dungeon in West Virginia, would be much too harsh for a delicate person such as himself. There had to be another way. He had to think fast, though. He considered her situation, a poor orphan girl knocked up and half out of her mind with worry. All these thoughts ran through his head while he took his time locking the door. Then he walked to the front of the church where she sat on one of the benches, tears running down her quivering face. He decided to begin talking, which was what he did best. He told her that he had heard of cases like hers, where the person was so deluded and sick over something they had done, some sin they had committed that was so terrible, that they started imagining things. Why, he'd read about people, just common folks, some of them barely able to write their own name, who became convinced that they were the president or the pope or even some famous movie star. Those kinds, Teagardin warned in a sad voice, usually ended up in a nuthouse, getting raped by the orderlies and forced to eat their own waste.

Lenora had quit sobbing by then. She wiped her eyes with the sleeve of her dress. "I don't understand what you're talking about," she said. "I'm pregnant with your baby."

He held out his hands, heaved a sigh. "That's part of it, the book says, not understanding. But you think about it. How could I be the daddy? I've never touched you, not once. Look at you. I've got a wife sitting at home that's a hundred times as pretty and she'll do anything I ask, and I do mean anything."

She looked up with a dumbfounded expression on her face. "You're saying you don't remember all the things we did in your car?"

"I'm saying that you must be crazy to come into the Lord's house and talk such trash. You think anyone's gonna believe you over me? I'm a preacher." Jesus, he thought, standing there looking down at this red-nosed, sniveling little hag, why hadn't he just held out and waited until the Reaster girl came around. Pamela had proved to be the finest piece he'd had since the early days with Cynthia.

"But you're the father," Lenora said in a soft, numb voice. "Hasn't been nobody else."

Teagardin looked at his watch again. He had to get rid of this wench fast, or his whole afternoon was going to be ruined. "My advice to you, girl," he said, his voice turning low and hateful, "is you figure some way to get rid of it, that is, if you even are knocked up like you say. It would just be some little bastard with a whore for a mother if you keep it. If nothing else, think of that poor old woman who's raised you, brings you to church here every Sunday. She'll die from the shame of it all. Now you get on out before you cause any more trouble."

Lenora didn't say another word. She looked at the wooden cross hanging on the wall behind the altar, then stood up. Teagardin unlocked the door and held it open, a scowl etched on his face, and she walked past him with her head down. She heard the door quickly close behind her. Though she felt faint, she managed to walk a couple hundred yards before she collapsed under a tree a few feet from the edge of the gravel road. She could still see the church, the one she had gone to all her life. She had felt the presence of God there many times, but not once, it occurred to her now, since the new preacher had arrived. A few minutes later, she watched Pamela Reaster come up the other end of the road and go inside, a look of happiness spread across her pretty face.

That evening, after supper, Arvin drove Emma to the church for the Thursday night service. Lenora had pleaded sick, said her head felt like it was splitting open. She hadn't touched her food. "Well, you don't look good, that's for sure," Emma said, feeling the girl's cheek for fever. "You go ahead and stay home tonight. I'll have 'em say a prayer for you." Lenora waited in her bedroom until she heard Arvin's car start up, then made sure Earskell was still asleep in his rocker on the porch. She went out to the smokehouse and opened the door. She stood and waited until her eyes adjusted to the gloom. She found a length of rope coiled in a corner behind some minnow traps and tied a crude noose on one end. Then she moved an empty lard bucket over to the center of the small shed. She stepped up on it and wrapped the other end of the rope seven or eight times around one of the support beams. Then she hopped off the bucket and closed the door. It was dark in the shed now.

Stepping back up on the metal bucket, she put the noose around her neck and tightened it. A trickle of sweat ran down her face, and she caught herself thinking that she should do this out in the sunlight, in the warm summer air, maybe even wait another day or two. Perhaps Preston would change his mind. That's what she would do, she thought. He couldn't have meant what he said. He was upset, that's all. She started to loosen the noose and the lard bucket began to wobble. Then her foot slipped and the bucket rolled away and left her dangling in the air. She had dropped only a few inches, not nearly enough to break her neck clean. She could almost touch her toes to the floor, just another inch or so. Kicking her legs, she grabbed hold of the rope, tried her best to raise herself up to the beam, but she didn't have enough strength. She tried to yell out, but the choking sounds wouldn't carry beyond the shed door. As the rope slowly squeezed her windpipe shut, she became more frantic, clawing at her neck with her fingernails. Her face turned purple. She was vaguely aware of urine running down her legs. The blood vessels in her eyes began to burst, and everything got darker and darker. No, she thought, no. I can have this baby, God. I can just leave this place, go away like my daddy did. I can just disappear.

37

A WEEK OR SO AFTER THE FUNERAL, Tick Thompson, the new sheriff of Greenbrier County, was waiting at Arvin's car when the boy got off work. "I need to talk to you, Arvin," the lawman said. "It's about Lenora." He had been one of the men who helped carry her body out of the smokehouse after Earskell saw the door unlatched and found her. He'd been called to a few suicides over the years, mostly men, though, blowing their brains out over some woman or a bad business deal, never a young girl hanging herself. When he'd asked, right after the ambulance pulled away that evening, Emma and the boy both said she had actually seemed happier lately. There was something about it that didn't add up. He hadn't had a decent night's sleep all week.

Arvin tossed his lunch bucket in the front seat of the Bel Air. "What about her?"

"I figured it might be best to tell you instead of your grandmother. From what I hear, she's not taking things too good."

"Tell me what?"

The sheriff took his hat off, held it in his hands. He waited until a couple of other men walked by and got in their vehicles, then cleared his throat. "Well, hell, I don't know how to say it, Arvin, other than just say it. Did you know Lenora was carrying a baby?"

Arvin stared at him for a long minute, a puzzled look on his face. "That's bullshit," he finally said. "Some sonofabitch is lying."

"I know how you must feel, I really do, but I just came from the coroner's office. Though ol' Dudley might be a drunk, he ain't no liar. Near as he can figure it, she was about three months along."

The boy turned away from the sheriff and reached in his back pocket for a dirty rag, wiped his eyes. "Jesus," he said, struggling to keep his upper lip from quivering.

"Do you think your grandmother knew?"

Shaking his head, Arvin took a deep breath and exhaled it slowly, then said, "Sheriff, my grandma would die if she heard that."

"Well, did Lenora have a boyfriend, someone she was seeing?" the sheriff asked.

Arvin thought about the night, just a few weeks ago, when Emma had asked that same question. "None that I know of. Hell, she was the most religious person I ever seen."

Tick put his hat back on. "Look, here's the way I see it," he said. "Ain't nobody has to know about this but you, me, and Dudley, and he won't say nothing, I guarantee it. So we'll just keep it quiet for now. How does that sound?"

Swiping at his eyes again, Arvin nodded. "I'd appreciate that," he said. "It's been bad enough everyone knowing what she did to herself. Hell, we couldn't even get that new preacher to—" His face suddenly grew dark, and he looked away toward Muddy Creek Mountain in the distance.

"What is it, son?"

"Ah, nothing," Arvin said, looking back at the sheriff. "We couldn't get him to say no words at the funeral, that's all."

"Well, some people have strong views on things like that."

"Yeah, I guess so."

"So you got no idea who she might have been messing with?"

"Lenora stayed to herself mostly," the boy said. "Besides, what could you do about it anyway?"

Tick shrugged. "Not much, I expect. Maybe I shouldn't have said nothing."

"I'm sorry, I didn't mean no disrespect," Arvin said. "And I'm glad you told me. At least now I know why she did it." He stuck the rag back in his pocket and shook Tick's hand. "And thanks for thinking about my grandma, too."

He watched the sheriff pull away, then got in his car and drove the fifteen miles back to Coal Creek. He played the radio as loud as it would go and stopped at the bootlegger's shack in Hungry Holler and bought two pints of whiskey. When he got home, he went in and checked on Emma. She hadn't been out of bed all week as far as he knew. She was starting to smell bad. He got her a glass of water and made her drink a little. "Look, Grandma," he said to her, "I expect you to get out of bed in the morning and fix me and Earskell breakfast, okay?"

"Just let me lay here," she said. She rolled over on her side, closed her eyes.

"One more day, that's it," he told her. "I'm not kidding around." He went in the kitchen and fried some potatoes, fixed bologna sandwiches for him and Earskell. After they ate, Arvin washed up the skillet and plates and looked in on Emma again. Then he took the two pints out on the porch and handed one to the old man. He sat down in a chair and finally allowed himself to consider what the sheriff had told him. Three months along. For sure, it hadn't been some boy from around here got Lenora pregnant. Arvin knew everybody, and he knew what they thought about her. The only place she liked to go was church. He thought back to when the new preacher first arrived. That would have been April, a little over four months ago. He recalled the way Teagardin got all excited when the two Reaster girls walked in the night of the potluck. Other than himself, nobody had seemed to notice except the young wife. Lenora had even put her bonnets away not long after Teagardin showed up. He had thought she was finally sick of being made fun of at school, but maybe she had another reason.

He shook two cigarettes out of his pack and lit them, handed one to Earskell. The day before the funeral, Teagardin told some of the church members that he didn't feel comfortable preaching over a suicide. Instead, he asked his poor sick uncle to say a few words in his place. Two men had carried Albert in on a wooden kitchen chair. It was the hottest day of the year, and the church was like a furnace, but the old man had risen to the occasion. A couple of hours later, Arvin went out driving around on the back roads, which was what he always did now when things didn't make any sense. He passed by Teagardin's house, saw the preacher walking to the outhouse in a pair of bedroom slippers and a floppy, pink hat like a woman might wear. His wife was sunbathing in a bikini, stretched out on a blanket in the weedy, overgrown yard.

"Damn, it's hot," Earskell said.

"Yeah," Arvin said after a minute or two. "Maybe we ought to sleep out here tonight."

"I don't see how Emma stands it in that bedroom. It's like an oven back there."

"She's gonna get up in the morning, fix us breakfast."

"Really?"

"Yeah," Arvin said, "really."

And she did, biscuits and eggs and sawmill gravy, was up an hour before they stirred from their blankets on the porch. Arvin noticed that she had washed her face and changed her dress, tied a clean rag around her thin, gray hair. She didn't say much, but when she sat down and began to fix herself a plate, he knew that he could stop worrying about her now. The next day, when the foreman got out of his pickup and pointed at his watch that it was quitting time, Arvin hurried to his car and drove by Teagardin's again. He parked a quarter of a mile down the road and walked back, cutting through the woods. Sitting in the fork of a locust tree, he watched the preacher's house until the sun went down. He didn't know what he was looking for yet, but he had an idea of where to find it.

38

THREE DAYS LATER AT QUITTING TIME, Arvin told the boss he wouldn't be back. "Aw, come on, boy," the foreman said. "Shit, you 'bout the best worker I got." He spit a thick string of tobacco juice against the front tire of his pickup. "Stay two more weeks? We be finishing up by then."

"It ain't the job, Tom," Arvin said. "I just got something else needs taking care of right now."

He drove to Lewisburg and bought two boxes of 9mm bullets and stopped at the house and checked on Emma. She was in the kitchen scrubbing the linoleum floor on her hands and knees. He went to his bedroom and got the German Luger from the bottom drawer of his dresser. It was the first time he'd touched it since Earskell had asked him to put it away over a year ago. After telling his grandmother he'd be back soon, he went over to Stony Creek. He took his time cleaning the gun, then loaded eight shells into the magazine and lined up some cans and bottles. He reloaded four more times over the next hour. By the time he put it back in the glove box, the pistol felt like a part of his hand again. He had missed only three times.

On his way back home, he stopped at the cemetery. They had buried Lenora beside her mother. The monument man hadn't put the stone up yet. He stood looking down at the dry, brown dirt that marked her place, remembering the last time he'd come here with her to see Helen's grave. He could vaguely recall how she had tried, in her own awkward way, to flirt with him that afternoon, talking about orphans and star-crossed lovers, and he had gotten aggravated with her. If only he had paid a little more attention, he thought, if only people hadn't made fun of her so much, maybe things wouldn't have turned out like they did.

The next morning, he left the house at the usual time, acting as if he was going to work. Though he was certain in his gut that Teagardin was the one, he had to be sure. He began keeping track of the preacher's every movement. Within a week, he had watched the bastard fuck Pamela Reaster three times in an old farm lane just off Ragged Ridge Road. She walked through the fields from her parents' house to meet him there, every other day at exactly noon. Teagardin sat in his sports car and studied himself in the mirror until she arrived. After the third time he saw them meet there, Arvin spent an afternoon piling up deadwood and horseweeds to make a blind just a few yards from where the preacher parked under the shade of a tall oak tree. It was Teagardin's custom to hustle the girl away as soon as he was finished with her. He liked to dawdle a bit alone under the tree, relieving his bladder and listening to bubble gum music on the car radio. Occasionally, Arvin heard him talking to himself, but he could never make out the words. After twenty or thirty minutes, the car would start up, and Teagardin would turn around at the end of the lane and go home.

The next week, the preacher added Pamela's younger sister to his roster, but the meetings with Beth Ann took place inside the church. By then, Arvin had no doubts, and when he woke up Sunday morning to the sound of the church bells tolling across the holler, he decided the time had come. If he waited any longer, he was afraid he would lose his nerve. He knew Teagardin always met the older girl on Mondays. At least the horny sonofabitch was regular in his habits.

Arvin counted the money he had managed to put back over the last couple of years. He had $315 in the coffee can under his bed. He drove over to Slot Machine's after Sunday dinner and bought a fifth of whiskey, spent the evening drinking with Earskell on the porch. "You sure are good to me, boy," the old man said. Arvin had to swallow several times to keep from crying. He thought about tomorrow. This was the last time they would ever share a bottle.

It was a beautiful evening, cooler than it had been for several months. He went inside and got Emma, and she sat with them for a while with her Bible and a glass of ice tea. She hadn't been back to the Coal Creek Church of the Holy Ghost Sanctified since the night that Lenora died. "I think fall's going to come early this year," she said, marking her place in the book with a bony finger and gazing out across the road at the leaves already beginning to turn rust-colored. "We're going to have to start thinking about getting some wood in before long, ain't we, Arvin?"

He looked over at her. She was still staring at the trees on the hillside. "Yeah," he said. "Be cold before you know it." He hated himself for deceiving her, pretending everything was going to be all right. He wanted so much to be able to tell them goodbye, but they would be better off not knowing anything if the law came hunting for him. That night, after they went to bed, he packed some clothes in a gym bag and put it in the trunk of his car. He leaned on the porch railing and listened to the faint rumble of a coal train over the next swath of hills heading north. Going back inside, he stuck a hundred dollars in the tin box that Emma kept her needles and thread in. He didn't sleep any that night, and in the morning he just drank some coffee for breakfast.

He had been sitting in the blind for two hours when the Reaster girl came hurrying across the field, maybe fifteen minutes early. She appeared worried, kept looking at her wristwatch. When Teagardin showed up, easing his car down the rutted road slowly, she didn't jump in like she had always done in the past. Instead, she stood a few feet away and waited for him to shut the engine off. "Well, get in, honey," Arvin heard the preacher say. "I got a full sack for you."

"I ain't staying," she said. "We got problems."

"What do you mean?"

"You were supposed to keep your hands off my sister," the girl said.

"Oh, shit, Pamela, that didn't mean anything."

"No, you don't understand," she said. "She told Mother about it."

"When?"

"About an hour ago. I didn't think I was going to be able to get away."

"That little bitch," Teagardin cursed. "I hardly touched her."

"That ain't the way she tells it," Pamela said. She looked toward the road nervously.

"What did she say exactly?"

"Believe me, Preston, she told everything. She got scared because the bleeding won't stop." The girl pointed her finger at him. "You better hope you didn't do something so she can't have kids."

"Shit," Teagardin said. He got out of the car and paced back and forth for several minutes, his hands clasped behind his back like a general in his tent planning a counterattack. He took a silk handkerchief out of his pants pocket and patted his mouth. "What do you think your old lady will do?" he finally said.

"Well, knowing her, after she takes Beth Ann to the hospital, the first thing she'll do is call the fucking sheriff. And just so you know, he's my mom's cousin."

Teagardin placed his hands on the girl's shoulders and looked into her eyes. "But you haven't said anything about us, right?"

"You think I'm crazy? I'd rather die first."

Teagardin let go of her and leaned against the car. He looked out over the field before them. He wondered why nobody was farming it anymore. He imagined an old two-story house in ruins, some rusted pieces of antique machinery sitting in the weeds, maybe a hand-dug well of cool, clean water, covered over with rotten boards. Just for a moment, he pictured himself fixing the place back up, settling down to a simple life, preaching on Sundays and working the farm with callused hands through the week, reading good books out on the porch in the evenings after a nice supper, some tender babes playing in the shaded yard. He heard the girl say she was leaving, and when he finally turned to look, she was gone. Then he considered the possibility that perhaps Pamela was lying to him, trying to scare him into keeping off her little sister. He wouldn't put anything past her, but if what she said was true, he had only an hour or two at best to pack and get out of Greenbrier County. He was just getting ready to start the car when he heard a voice say, "You ain't much of a preacher, are you?"

Teagardin looked up and saw the Russell boy standing right outside the door of the car pointing a pistol of some kind at him. He'd never owned a gun, and the only thing he knew about them was that they usually caused trouble. The boy looked bigger up close. Not an ounce of fat on him, he noticed, dark hair, green eyes. He wondered what Cynthia would think of him. Though he knew it was ridiculous, with all the young pussy he was getting, he felt a pang of jealousy just then. It was sad to realize that he'd never look anything like this boy. "What the hell are you doing?" the preacher said.

"Been watching you screw that Reaster girl that just left. And if you try to start that car, I'm gonna blow your fucking hand off."

Teagardin let go of the ignition key. "You don't know what you're talking about, boy. I didn't touch her. All we did was talk."

"Maybe not today, but you been plowing her pretty steady."

"What? You been spying on me?" Maybe the boy was one of those voyeurs, he thought, recalling the term from his collection of nudist magazines.

"I know every fuckin' move you've made for the last two weeks."

Teagardin looked out the windshield toward the big oak at the end of the lane. He wondered if it could be true. In his head, he counted the number of times he'd been here with Pamela over the last couple of weeks. At least six. That was bad enough, but at the same time he felt a little relieved. At least the boy hadn't seen him banging his sister. Hard to tell what the crazy hillbilly might have done. "It ain't what it looks like," he said.

"What is it then?" Arvin asked. He flipped the safety off the gun.

Teagardin started to explain that the little slut wouldn't leave him alone, but then he reminded himself to be careful with his words. He considered the possibility that maybe this hoodlum had a crush on Pamela. Perhaps that's what this was all about. Jealousy. He tried to recall what Shakespeare had written about it, but the words wouldn't come to him. "Say, ain't you Mrs. Russell's grandson?" the preacher asked. He looked down at the clock on the dash. He could have been halfway home by now. Rivulets of greasy sweat began to run down his pink, clean-shaven face.

"That's right," Arvin said. "And Lenora Laferty was my sister."

Teagardin turned his head slowly, his eyes focused on the boy's belt buckle. Arvin could almost see the wheels spinning inside his head, watched him swallow several times. "That was a shame, what that poor girl did," the preacher said. "I pray for her soul every night."

"You pray for the baby's, too?"

"Now you got it all wrong there, my friend. I didn't have nothing to do with that."

"Do with what?"

The man squirmed around in the car's tight seat, glanced at the German Luger. "She came to me, said she wanted to make a confession, told me she was with child. I promised her I wouldn't tell anybody."

Arvin took a step back and said, "I'll bet you did, you fat sonofabitch." Then he fired three shots, blew out the tires on the driver's side and put the last one through the back door.

"Stop!" Teagardin yelled. "Stop, goddamn it!" He threw his hands up.

"No more lies," Arvin said, moving forward and jamming the pistol against the preacher's temple. "I know you was the one got her that way."

Teagardin jerked his head away from the gun. "Okay," he said. He took a deep breath. "I swear, I was going to take care of everything, I really was, and then . . . and then the next thing I know she'd done herself in. She was crazy."

"No," Arvin said, "she was just lonely." He pressed the barrel against the back of Teagardin's head. "But don't worry, I ain't gonna make you suffer like she did."

"Now hold on here, goddamn it. Jesus Christ, man, you wouldn't kill a preacher, would you?"

"You ain't no preacher, you worthless piece of shit," Arvin said.

Teagardin began crying, true tears running down his face for the first time since he was a little boy. "Let me pray first," he sobbed. He started to put his hands together.

"I already did it for you," Arvin said. "Put in one of them special requests you fuckers are always talking about, asked Him to send you straight to hell."

"No," Teagardin said, right before the gun went off. A fragment of the bullet came out right above his nose and landed with a ping on the dashboard. His big body pitched forward, and his face banged against the steering wheel. His left foot kicked the brake pedal a couple of times. Arvin waited until he stopped moving, then reached inside and picked the sticky shell fragment up off the dash and threw it into the weeds. He regretted shooting those other rounds off now, but there wasn't time to dig around for them. He hurriedly scattered the blind that he'd built and picked up the can he'd used for his cigarette butts. In five minutes, he was back at his car. He tossed the butt can in the ditch. As he stuck the German Luger up under the dash, he suddenly thought of Teagardin's young wife. She was probably sitting over in their little house right now, waiting for him to get home, the same as Emma would be doing for him tonight. He leaned back in the seat and shut his eyes for a moment, tried to think of other things. He started the engine and drove out to the end of Ragged Ridge, made a left toward Route 60. The way he had it figured, he could be in Meade, Ohio, sometime tonight if he didn't stop. He hadn't planned any further ahead than that.

Four hours later, about fifty miles outside of Charleston, West Virginia, the Bel Air began making a thumping noise underneath. He managed to get off the highway and into a filling station lot before the transmission went out completely. He got down on his hands and knees and watched the last of the fluid drip from the casing. "Motherfucker," he said. Just as he started to get up, a thin man in baggy blue coveralls came out and asked if he needed any help. "Not unless you got a transmission you can put in this thing," Arvin said.

"She went out on ye, huh?"

"It's shot," Arvin said.

"Where you headed?"

"Michigan."

"You welcome to use the phone if you want to call someone," the man said.

"Ain't no one to call." As soon as he said it, Arvin realized how true that statement really was. He thought for a minute. Though he hated the thought of giving the Bel Air up, he had to keep moving. He was going to have to make a sacrifice. He turned to the man and tried to smile. "How much would you give me for her?" he asked.

The man glanced at the car and shook his head. "I got no use for it."

"The engine's good. I just changed the points and plugs a couple days ago."

The man began walking the Chevy, kicking the tires, checking for putty. "I don't know," he said, rubbing the gray stubble on his chin.

"How about fifty bucks?" Arvin said.

"It ain't hot, is it?"

"The title's in my name."

"I'll give you thirty."

"Is that the best you can do?"

"Sonny, I got five kids at home," the man said.

"Okay, it's yours," Arvin said. "Just let me get my stuff." He watched the man go back inside the station. He took his bag out of the trunk and then sat down in the car one last time. The day he'd bought it, he and Earskell had burned up a whole tank of gas riding around, drove clear over to Beckley and back. He had a sudden feeling that he was going to lose a lot more before this was over. Reaching under the dash, he got the Luger, stuck it in his waistband. Then he took the title and a box of shells from the glove compartment. When he went inside, the man laid the thirty dollars on the counter. Arvin signed the title and dated it, then put the money in his wallet. He bought a Zagnut and a bottle of RC Cola. It was the first he'd eaten or drunk since the coffee that morning in his grandmother's kitchen. He looked out the window at the endless stream of cars going by on the highway while he chewed on the candy bar. "You ever hitchhike?" he asked the man.

39

ROY FINISHED PICKING ORANGES THAT DAY around five o'clock and collected his pay, which was thirteen dollars. He went to the store at the intersection and bought half a pound of pickle loaf and half a pound of cheese and a loaf of rye bread and two packs of Chesterfields and three fifths of White Port. It was nice getting paid every day. He felt like a rich man walking back to the spot where he and Theodore were camping. The boss was the best one he'd ever had, and Roy had been picking steady for three weeks. The man had told him today that there was maybe only another four or five days of work left. Theodore would be glad to hear that. He wanted to get back to the ocean awful bad. They had put away almost a hundred dollars in the last month, more money than they had had in a long, long time. Their plan was to buy some decent clothes and start preaching again. Roy thought they could find a couple of suits at the Goodwill for maybe ten or twelve bucks. Theodore couldn't play the guitar like he used to, but they could get along all right.

Roy crossed a drainage ditch and headed for their campsite under a small stand of stunted magnolia trees. He saw Theodore asleep on the ground next to his wheelchair, his guitar lying beside him. Roy shook his head and pulled out one of the bottles of wine and a pack of the smokes. He sat down on a stump and took a drink before he lit a cigarette. He had killed half the fifth before he finally noticed that the cripple's face was crawling with ants. Rushing to his side, Roy rolled him over on his back. "Theodore? Hey, come on, buddy, wake up," Roy pleaded, shaking him and slapping at the bugs. "Theodore?"

As soon as he tried to lift the man, Roy knew that he was dead, but he still struggled for fifteen minutes to get him back up in the wheelchair. He began pushing him through the sandy soil toward the highway, but went only a few feet before he stopped. The authorities would ask a lot of questions, he thought, as he watched a fancy car pass by in the distance. He looked around at the campsite. Maybe it would be better just to stay here. Theodore loved the ocean, but he liked the shade, too. And this grove of trees was as much a home as anything they'd had since their days with Bradford Amusements.

Roy sat down on the ground beside the wheelchair. They had done a lot of bad things over the years, and he spent the next several hours praying for the cripple's soul. He hoped someone would do the same for him when it came his time. Around sundown, he finally got up and fixed himself a sandwich. He ate part of it and tossed the rest in the weeds. Halfway through another cigarette, it dawned on him that he didn't have to run anymore. He could go back home now, turn himself in. They could do whatever they wanted to, as long as he got to see Lenora one more time. Theodore had never been able to understand that, how Roy could miss somebody he didn't really know. It was true that he could barely recall what his little girl's face had looked like, but even so, he had wondered a thousand times how her life had turned out. By the time he finished the smoke, he was already rehearsing some words he would say to her.

That night, he got drunk with his old friend one last time. He built a fire and talked to Theodore like he was still alive, told the same stories over again, the ones about Flapjack, and the Flamingo Lady, and the Zit-Eater, and all those other lost souls they had run into on the road. Several times he caught himself waiting on Theodore to laugh or add something that he'd forgotten. After a few hours, there were no more tales to tell, and Roy felt lonelier than he had ever felt in his life. "Hell of a long way from Coal Creek, ain't it, boy?" was the last thing he said before he lay down on his blanket.

He woke right before dawn. He wet a rag with some water from the gallon jug they always kept tied to the back of the wheelchair. He wiped the grime off Theodore's face and combed his hair, pressed his eyes shut with his thumb. There was a splash of wine left in the last bottle and he set it in the cripple's lap, placed his ragged straw hat on his head. Then Roy wrapped his few belongings in a blanket and stood with his hand on the dead man's shoulder. He closed his eyes and said a few more words. He realized that he would never preach again, but that was all right. He'd never been much good at it anyway. Most people just wanted to hear the cripple play. "I wish you was going with me, Theodore," Roy said. By the time he managed to catch a ride, he was already two miles down the road.

Serpents

PART SIX

40

THANK GOD, JULY WAS COMING TO AN END. Carl could hardly wait to get out on the road again. He hauled the two jars filled with Sandy's tips to the bank and turned it into paper money, then spent the next few days leading up to the vacation buying supplies—two new outfits and some frilly underwear from JC Penney for Sandy, a gallon of motor oil, spare spark plugs, a hacksaw he found on sale and bought on a whim, fifty feet of rope, a set of road maps of the southern states from the AAA office, two cartons of Salem, and a dozen dog dicks. By the time he finished shopping and had a mechanic put a set of brake pads on the car, they were down to $134, but that would take them far. Hell, he thought, as he sat at the kitchen table and counted again, they could live like kings for a week on this much money. He recalled the summer two years ago, when they had left Meade with $40. It was potted meat and stale chips and siphoned gas and sleeping in the sweltering car the whole way, but they had managed to stay out sixteen days with the money they scrounged off the models. Compared to that, they were in fine shape this time.

Still, there was something bothering him. He'd been looking through his photos one evening, trying to get pumped up for the hunt, when he came across one of Sandy holding on to last summer's army boy. He'd been vaguely aware that she hadn't acted quite the same since he had killed that one, like he had taken something precious from her that night. But in the picture he held in his hand was a look of disgust and disappointment in her face that he hadn't noticed before. As he sat there staring at it, he began to wish that he'd never bought her that gun. There was also the business with the waitress at the White Cow. Sandy had started asking him where he went in the evenings while she was at work, and though she had never come right out and accused him of anything, he was beginning to wonder if she might have heard something. The waitress didn't act as friendly as she used to, either. He was probably just being paranoid, but it was hard enough handling the models without having to worry about the bait turning on him, too. The next day, he paid a visit to the hardware store in Central Center. That night after she went to bed, he unloaded her pistol—she'd started carrying it in her purse—and replaced the hollow points with blanks. The more he thought about it, the less he could imagine a situation in which she would have to fire it anyway.

One of the last things he did in preparation for the trip was make a new print of his favorite photograph. He folded it and put it in his wallet. Sandy didn't know, but he always carried a copy when they went back out. It was a picture of her cradling the head of a model in her lap, one they had worked with on their first hunt, the summer after they killed the sex fiend in Colorado. It wasn't one of his best, but it was good for someone who was still learning. It reminded Carl of one of those paintings of Mary with the baby Jesus, the way Sandy was looking down at the model with a sweet, innocent look on her face, a look that he'd been able to catch a couple of times that first year or two, but then was gone forever. And the boy? The way he remembered it, they had gone five days without a single hitcher. They were broke and arguing with each other, Sandy wanting to go home and him insisting that they keep on. Then they came around a bend on some potholed two-lane just below Chicago and there he was with his thumb out, like a gift straight out of heaven. He was a big cutup, that boy, full of fun and dumb jokes, and if Carl peered hard enough at the picture, he could still see that orneriness in his face. And every time he looked at it, he was also reminded that he could never find another girl to work with who would be as good as Sandy.

41

IT WAS A HOT SUNDAY MORNING, the first of August, and Carl's shirt was already soaked with sweat. He sat in the kitchen staring at the grimy woodwork and the coat of rancid grease on the wall behind the stove. He checked his watch, saw that it was noon. They should have been on the road four hours ago, but Sandy had come home stinking of booze last night, barging through the door with an ugly look on her red face and going on and on about this being the last trip for her. It had taken her all morning to get straightened up. When they walked outside to get in the car, she stopped and fumbled in her purse for her sunglasses. "Jesus Christ," she said. "I'm still sick."

"We got to stop and fill the gas can before we leave town," he said, ignoring her. He'd decided while waiting on her to get ready that he wasn't going to let her ruin the trip. If need be, he'd get rough with her once they got away from Ross County and that nosy fucking brother of hers.

"Shit, you had all week to do that," she said.

"I'm telling you, girl, you better watch it."

At the Texaco on Main Street, Carl got out and started filling the can. When the high, sharp sound of a siren cut through the air, he nearly jumped out in front of a Mustang leaving the pumps. Turning around, he saw Bodecker sitting in his cruiser behind the station wagon. The sheriff shut the siren off and got out of the car laughing. "Damn, Carl," he said, "I hope you didn't make a mess in your pants." He glanced in their car as he walked past, saw their stuff piled up in the back. "You all taking a trip?"

Sandy opened the door and stepped out. "Going on vacation," she said.

"Where to?" Bodecker asked.

"Virginia Beach," Carl said. He felt something wet and looked down, saw that he'd soaked one of his shoes with gasoline.

"I thought you went there last year," Bodecker said. He wondered if his sister had started up whoring again. If so, she was evidently being more careful about it. He hadn't heard any complaints about her since the woman's phone call last summer.

Carl glanced over at Sandy, then said, "Yeah, we like it there."

"I been thinking about taking me a little respite," Bodecker said. "So it's a good place to go, huh?"

"It's nice," Sandy said.

"What is it you like about it?"

She looked back toward Carl for help, but he was already bent over the can again, topping it off. His pants were hanging low, and she hoped Lee didn't notice the crack of his white ass showing. "It's just nice, that's all."

Bodecker pulled a toothpick out of his shirt pocket. "How long you gonna be gone?" he said.

Sandy crossed her arms in front of herself and gave him a dirty look. "Why all the fuckin' questions?" Her head was starting to pound again. She should have never mixed beer with the vodka.

"No reason, sis," he said. "Just curious."

She stared at him for a minute. She tried to imagine the look on his smug face if she told him the truth. "About two weeks," she said.

They stood and watched Carl tighten the cap on the gas can. When he went inside the station to pay, Bodecker pulled the toothpick out of his mouth and snorted, "Vacation."

"Knock it off, Lee. What we do is our own business."

42

JAMIE JOHANSEN WAS THE FIRST OF HIS KIND that they ever picked up, hair down to his shoulders, a set of thin gold hoops hanging from his earlobes. That's what the woman told him as soon as he got in their filthy car, like it was the most exciting thing that had ever happened to her. Jamie had run away from home in Massachusetts the year before, which was also the last time he'd been to a barbershop. He didn't consider himself a hippie—the few whom he'd met on the streets acted retarded—but what the fuck? Let her think what she wanted. For the past six months, he'd been living with a family of transvestites in a run-down, cat-infested house in Philadelphia. He had finally split when two of the older sisters decided Jamie needed to share more of the money he was making in the bus station restroom over on Clark Street. Fuck these hags, Jamie figured. Just a bunch of losers in bad makeup and cheap wigs. He'd go to Miami and find himself a rich old fag who would be thrilled just to play with his long, beautiful hair and show him off on the beach. He looked out the car window at a sign that said something about Lexington. He couldn't even remember how he had ended up in Kentucky. Who the fuck goes to Kentucky?

And these two who just picked him up, another couple of losers. The woman seemed to think she was sexy or something, the way she kept smiling at him in the mirror and licking her lips, but just looking at her gave him the willies. There was a ripe, fishy smell coming from somewhere in the car, and he figured it had to be her. He could tell the fat man was dying to suck his dick, the way he kept turning around in the front seat and asking stupid questions so he could take another look at his crotch. They hadn't gone but five or six miles when Jamie decided that, if he got the chance, he was going to steal their car. Even this piece of junk would be better than hitchhiking. The man who picked him up last night, stiff black hat, long white fingers, had scared the shit out of him, talking about gangs of rabid rednecks and tribes of half-starved hoboes and the awful things they did to sweet, young waifs they caught out on the road. After relating a number of stories he had heard—boys buried alive, tamped down headfirst into tight holes like fence posts, others turned into a gooey mulligan stew seasoned with wild onions and windfall apples—the man had offered good money and a night in a nice motel for a special kind of party, one that involved a bag of cotton balls and a funnel in some way, but for the first time since he had left home, Jamie turned the good money down, could see the maid finding him the next morning hollowed out like a Beggar's Night pumpkin in the bathtub. These two here were like Ma and Pa Kettle compared to that crazy bastard.

Still, it surprised him when the woman turned off the highway and the man asked him straight out if he would be interested in fucking his wife while he took a few photographs. He hadn't seen that one coming, but he played it cool. Jamie wasn't really into women, especially ugly ones; but if he could talk the fat man into taking his clothes off too, stealing the car should be a piece of cake. He'd never had his own set of wheels before. He told the man, sure, he was interested, that is, if they were willing to pay for it. He looked past the man out the windshield smeared with the guts of dead insects. They were on a gravel road now. The woman had slowed down to a crawl and was evidently looking for a place to park.

"I thought your kind believed in that free love shit," the man said. "That's what Walter Cronkite said on the news the other night."

"A boy's still got to make a living, right?" Jamie said.

"I guess that's fair enough. How's twenty bucks sound?" The woman put the car in park and shut off the engine. They were sitting at the edge of a soybean field.

"Heck, I'll take you both on for twenty dollars," Jamie said with a smile.

"Both of us?" The fat man turned and looked at him with cold, gray eyes. "It sounds like you think I'm pretty." The woman gave a little giggle.

Jamie shrugged. He wondered if they would still be laughing when he drove away in their car. "I've had worse," he said.

"Oh, I doubt that," the man said, shoving his car door open.

43

"YOU ONLY BROUGHT THE ONE SHIRT?" Sandy asked him. They had been on the road six days, and had worked with two models, the kid with all the hair and a man with a harmonica who thought he was going to Nashville to become a country music star, that is, right up until a few minutes after they listened to him completely butcher Johnny Cash's "Ring of Fire," which happened to be Carl's favorite song that summer.

"Yeah," Carl said.

"Okay, we're gonna have to do some laundry," she said.

"Why?"

"You stink, that's why."

They came across a Laundromat in a small town in South Carolina a couple of hours later. Sandy made him take the shirt off. She carried a grocery bag of dirty clothes in and put them in a washer. He sat on a bench out front, watching the occasional car drive past and chewing on a cigar, his saggy tits nearly hanging to his fishy-white paunch. Sandy came out and sat on the other end of the bench and hid behind her sunglasses. Her blouse was plastered to her back with sweat. She rested her head against the building and shut her eyes.

"What we did was the best thing that could have happened to him," Carl said.

Jesus, Sandy thought, he's still talking about that fucker with the mouth harp. He had been yapping about him all morning. "I've already heard it," she said.

"I'm just saying, for one, he couldn't sing worth a shit. And he had, what, maybe three fucking teeth in his head? You ever look at them country music stars? Those people got expensive teeth. No, they would have laughed him right out of town, and then he would have went home and knocked up some old cow and been tied down by a bunch of brats, and that would have been the end of it."

"The end of what?" Sandy said.

"The end of his dream, that's what. Maybe he couldn't see it last night, but I did that boy a big favor. He died with that dream still alive in his head."

"Jesus, Carl, what the hell's got into you?" She heard the washer stop and stood up, held out her hand. "Give me a quarter for the dryer."

He handed her some change, then bent down and untied his shoes, kicked them off. He wasn't wearing any socks. He was down to his trousers now. Taking his pocketknife out, he started cleaning his toenails. Two young boys, maybe nine or ten years old, came speeding around the corner on bicycles just as he smeared a gob of gray gunk on the seat of the bench. They both waved to him and smiled when he looked up. Just for a second, they made him wish, as they flew by pumping their legs and laughing as if they didn't have a care in the world, that he was somebody else.

44

ON THEIR TWELFTH DAY OUT, ONE GOT AWAY. That had never happened before. He was an ex-con named Danny Murdock, the fourth model they had picked up this trip. On his right forearm, he had a tattoo of two scaly serpents wrapped around a tombstone that Carl imagined doing something special with once they had him down. They had been riding around all afternoon drinking beer and sharing a jumbo bag of pork rinds and getting him relaxed. They found a spot to park along a long, narrow lake just a mile or so inside the Sumter National Forest. As soon as Sandy shut the engine off, Danny flung the door open and got out of the car. He stretched and yawned, then started ambling toward the water, shucking off his clothes as he went. "What are you doing?" Carl yelled.

Danny tossed his shirt on the ground and turned to look back at them. "Hey, I got no problem giving your old lady the cock, but let me get cleaned up first," he said, jerking his underwear down. "I'm warning you, though, ol' buddy, I get past the used part, she ain't gonna be happy with your ass no more."

"Boy, he's got a mouth on him, don't he?" Sandy said, as she walked around the front of the station wagon. She leaned against the fender and watched the man jump into the water.

Carl set the camera on the hood and smiled. "Not for long, he ain't." They shared another beer and watched him swim, arms pumping and feet kicking, out to the middle of the lake and then roll over on his back.

"I gotta say, that looks like fun," Sandy said. She kicked off her sandals and spread the blanket on the grass.

"Shit, hard to tell what's in that mud hole," Carl said. He opened another beer, tried to enjoy being out of the stinking car for a while.

Eventually though, his patience with the swimmer wore thin. He had been out there playing over an hour. He went to the edge of the beach and started yelling and motioning for Danny to come in, and each time the man dove under and came back up whooping and splashing water like some schoolboy, Carl got a little more pissed. When Danny finally walked up out of the lake grinning with his dick hanging halfway to his knees and the evening sun sparkling all over his wet skin, Carl pulled the gun out of his pocket and said, "Are you clean enough yet?"

"What the hell?" the man said.

Carl motioned with the gun. "Goddamn it, get over there on that blanket like we talked about. Shit, we're losing the light here." He looked back at Sandy and nodded. She reached behind her head and started to undo her ponytail.

"Go fuck yourself!" Carl heard the man yell.

By the time he realized what was happening, Danny Murdock was already bolting into the woods on the other side of the road. Carl fired twice wildly and took after him. Slipping and stumbling, he went deep into the woods, until he was afraid he'd never find his way back to the car. He stopped and listened, but couldn't hear a thing except for the sound of his own raspy breathing. He was too fat and slow to be chasing anyone, let alone a long-legged prick who had bragged to them all afternoon about outrunning three squad cars on foot through downtown Spartanburg the week before. By then, it was near dusk, and he suddenly realized that the man might have circled back around to where Sandy was waiting at the car. But even with blanks in her gun, he should have heard a shot, that is, unless the fucker took her by surprise. Goddamn that sneaking sonofabitch. He hated going back to the car empty-handed. Sandy would never let him hear the end of it. He hesitated a second, then pointed the pistol up in the air and fired twice.

She was standing by the open driver's door holding the .22 in her hands when he came crashing through the brush at the edge of the road, red-faced and panting. "We got to get out of here," he yelled. He grabbed the blanket they had spread on the ground behind the car and hurried over and scooped up the man's clothes and shoes out of the grass. He tossed them in the backseat and climbed in the front.

"Jesus, Carl, what happened?" she said as she started the car.

"Don't worry, I got the bastard," he said. "Put two through his stupid head."

She looked over at him. "You chased that fucker down?"

He heard the doubt in her voice. "Be quiet for a minute," he said. "I got to think." He pulled out a map and studied it for a minute or so, tracing his finger back and forth. "The way it looks we're maybe ten miles from the border. Just turn around and make a left where we came in, and we oughta run into the highway."

"I don't believe you," she said.

"What?"

"That guy took off like a deer. Ain't no way you caught up with him."

Carl took a couple of deep breaths. "He was hiding under a log. I damn near stepped on him."

"What's the hurry then?" she said. "Let's go back and take some pictures."

Carl laid the .38 on the dash and pulled his shirt up, wiped the sweat off his face. His heart was still beating like a hammer in his chest. "Sandy, just drive the goddamn car, okay?"

"He got away, didn't he?"

He looked out the passenger window into the darkening woods. "Yeah, the bastard got away."

She put the car in drive. "Don't lie to me no more, Carl," she said. "And another thing, while we're on the subject, if I hear about you messing around with that little cunt at the White Cow again, you're gonna be sorry." Then she pressed her foot to the accelerator, and twenty minutes later, they crossed the state line into Georgia.

45

LATER THAT NIGHT, SANDY PARKED at the edge of a truck stop a few miles south of Atlanta. She ate a piece of beef jerky and crawled in the backseat to sleep. Around three AM, it began to rain. Carl sat in the front and listened to it beat on top of the car and thought about the ex-con. There's a lesson to be learned from this, he thought. He had just turned his back on the cowardly fucker for a second, but that had been long enough to screw everything up. He pulled the man's clothes from underneath the seat and started going through them. He found a broken switchblade and a Greenwood, South Carolina, address written inside a matchbook and eleven dollars in his wallet. Underneath the address were the words GOOD HEAD. He put the money in his pocket and rolled everything else up into a ball, then walked across the lot and tossed it in a trash barrel.

The rain was still coming down when she woke the next morning. Eating breakfast with Sandy at the truck stop, he wondered if any of the drivers sitting around them had ever killed a hitchhiker. It would be an excellent job for that sort of thing if a person was so inclined. As they started on their third cup of coffee, the rain let up and the sun popped out like a big, festering boil in the sky. By the time they paid the bill, wisps of steam were already rising up off the blacktopped parking lot. "About what happened yesterday," Carl said, as they walked back to the car, "I shouldn't have done that."

"Like I said," Sandy told him, "don't lie to me no more. We get caught, it's my ass in the sling just as much as yours."

Carl thought again about the blanks he'd stuck in her gun, but decided it would be better not to say anything about that. They would be home soon, and he could replace them without her ever knowing. "Ain't nobody gonna catch us," he said.

"Yeah, well, you probably didn't think one would ever get away, either."

"Don't worry," he said, "that won't ever happen again."

They drove around Atlanta and stopped in a place called Roswell for gas. They had twenty-four dollars and some change to get home on. Just as Carl was getting back in the station wagon after paying the cashier, a gaunt man in a worn black suit timidly approached. "You wouldn't be headin' north by any chance, would you?" he asked. Carl went ahead and picked his cigar up out of the ashtray before he turned to look the man over. The suit was several sizes too big. The cuffs of the pants were turned up several times to keep them from dragging on the ground. He could see a little paper price tag still attached to the sleeve of the coat. The man was packing a flimsy bedroll; and though he could have easily passed for sixty, Carl figured the wayfarer at least a few years younger than that. For some reason, he reminded Carl of a preacher, one of the real ones that you seldom run into anymore: not one of those greedy, sweet-smelling bastards just out to take people's money and make a fat fucking living off God, but a man who truly believed in the teachings of Jesus. On second thought, that was probably taking things a bit too far; the old boy was probably just another bum.

"Might be," Carl said. He looked over at Sandy for some indication that she was on board, but she just shrugged and put her sunglasses back on. "Where you going?"

"Coal Creek, West Virginia."

Carl thought about the one who got away last night. That big-dicked sonofabitch was going to leave a bad taste in his mouth for a long time. "Aw, hell, why not?" he told the man. "Get in the back."

Once they pulled out on the highway, the man said, "Mister, I do appreciate this. My poor feet are 'bout wore out."

"Been having trouble getting rides, huh?"

"I've did more walking than riding, I can tell you that."

"Yeah," Carl said, "I don't understand people who won't pick up strangers. That should be a good thing, helping someone out."

"You sound like you a Christian," the man said.

Sandy choked back a laugh, but Carl ignored her. "In some ways, I suppose," he told the man. "But I have to admit, I don't follow it quite as close as I used to."

The man nodded and stared out the window. "It's hard to live a good life," he said. "It seems like the Devil don't ever let up."

"What's your name, honey?" Sandy asked. Carl glanced at her and smiled, then reached over and touched her leg. He'd been afraid, after the way he fucked up last night, that she was going to be a first-class bitch the rest of the trip.

"Roy," the man said, "Roy Laferty."

"So what's in West Virginia, Roy?" she said.

"Going home to see my little girl."

"That's nice," Sandy said. "When did you see her last?"

Roy thought for a minute. Lord, he'd never felt so tired. "It's been seventeen years almost." Riding in the car was making him sleepy. He hated to be impolite, but as hard as he tried, he couldn't keep his eyes open.

"What you been doing away from home that long?" Carl said. After waiting for a minute or so for the man to answer, he turned around and looked in the backseat. "Shit, he's passed out," he told Sandy.

"Just let him be for now," she said. "And as far as me actually fucking him, you can forget that. He smells worse than you do."

"All right, all right," Carl said, pulling the Georgia highway map out of the glove box. Thirty minutes later, he pointed at an exit ramp, told Sandy to take it. They drove two or three miles down a dusty clay road, eventually found a pull-off littered with party trash and a busted-up piano. "This is gonna have to do," Carl said, stepping out of the car. He opened the hitcher's door and shook his shoulder. "Hey there, buddy," he said, "come on, I want to show you something."

A couple of minutes later, Roy found himself in a stand of tall loblolly pines. The ground underneath them was carpeted with dry, brown needles. He couldn't recall exactly how long he had been traveling, maybe three days. He hadn't had much luck with rides, and he had walked until his feet were raw with blisters. Though he didn't think he could take another step, he didn't want to stop moving either. He wondered if the animals had gotten to Theodore yet. Then he saw that the woman was taking her clothes off, and that confused him. He looked around for the car he'd been riding in and saw the fat man pointing a pistol at him. There was a black camera hanging from his neck by a cord, an unlit cigar stuck between his thick lips. Maybe he was dreaming, Roy thought, but, damn, it seemed so real. He could smell the sap seeping from the trees in the heat. He saw the woman get down on a red plaid blanket, like the kind people might use for a picnic, and then the man said something that woke him up. "What?" Roy asked.

"I said I'm giving you a good thing here," Carl repeated. "She likes lanky ol' studs like you."

"What's going on here, mister?" Roy said.

Carl heaved a sigh. "Jesus Christ, man, pay attention. Like I said, you're gonna fuck my wife, and I'm going to take some pictures, that's all."

"Your wife?" Roy said. "I've never heard of such a thing. Here I thought you was a good feller."

"Just shut up and get that welfare suit off," Carl said.

Looking over at Sandy, Roy held his hands out. "Lady," he said, "I'm sorry, but I promised myself when Theodore died that I was gonna live right from now on, and I intend to stick to that."

"Oh, come on, sweetie," Sandy said. "We'll just take a few pictures and then the big dumb bastard will leave us alone."

"Woman, look at me. I been run through the ringer. Hell, I don't even know half the places I been. Do you really want these hands touching you?"

"You sonofabitch, you're going to do what I say," Carl said.

Roy shook his head. "No, mister. The last woman I was with was a bird, and that's the way it's going to stay. Theodore was afraid of her, so I didn't let on, but Priscilla, she really was a flamingo."

Carl laughed and threw his cigar down. Jesus Christ, what a mess. "Okay, looks like we got us a fruitcake."

Sandy stood up and started pulling her clothes back on. "Let's get the hell out of here," she said.

Just as Roy turned and watched her start to walk toward the car sitting out by the road, he felt the barrel of the gun press against the side of his head. "Don't even think about running," Carl told him.

"You don't have to worry about that," Roy said. "My runnin' days are over with." He raised his eyes and searched out a small patch of blue sky visible through the dense, green branches of the pines. A white wisp of a cloud drifted by. That's what dying will be like, he told himself. Just floating up in the air. Nothing bad about that. He smiled a little. "I don't reckon you're gonna let me back in the car, are you?"

"You got that right," Carl said. He started to squeeze the trigger.

"Just one thing," Roy said, his voice filled with urgency.

"What's that?"

"Her name's Lenora."

"Who the fuck you talking about?"

"My little girl," Roy said.

46

IT WAS HARD TO BELIEVE, but the crazy bastard in the dirty suit was carrying almost a hundred dollars in his pocket. They ate barbecue and coleslaw at a pig shack in a colored section of Knoxville, and that night they stayed in a Holiday Inn in Johnson City, Tennessee. As usual, Sandy took her sweet time the next morning. By the time she announced that she was ready to go, Carl was sinking into a foul mood. Except for the photos of the boy in Kentucky, most of the others he had taken this time out were slop. Nothing had turned out right. He had sat up all night dwelling on it in a chair by the third-floor window, looking down on the parking lot and rolling a dog dick cigar between his fingers until it fell apart. He kept considering signs, maybe something he had missed. But nothing stood out, except for Sandy's mostly piss-poor attitude and the ex-con who got away. He swore he'd never hunt in the South again.

They entered southern West Virginia around noon. "Look, we still got the rest of today," he said. "If there's any fucking way possible, I want to shoot another roll of film before we get home, something good." They had pulled into a rest stop so he could check the oil in the car.

"Go ahead," Sandy said. "There's all kinds of pictures out there." She pointed out the window. "See, there's a bluebird just landed in that tree."

"Funny," he said. "You know what I mean."

She put the car into gear. "I don't care what you do, Carl, but I want to sleep in my own bed tonight."

"Good enough," he said.

Over the next four or five hours, they didn't come across a single hitchhiker. The closer they got to Ohio, the more agitated Carl became. He kept telling Sandy to slow down, made her stop and stretch her legs and drink coffee a couple of times just to keep his hopes alive a little while longer. By the time they drove through Charleston and headed toward Point Pleasant, he was filled with disappointment and doubt. Maybe the ex-con really was a sign. If so, Carl thought, it could mean only one thing: they should quit while they were ahead. That's what he was thinking, as they approached the long line of traffic waiting to go over the silver metal bridge that would take them into Ohio. Then he saw the handsome, dark-haired boy with the gym bag standing on the walkway seven or eight car lengths up ahead. He leaned forward, breathed in the car exhaust and the stink from the river. The traffic moved a few feet, then stopped again. Somebody behind them in the line honked his horn. The boy turned and looked back toward the end of the line, his eyes squinting in the sun.

"Do you see that?" Carl said.

"But what about your fucking rules? Shit, we're heading back into Ohio."

Carl kept his eyes on the boy, prayed that nobody offered him a ride before they got close enough to pick him up. "Let's just see where's he's going. Hell, that can't hurt nothing, can it?"

Sandy took off her sunglasses, gave the boy a closer look. She knew Carl well enough to know that it wasn't going to stop with just giving him a ride, but from what she could see, he was maybe nicer than anything they'd ever come across before. And there certainly hadn't been any angels this trip. "I guess not," she said.

"But I need you to do some talking, okay? Give him that smile of yours, make him want it. I hate to point it out, but you been dropping the ball this trip. I can't do it alone."

"Sure, Carl," she said. "Anything you say. Hell, I'll offer to suck him off as soon as he plops his ass down in the backseat. That ought to do it."

"Jesus, you got a filthy mouth on you."

"Maybe so," she said. "But I just want to get this over with."

PART SEVEN

Ohio

47

IT SEEMED THAT THERE MUST BE a wreck up ahead, as slow
as the traffic was moving. Arvin had just made up his mind to walk
across the bridge when the car pulled up and the fat man asked him
if he needed a ride. After selling the Bel Air, he'd walked out to the
highway and caught a lift through Charleston with a fertilizer salesman—rumpled white shirt, gravy-stained tie, the stink of last night's
alcohol seeping from his big pores—on his way to a feed and seed
convention in Indianapolis. The salesman let him off on Route 35
at Nitro; and a few minutes later, he got another ride with a colored
family in a pickup truck that took him to the edge of Point Pleasant.
He sat in the back with a dozen baskets of tomatoes and green beans.
The black man pointed the way to the bridge, and Arvin began walking. He could smell the Ohio River several blocks before he saw its
greasy, blue-gray surface. A clock on a bank said 5:47. He could hardly
believe that a person could travel so fast with just his thumb.

When he got in the black station wagon, the woman behind the
wheel looked back at him and smiled. It seemed like she was almost
happy to see him. Their names were Carl and Sandy, the fat man told
him. "Where you going?" Carl asked.

"Meade, Ohio," Arvin said. "Ever hear of it?"

"We—" Sandy began to say.

"Sure," Carl interrupted. "If I'm not mistaken, I think it's a paper
mill town." He took his cigar out of his mouth and looked over at the
woman. "In fact, we're going right by there this trip, ain't we, babe?"
This had to be a sign, Carl thought, picking up a fine-looking boy like
this who was headed for Meade clear down here among the river rats.

"Yeah," she said. The traffic started moving again. The holdup was
an accident on the Ohio side, two crumpled cars and a scattering of

broken glass on the pavement. An ambulance turned its siren on and pulled out in front of them, barely avoiding a collision. A policeman blew a whistle, held his hand up for Sandy to stop.

"Jesus Christ, be careful," Carl said, shifting in his seat.

"Do you want to drive?" Sandy said, hitting the brakes too hard. They sat there for another few minutes while a man in coveralls hurriedly swept up glass. Sandy adjusted her rearview, took another look at the boy. She was so glad that she had gotten to take a bath this morning. She'd still be nice and clean for him. When she reached in her purse for a fresh pack of cigarettes, her hand brushed against the pistol. As she watched the man finish the cleanup, she fantasized about killing Carl and taking off with the boy. He was probably only six or seven years younger than she was. She could make something like that work. Maybe even have a couple of kids. Then she closed the purse and started peeling the pack of Salems open. She'd never do it, of course, but it was still nice to think about.

"What's your name, honey?" she asked the boy, after the policeman waved them on through.

Arvin allowed himself a sigh of relief. He thought for sure the woman was going to get them pulled over. He looked at her again. She was rail thin and dirty-looking. Her face was caked with too much makeup, and her teeth were stained a dark yellow from too many years of cigarettes and neglect. A strong odor of sweat and filth was coming from the front seat, and he figured both of them were in bad need of a bath. "Billy Burns," he told her. That was the fertilizer salesman's name.

"That's a nice name," she said. "Where you coming from?"

"Tennessee."

"So what you going to Meade for?" Carl asked.

"Oh, just visiting, that's all."

"You got family there?"

"No," Arvin said. "But I used to live there a long time ago."

"Probably ain't changed much," Carl said. "Most of them little towns never do."

"Where is it you all live?" Arvin asked.

"We're from Fort Wayne. Been on vacation down in Florida. We like to meet new people, don't we, hon?"

"We sure do," Sandy said.

Just as they passed the sign that marked the Ross County line, Carl looked at his watch. They probably should have stopped before they got this far, but he knew a safe spot nearby where they could take the boy. He'd come across it last winter on one of his drives. Meade was just ten miles away now, and it was after six o'clock. That meant they had only another ninety or so minutes of decent light left. He had never broken any of the major rules before, but he'd already made up his mind. Tonight, he was going to kill a man in Ohio. Shit, if this worked out, he might even do away with that rule altogether. Maybe that's what this boy was all about, maybe not. There wasn't enough time to think about it. He shifted in his seat and said, "Billy, my old bladder don't work like it used to. We're gonna pull over so I can take a leak, okay?"

"Yeah, sure. I just appreciate you givin' me a ride."

"There's a road up here to the right," Carl said to Sandy.

"How far?" Sandy asked.

"Maybe a mile."

Arvin leaned over just a little, looked past Carl's head out the windshield. He didn't see any indication of a road, and he thought it a bit odd that the man knew there was one up ahead if he wasn't from around here. Maybe he's got a map, the boy told himself. He sat back in his seat again and watched the scenery going by. Except for the hills being smaller and more rounded off, it looked a lot like West Virginia. He wondered if anyone had found Teagardin's body yet.

Sandy turned off Route 35 onto a dirt and gravel road. She drove past a big farm that sat on the corner. After another mile or so, she slowed and asked Carl, "Here?"

"No, keep going," he said.

Arvin straightened up and looked around. They hadn't passed another house since the farm. The Luger was pressing against his groin, and he adjusted it a little.

"This looks like a good spot," Carl finally said, pointing at the vague remains of a driveway that led to a run-down house. It was obvious that the place had been empty for years. The few windows were busted out and the porch was caving in on one end. The front door was standing open, hanging crooked from one hinge. Across the road was a cornfield, the stalks withered and yellow from the hot, droughty weather. As soon as Sandy shut the engine off, Carl opened the glove compartment. He pulled out a fancy-looking camera, held it up for Arvin to see. "Bet you never would have guessed I'm a photographer, would you?" he said.

Arvin shrugged. "Probably not." He could hear the hum of insects outside the car in the dry weeds. Thousands of them.

"But look, I'm not one of them jackasses that shoot dumb pictures like you see in the newspaper, am I, Sandy?"

"No," she said, looking back at Arvin, "he's not. He's really good."

"You ever hear of Michelangelo or Leonardo . . . ? Oh, hell, I've done forgot his name. You know who I mean?"

"Yeah, I think so," Arvin said. He thought about the time Lenora showed him a painting called *Mona Lisa* in a book. She had asked him if he thought she looked anything like the pale woman in the picture, and he was glad he'd told her that she was prettier than that.

"Well, I like to think that someday people are gonna look at my photographs and think they're just as good as anything them guys ever made. The pictures I take, Billy, they're like art, like you see in a museum. You ever been to a museum?"

"No," Arvin said. "Can't say that I have."

"Well, maybe you will someday. So how about it?"

"How about what?" Arvin said.

"Why don't we get out here and you let me take some pictures of you with Sandy?"

"No, mister, I better not. It's been a long day for me, and I'd just as soon keep moving. I just want to get to Meade."

"Oh, come on, son, won't take but a few minutes. How about this? What if she got naked for you?"

Arvin reached for the door handle. "That's all right," he said. "I'm just gonna walk back up to the highway. You stay back here and take all the pictures you want."

"Now wait up, goddamn it," Carl said. "I didn't mean to get you all upset. But shit, wasn't no harm in me asking, was there?" He laid the camera down on the seat and sighed. "All right, just let me take my piss and we'll get on out of here."

Carl heaved his big body out of the car, walked around to the back. Sandy took a cigarette from her pack. Looking over, Arvin watched her hands tremble as she tried several times to strike a match. A feeling, one that he couldn't quite put a name on, suddenly twisted in his gut like a knife. He was already pulling the Luger from the waistband of his overalls when he heard Carl say, "Get out of the car, boy." The fat man was standing five feet away from the back door pointing a long-barreled pistol at him.

"If it's money you want," Arvin said, "I got a little bit." He eased the safety off the gun. "You can have it."

"Being nice now, huh?" Carl said. He spat in the grass. "I'll tell you what, you little cocksucker, you just hang on to that money for right now. Sandy and me will sort it out after we take my goddamn pictures."

"Better go ahead and do what he says, Billy," Sandy said. "He can get pretty excited if things don't go his way." When she glanced back at him and smiled with all her rotten teeth, Arvin nodded to himself and shoved his door open. Before it registered in Carl's mind what the boy held in his hand, the first blast had torn through his stomach. The force of the bullet started to spin him around. He staggered back three or four feet and caught himself. He tried to raise his gun and aim at the boy, but then another round hit him in the chest. He landed on his back in the weeds with a heavy thump. Though he could still feel the .38 in his hand, his fingers wouldn't work. Somewhere far off, he could hear Sandy's voice. It sounded like she was saying his name over and over again: Carl, Carl, Carl. He wanted to answer her, thought that if he just rested a minute, he could still straighten this mess out. Something cold began to crawl over him. He felt his body start to sink into a hole that seemed to be opening up beneath him in the ground, and it scared him, that feeling, the way it sucked the breath right out of him. Gritting his teeth, he fought to climb out before he sank in too deep. He felt himself rising. Yes, by God, he could still fix things, and then they would quit. He saw those two little boys on their bicycles riding by waving at him. No more pictures, he wanted to tell Sandy, but he was having trouble finding the air. Then something with huge black wings settled on top of him, pushing him down again, and even though he grabbed frantically at the grass and dirt with his left hand to keep from slipping, he couldn't stop himself this time.

When the woman started screaming the man's name, Arvin turned and saw her in the front seat digging something out of her purse. "Don't do that," he said, shaking his head. He stepped back from the car and pointed the Luger at her. "I'm begging you." Black streaks of mascara were running down her face. She cried the man's name one more time, and then stopped. Taking several deep breaths, she stared at the soles of Carl's shoes while she quieted down. One of them, she noticed, had a hole in it as big around as a fifty-cent piece. He hadn't mentioned it the whole trip. "Please, lady," Arvin said when he saw her smile.

"Fuck it," she said quietly, just before she drew a pistol up over the seat and fired. Though she aimed directly at the middle of the boy's body, he just stood there. Frantically, she pulled the hammer back again with her thumbs, but before she could get off the second round, Arvin shot her in the neck. The .22 dropped to the floorboards as the bullet knocked her against the driver's-side door. Pressing her hands against her throat, she tried to stop the red stream that was spurting from the wound. She began to choke, and coughed a gush of blood out on the seat. Her eyes settled on his face. They grew big for a few seconds and then slowly closed. Arvin listened to her take a few ragged breaths and then one last sticky heave. He couldn't believe that the woman had missed him. Jesus Christ, she was so close.

He sat down on the edge of the backseat and puked a little in the grass between his feet. A numbing despair began to settle over him, and he tried to shake it off. He stepped out into the dirt road and paced around in a circle. He put the Luger back in his pants and knelt down beside the man. He reached underneath him and pulled the wallet out of his back pocket and glanced through it quickly. He didn't see any driver's license, but he found a photograph behind some paper money. Suddenly he felt sick all over again. It was a picture of the woman cradling a dead man in her arms like a baby. She was wearing only a black bra and panties. There was what appeared to be a bullet hole above the man's right eye. She was looking down at him with a hint of sorrow on her face.

Arvin put the photograph in his shirt pocket and dropped the wallet on the fat man's chest. Then he opened the glove compartment, finding nothing but road maps and rolls of film. He listened again for any cars coming, wiped the sweat out of his eyes. "Think, goddamn it, think," he told himself. But the only thing he knew for sure was that he had to get out of this place fast. Picking up his gym bag, he took off walking west through the parched rows of corn. He was twenty yards out in the field when he stopped and turned around. He hurried back to the car and took two of the film canisters out of the glove box, stuck them in his pants pocket. Then he got a shirt out of his bag and wiped off everything that he might have touched. The insects resumed their humming.

48

HE DECIDED TO STAY OFF THE ROADS, and it was after midnight
when Arvin finally walked into Meade. In the middle of town, right
off Main Street, he found a squat brick motel called the Scioto Inn
that still had its VACANCY sign on. He had never stayed in a motel
before. The clerk, a boy not much older than himself, was gazing wea-
rily at an old movie, *Abbott and Costello Meet the Mummy*, on a small
black-and-white TV sitting in the corner. The room was five bucks a
night. "We change the towels every other day," the clerk said.

In his room, Arvin stripped off his clothes and stood in the
shower for a long time trying to get clean. Nervous and exhausted,
he lay down on top of the bedspread and sipped a pint of whiskey.
He was goddamn glad he'd remembered to bring it along. He noticed
on the wall a small picture of Jesus hanging from the cross. When he
got up to take a leak, he turned the picture over. It reminded him too
much of the one in his grandmother's kitchen. By three o'clock in the
morning, he was drunk enough to go to sleep.

He woke around ten the next morning after dreaming about the
woman. In the dream, she fired the pistol at him just like she did yesterday afternoon, only this time she hit him squarely in the forehead,
and he was the one who died instead of her. The other details were
vague, but he thought maybe she took his picture. He almost wished
that had happened as he went to the window and peeked out the
curtain, half expecting the parking lot to be filled with police cruisers. He watched the traffic go by on Bridge Street while he smoked a
cigarette, then he took another shower. After he got dressed, he went
over to the office and asked if he could keep the room another day.
The boy from last night was still on duty. He was half asleep, listlessly
chewing a wad of pink bubble gum. "You must put in a lot of hours,"
Arvin said.

The boy yawned and nodded, rang up another night in the register. "Don't I know it," he said. "My old man owns the place, so I'm pretty much his slave when I'm not in college." He handed back the change from a twenty. "Better than getting shipped off to Vietnam, though."

"Yeah, I expect so," Arvin said. He put the loose bills in his wallet. "Used to be an eating place around here called the Wooden Spoon. Is it still in business?"

"Sure." The boy walked over to the door and pointed up the street. "Just walk over there to the light and turn left. You'll see it across from the bus station. They got good chili."

He stood outside the door of the Wooden Spoon a few minutes, looking across at the bus station trying to imagine his father getting off a Greyhound and seeing his mother for the first time, over twenty years ago. Once inside, he ordered ham and eggs and toast. Though he hadn't eaten anything since the candy bar yesterday afternoon, he found that he wasn't very hungry. Eventually the old, wrinkled waitress came over and picked up his plate without a word. She barely looked at him, but when he got up, he left her a dollar tip anyway.

Just as he walked outside, three cruisers sped past going east with their lights flashing and sirens blaring. His heart seemed to stop for a moment in his chest, and then began to race. He leaned against the side of the brick building and tried to light a cigarette, but his hands were shaking too much to strike a match, just like the woman yesterday evening. The sirens faded into the distance, and he calmed down enough to get it lit. A bus pulled into the alley beside the station just then. He watched a dozen or so people get out. A couple of them wore military uniforms. The bus driver, a heavy-jowled, sour-faced man in a gray shirt and black tie, leaned back in his seat and pulled his cap down over his eyes.

Arvin walked back over to the motel and spent the rest of the day pacing the green, threadbare carpet. It was only a matter of time before the law figured out he was the one who killed Preston Teagardin. Taking off from Coal Creek so suddenly, he realized, was the dumbest damn thing he could have done. How much more obvious could he have been? The longer he walked the floor, the clearer it became that when he shot that preacher he had set something in motion that was going to follow him for the rest of his life. He knew in his gut that he should attempt to get out of Ohio immediately, but he couldn't bear the thought of leaving without seeing the old house and the prayer log one more time. No matter what else happened, he told himself, he had to try to set right those things about his father that still ate at his heart. Until then, he'd never be free anyway.

He wondered if he would ever feel clean again. There was no TV in the room, just a radio. The only station he could find without static was country and western. He let it play softly while he tried to go to sleep. Every once in a while, someone in the next room coughed, and the sound made him think of the woman choking on her blood. He was still thinking of her when morning came.

49

"I'm sorry, Lee," Howser said as Bodecker approached. "This is all fucked up." He was standing next to Carl and Sandy's station wagon. It was Tuesday around noon. Bodecker had just arrived. A farmer had found the bodies approximately an hour ago, flagged down a Wonder Bread truck out along the highway. There were four cruisers lined up behind one another on the road, and men in gray uniforms standing around fanning themselves with their hats, waiting for orders. Howser was Bodecker's chief deputy, the only man he could depend on with anything beyond petty theft and writing speeding tickets. As far as the sheriff was concerned, the rest of them weren't fit to be crossing guards in front of a one-room schoolhouse.

He glanced down at Carl's body, and then looked in at his sister. The deputy had already told him on the radio that she was dead. "Jesus," he said, his voice nearly breaking. "Jesus Christ."

"I know," Howser said.

Bodecker took several deep gulps of air to steady himself and stuck his sunglasses in his pocket. "Give me a couple minutes here alone with her."

"Sure," the deputy said. He walked over to where the other men were standing, said something to them in a low voice.

Squatting down beside the open passenger door, Bodecker studied Sandy closely, the lines in her face, the bad teeth, the faded bruises on her legs. She'd always been a little fucked-up, but she was still his sister. He pulled his handkerchief out and wiped at his eyes. She was wearing a pair of skimpy shorts and a tight blouse. Still dressing like a whore, he thought. He climbed in the front seat, pulled her close, and looked over her shoulder. The bullet had gone through her neck and come out at the top of her back, just to the left of her spine, a couple of inches below the entry wound. It was buried in the padding of the driver's-side door. He used his penknife to dig out the slug. It looked like a 9 millimeter. He saw a .22 pistol lying near the brake pedal. "Was that back door open like that when you got here?" he called out to Howser.

The deputy left the men in the road and jogged back to the station wagon. "We ain't touched a thing, Lee."

"Where's the farmer that found 'em?"

"Said he had a sick heifer to tend to. But I questioned him pretty good before he left. He don't know nothing."

"You already take pictures?"

"Yeah, just got done when you pulled in."

He handed Howser the bullet, then leaned across the front seat again, picked up the .22 with his handkerchief. He sniffed the barrel, then released the cylinder, saw that it had been fired once. Pushing the extractor back, five shells fell out into his hand. The ends were crimped. "Hell, these are blanks."

"Blanks? Why the hell would a person do that, Lee?"

"I don't know, but it was a bad mistake, that's for certain." He set the gun on the seat next to the purse and the camera. Then he got out of the car and stepped over to where Carl lay. The dead man still had hold of the .38 in his right hand, some grass and dirt in the other. It looked like he had been clawing at the ground. Several flies crawled around his wounds and another rested on his lower lip. Bodecker checked the gun. "And this fucker, he didn't fire a shot."

"Either one of them holes he's got in him would account for that," Howser said.

"Wouldn't take much to put Carl down anyway," Bodecker said. He turned his head and spat. "He was about as worthless as they come." He picked up the wallet lying on top of the body and counted fifty-four dollars. He scratched his head. "Well, I guess it wasn't robbery, was it?"

"Any chance Tater Brown could have something to do with this?"

Bodecker's face reddened. "What the hell makes you think that?"

The deputy shrugged. "I don't know. I'm just throwing stuff out. I mean, who else does this kind of shit around here?"

Standing up, Bodecker shook his head. "No, this kind of thing's

too out in the open for that slimy cocksucker. If he was the one done
it, we wouldn't have come across them this easy. He'd have made sure
the maggots got a few days alone with them."

"Yeah, I guess," the deputy said.

"What about the coroner?" Bodecker said.

"He's supposed to be on his way."

Bodecker nodded over at the other deputies. "Have them look
around in that cornfield, see if they can find something, then you keep
watch for that coroner." He wiped the sweat off his neck with his
handkerchief. He waited until Howser walked away, then sat down in
the passenger's seat of the station wagon. A camera was lying beside
Sandy's purse. The dash was open. Underneath some wadded-up
maps were several rolls of film, a box of .38 shells. Glancing around to
make sure Howser was still talking to the deputies, Bodecker stuffed
the film in his pants pocket, looked through the purse. He found a
receipt from a Holiday Inn in Johnson City, Tennessee, dated two
nights ago. He thought back to the day he'd seen them at the gas
station. Sixteen days ago now, he figured. They had almost made it
home.

Eventually he noticed what appeared to be dried vomit in the
grass, ants crawling over it. He sat down on the backseat and placed
his feet out on the ground, on both sides of the mess. He looked over
where his brother-in-law lay in the grass. Whoever got sick was sitting right here in this seat when they did it, Bodecker said to himself.
So Carl's standing outside with a gun and Sandy's in the front, and
somebody else is in the back. He stared down at the puke for a few
more seconds. Carl didn't even get a chance to fire before somebody
got three shots off. And sometime in there, probably after the shooting was over, whoever it was got awful shook up. He thought back
to the first time he'd killed a man for Tater. He'd nearly gotten sick
himself that night. Chances are, then, he thought, whoever done this
wasn't used to killing, but the fucker definitely knew how to handle
a gun.

Bodecker watched the deputies cross the ditch and start moving
slowly through the cornfield, the backs of their shirts dark with sweat.
He heard a car coming, turned and saw Howser start walking up the

road to meet the coroner. "Goddamn it, girl, what the hell were you doing out here?" he said to Sandy. Reaching across the seat, he hurriedly removed a couple of keys hanging on the same metal ring as the ignition key, put them in his shirt pocket. He heard Howser and the coroner behind him. The doctor stopped when he got close enough to see Sandy in the front seat. "Good Lord," he said.

"I don't think the Lord's got anything to do with this, Benny," Bodecker said. He looked over at the deputy. "Get Willis out here to help you dust for prints before we move the car. Go over that backseat real close."

"What you figure happened?" the coroner asked. He set his black bag on the hood of the car.

"The way it looks to me, Carl got shot by somebody sitting in the back. Then Sandy managed to get one round off with that .22, but, hell, she didn't have a chance. That fucking thing's loaded with blanks. And I think, judging from the place where the bullet came out her, whoever shot her was standing up by that time." He pointed at the ground a few feet from the back door. "Probably right here."

"Blanks?" the coroner said.

Bodecker ignored him. "How long you figure they been dead?"

The coroner got down on one knee and raised Carl's arm up, tried to move it around a little, pressed on the mottled blue and gray skin with his fingers. "Oh, yesterday evening, I'd say. Thereabouts, anyway."

They all stood looking at Sandy silently for a minute or so, then Bodecker turned to the coroner. "You make sure she gets took good care of, okay?"

"Absolutely," Benny said.

"Have Webster's pick her up when you're done. Tell 'em I'll be over later to talk about the arrangements. I'm gonna head back to the office."

"What about the other one?" Benny asked, as Bodecker started to walk away.

The sheriff stopped and spit on the ground, looked over at the fat man. "However you got to work it, Benny, you make sure that one gets a pauper's grave. No marker, no name, no nothing."

50

"LEE," THE DISPATCHER SAID. "Had a call from a Sheriff
Thompson in Lewisburg, West Virginia. He wants you to call him
back soon as possible." He handed Bodecker a piece of paper with a
number scrawled on it.

"Willis, is that a five or a six?"

The dispatcher looked at the paper. "No, that's a nine."

Bodecker shut the door of his office and sat down, opened a desk
drawer, and took out a piece of hard candy. After seeing Sandy dead,
the first thing he had thought about was a glass of whiskey. He stuck
the candy in his mouth and dialed the number. "Sheriff Thompson?
This is Lee Bodecker up in Ohio."

"Thanks for calling me back, Sheriff," the man said with a hillbilly
drawl. "How you all doing up there?"

"I ain't bragging."

"The reason I called, well, it might not be nothing, but someone
shot a man down here yesterday morning sometime, a preacher, and
the boy we suspect might have been in on it used to live up in your
parts."

"That right? How did he kill this man?"

"Shot him in the head while he was sitting in his car. Held the
gun right up to the back of his skull. Made a hell of a mess, but at
least he didn't suffer none."

"What kind of gun did he use?"

"Pistol, probably a Luger, one of them German guns. The boy was
known to have one. His daddy brought it back from the war."

"That's a nine millimeter, ain't it?"

"That's right."

"What did you say his name is?"

"Didn't say, but the boy's name is Arvin Russell. Middle name's Eugene. His parents both died up around there the way I understand it. I think his daddy might have killed himself. He's been living with his grandmother down here in Coal Creek for maybe the past seven, eight years."

Bodecker frowned, stared across the room at the posters and flyers tacked on the wall. Russell. Russell? How did he know that name? "How old is he?" he asked Thompson.

"Arvin's eighteen. Listen, he ain't a bad sort, I've known him for a long time. And from what I've been hearing, this preacher might have deserved killing. Seems he was messing with young girls. But that still don't make it right, I guess."

"This boy driving?"

"He's got a blue Chevy Bel Air, a '54 model."

"What does he look like?"

"Oh, average build, dark hair, good-looking feller," Thompson said. "Arvin's quiet, but he ain't the type to take no shit, either. And, hell, he might not even be involved in this, but I can't find him right now, and he's the only good lead I got."

"You send us any information you got as far as the tags on the car or whatever, and we'll keep an eye out for him. And how about you letting me know if he shows up back down there, okay?"

"I'll do that."

"One more thing," Bodecker said. "You got a picture of him?"

"Not yet, I don't. I'm sure his grandmother's got a couple, but she ain't in the mood to cooperate right now. I get one, we'll make sure you get a copy."

By the time Bodecker hung up the phone, it was all coming back to him, the prayer log and those dead animals and that young kid had the pie juice smeared on his face. Arvin Eugene Russell. "I remember you now, boy." He walked over to a big map of the United States on the wall. He found Johnson City and Lewisburg, and traced his finger up through West Virginia and crossed over into Ohio on Route 35 at Point Pleasant. He stopped in the general spot off the highway where Carl and Sandy had been killed. So if it was this Russell boy, they must have met somewhere along in there. But Sandy had told him she was going to Virginia Beach. He studied the map some more. It didn't make sense, them staying in Johnson City. That was surely taking the long way around to get home. And besides that, what the fuck were they doing packing those guns?

He drove over to their apartment with the keys he'd taken from the ring. The smell of rotten garbage hit him when he opened the door. After raising a couple of windows, he looked through the rooms, but didn't find anything out of the ordinary. What the fuck am I looking for anyway? he thought. He sat down on the couch in the living room. Pulling out one of the canisters of film he had sneaked from the glove box, he rolled it around in his hand. He'd been sitting there maybe ten minutes when it finally occurred to him that something wasn't right about the apartment. Going through the rooms again, he couldn't find a single photograph. Why wouldn't Carl have any pictures hanging on the walls or at least lying around? That's all the shutterbug sonofabitch thought about. He started searching again, now in earnest, and soon found a shoe box under the bed, hidden behind some spare blankets.

Later, he sat on the couch staring numbly at a hole in the ceiling where the rain had leaked through. Chunks of plaster lay beneath it in a pile on the braided rug. He thought back to a day in the spring of 1960. By then, he'd been a deputy almost two years, and, because their mother had finally agreed with him to let her quit school, Sandy was working full-time at the Wooden Spoon. From what he could see, the job had done little to bring her out of her shell; she seemed as backward and forlorn as ever. But he'd heard stories about boys coming by at closing time and coaxing her into their cars for a quickie, then dumping her off in the sticks to find her own way home. Every time he stopped by the diner to check on her, he looked for her to announce a bastard on the way. And he guessed she did that day, just not the kind he was figuring on.

It was "All You Can Eat Fish" day. "Be right back," Sandy told him, as she hurried past with another plate piled high with perch for Doc Leedom. "I got something to tell you." The foot doctor came in every Friday and tried to kill himself with fried fish. It was the only time he ever stopped at the diner. All you could eat anything, he told his patients, was the dumbest idea a restaurant owner could ever come up with.

She grabbed the coffeepot, poured Bodecker a cup. "That fat ol' sonofabitch is running my legs off," she whispered.

Bodecker turned and watched the doctor cram a long piece of breaded fish into his mouth and swallow. "Heck, he don't even chew it, does he?"

"And he can do it all goddamn day," she said.

"So what's going on?"

She pushed back a loose lock of hair. "Well, I figured I should tell you before you hear it from someone else."

This was it, he thought, one in the oven, another worry to pour on his ulcer. Probably doesn't even know the daddy's name. "You ain't in trouble, are you?" he said.

"What? You mean pregnant?" She lit a cigarette. "Jesus, Lee. You never give me a break."

"Okay, what is it then?"

She blew a smoke ring over his head and winked. "I got myself engaged."

"You mean to be married?"

"Well, yeah," she said with a little laugh. "What other kind is there?"

"I'll be damned. What's his name?"

"Carl. Carl Henderson."

"Henderson," Bodecker repeated, as he poured some cream in his coffee from a tiny metal pitcher. "He one of them you went to school with? That bunch over off Plug Run?"

"Oh, shit, Lee," she said, "them boys are half retarded, you know that. Carl ain't even from around here. He grew up on the south side of Columbus."

"What's he do? For a living, I mean."

"He's a photographer."

"Oh, so he's got one of those studios?"

She stubbed out the cigarette in the ashtray and shook her head. "Not right now," she said. "A setup like that don't come cheap."

"Well, how does he make his money then?"

She rolled her eyes, let out a sigh. "Don't worry, he gets by."

"In other words, he ain't working."

"I seen his camera and everything."

"Shit, Sandy, Florence has got a camera, but I sure wouldn't call her a photographer." He looked back into the kitchen, where the grill cook was standing at an open refrigerator with his T-shirt pulled up, trying to get cooled off. He couldn't help but wonder if Henry had ever fucked her. People said he was hung like a Shetland pony. "Where in the hell did you meet this guy?"

"Right over there," Sandy said, pointing at a table in the corner.

"How long ago was that?"

"Last week," she said. "Don't worry, Lee. He's a nice guy." Within a month they were married.

Two hours later, he was back at the jail. He had a bottle of whiskey in a brown paper bag. The shoe box of photographs and the rolls of film were in the trunk of his cruiser. He locked the door to his office and poured himself a drink in a coffee cup. It was the first one he'd had in over a year, but he couldn't say that he enjoyed it. Florence called just as he was getting ready to have another. "I heard what happened," she said. "Why didn't you call me?"

"I know I should have."

"So it's true? Sandy's dead?"

"Her and that no-good sonofabitch both."

"My God, it's hard to believe. Weren't they on vacation?"

"I believe Carl was a lot worse than I ever gave him credit for."

"You don't sound right, Lee. Why don't you come on home?"

"I still got some work to do. Might be at it all night, the way things look."

"Any idea who did it?"

"No," he said, looking at the bottle sitting on the desk, "not really."

"Lee?"

"Yeah, Flo."

"You haven't been drinking, have you?"

51

ARVIN SAW THE NEWSPAPER IN THE RACK outside the doughnut shop when he went to get some coffee the next morning. He bought a copy and took it back to his room and read that the local sheriff's sister and husband had been found murdered. They were returning from a vacation in Virginia Beach. There was no mention of a suspect, but there was a photo of Sheriff Lee Bodecker alongside the story. Arvin recognized him as the same man who was on duty the night his father killed himself. Goddamn, he whispered. Hurriedly, he packed his stuff and started out the door. He stopped and went back inside. Taking the Calvary picture down off the wall, he wrapped it in the newspaper and stuck it in his bag.

Arvin began walking west on Main Street. At the edge of town, a logging truck headed for Bainbridge picked him up and dropped him off at the corner of Route 50 and Blaine Highway. On foot, he crossed Paint Creek at Schott's Bridge, and an hour later, he arrived at the edge of Knockemstiff. Except for a couple of new ranch-style houses standing in what had once been a cornfield, everything looked pretty much as he remembered it. He walked a bit farther, and then dropped over the small hill in the middle of the holler. Maude's store still sat on the corner, and behind it was the same camper that had been there eight years ago. He was glad to see it.

The storekeeper was sitting on a stool behind the candy case when he went inside. It was still the same Hank, just a little older now, a little more frazzled. "Howdy," he said, looking down at Arvin's gym bag.

The boy nodded, set the bag on the concrete floor. He slid the door open on top of the pop case, searched out a bottle of root beer. He opened it and took a long drink.

Hank lit a cigarette and said, "You look like you been traveling."

"Yeah," Arvin said, leaning against the cooler.

"Where you headed?"

"Not sure exactly. There used to be a house on top of the hill behind here some lawyer owned. You know the one I'm talkin' about?"

"Sure, I do. Up on the Mitchell Flats."

"I used to live there." As soon as he said it, Arvin wished he could take it back.

Hank studied him for a moment, then said, "I'll be damned. You're that Russell boy, ain't you?"

"Yeah," Arvin said. "I thought I'd just stop and see the old place again."

"Son, I hate to tell you, but that house burned down a couple year ago. They think some kids did it. Wasn't nobody ever lived there after you and your folks. That lawyer's wife and her buck boyfriend went to prison for killing him, and as far as I know, it's been tied up in court ever since."

A wave of disappointment swept over Arvin. "Is there anything left of it at all?" he asked, trying to keep his voice steady.

"Just the foundation mostly. I think maybe the barn's still there, part of it anyway. Place is all growed up now."

Arvin stared out the big plate-glass window up toward the church while he finished the pop. He thought about the day his father ran the hunter down in the mud. After everything that had happened the last couple of days, it didn't seem like such a good memory now. He laid some saltines on the counter and asked for two slices of bologna and cheese. He bought a pack of Camels and a box of matches and another bottle of pop. "Well," he said, when the storekeeper finished putting the groceries in a sack, "I figure I'll walk on up there anyway. Heck, I come this far. Is it still okay to go up through the woods behind here?"

"Yeah, just cut across Clarence's pasture. He won't say nothing."

Arvin put the sack in his gym bag. From where he stood, he could see the top of the Wagners' old house. "There a girl named Janey Wagner still live around here?" he asked.

"Janey? No, she got married a couple year ago. Lives over in Massieville the last I heard."

The boy nodded and started for the door, then stopped. He turned back and looked at Hank. "I never did get to thank you for that night my dad died," he said. "You was awful good to me, and I want you to know I ain't forgot it."

Hank smiled. Two of his bottom teeth were missing. "You had that pie on your face. Damn Bodecker thought it was blood. Remember that?"

"Yeah, I remember everything about that night."

"I just heard on the radio where his sister got killed."

Arvin reached for the doorknob. "Is that right?"

"I didn't know her, but it probably should have been him instead. He's about as no-good as they come, and him the law in this county."

"Well," the boy said, pushing the door open. "Maybe I'll see you later."

"You come back this evening, we'll sit out by the camper and drink some beer."

"I'll do that."

"Hey, let me ask you something," Hank said. "You ever been to Cincinnati?"

The boy shook his head. "Not yet, but I've heard plenty about it."

52

A FEW MINUTES AFTER BODECKER got off the phone with his wife, Howser came in with a manila envelope that contained the slugs the coroner had dug out of Carl. They were both 9 millimeter. "Same as the one that hit Sandy," the deputy said.

"I figured as much. Just the one shooter."

"So, Willis told me some lawman down in West Virginia called you. Did it happen to have anything to do with this?"

Bodecker glanced over at the map on the wall. He thought about the photographs in the trunk of his car. He needed to get to that boy before anyone else did. "No. Just some bullshit about a preacher. To tell you the truth, I'm really not sure why he wanted to talk to us."

"Well."

"Get any prints off that car?"

Howser shook his head. "Looks like the back was wiped clean. All the others we found belonged to Carl and Sandy."

"Find anything else?"

"Not really. There was a gas receipt from Morehead, Kentucky, under the front seat. Shitload of maps in the glove box. Bunch of junk in the back, pillows, blankets, gas can, that kind of stuff."

Bodecker nodded and rubbed his eyes. "Go on home and get some rest. It looks like right now all we can do is hope that something pops up."

He finished off the fifth of whiskey in his office that night, and woke the next morning on the floor with dry pipes and a sick headache. He could remember that sometime during the night he had dreamed of walking in the woods with the Russell boy and coming upon all those decayed animals. He went into the restroom and washed up, then asked the dispatcher to bring him the newspaper and some coffee and a couple of aspirins. On his way out to the parking lot, Howser caught him and suggested they check the motels and the bus station. Bodecker thought for a moment. Though he wanted to take care of this problem himself, he couldn't be too obvious about it. "That's not a bad idea," Bodecker said. "Go ahead and send Taylor and Caldwell around."

"Who?" Howser said, a frown breaking out on his face.

"Taylor and Caldwell. Just make sure they understand this crazy sonofabitch would just as soon blow their heads off as look at them." He turned and went on out the door before the deputy could protest. As chickenshit as those two were, Bodecker didn't figure they would even get out of their cruiser after hearing that.

He drove to the liquor store, bought a pint of Jack Daniel's. Then he stopped at the White Cow to get a coffee to go. Everybody quit talking when he walked in. As he turned to leave, he thought maybe he should say something, about how they were doing everything possible to catch the killer, but he didn't. He poured some whiskey in his coffee and drove to the old dump on Reub Hill Road. Opening the trunk, he took the shoe box of photographs out and looked through them one more time. He counted twenty-six different men. There were at least a couple hundred different shots, maybe more, bundled together with rubber bands. Setting the box on the ground, he tore a few stained and crinkled pages from a Frederick's of Hollywood catalog he found in the trash pile and stuffed them down in the box. Then he dropped the three film canisters on top and lit a match. Standing there in the hot sun, he drank the rest of his coffee and watched the pictures turn to ashes. When the last of them burned up, he took an Ithaca 37 from the trunk. He checked to make sure the shotgun was loaded and laid it on the backseat. He could smell last night's booze coming out of his skin. He ran a hand over his beard. It was the first morning he'd forgotten to shave since his army days.

When Hank saw the cruiser pull in the gravel lot, he folded the newspaper and set it on the counter. He watched Bodecker tip up a bottle. The last time Hank could recall seeing the sheriff in Knockemstiff was the evening he handed out wormy apples in front of the

church to the kids on Halloween when he was running for election.
He reached over and turned down his radio. The last few notes of
Sonny James's "You're the Only World I Know" ended just as the
sheriff came in the screen door. "I was hoping you'd still be around,"
he said to Hank.

"Why's that?" the storekeeper asked.

"You recall the time that crazy Russell bastard killed himself up in
the woods behind here? You had his boy with you that night. Arvin
was his name."

"I remember."

"That boy come through here maybe last night or this morning?"

Hank looked down at the counter. "I was sorry to hear about your
sister."

"I asked you a question, goddamn it."

"What did he do? Get in some trouble?"

"You might say that," Bodecker said. He grabbed the newspaper
off the counter, held the front page up in front of Hank's face.

The storekeeper's brow wrinkled as he read the black headlines
once again. "He ain't the one done that, is he?"

Bodecker dropped the paper on the floor and pulled out his
revolver, pointed it at the storekeeper. "I ain't got time to fuck around,
you dumb bastard. Have you seen him?"

Hank swallowed and turned his eyes toward the window, watched
Talbert Johnson's hot rod slow down as it passed the store. "What you
gonna do, shoot me?"

"Don't think I won't," Bodecker said. "After I splatter your little
bit of brains all over the candy case, I'll put that butcher knife in your
hand you got laying over there by your scroungy meat slicer. It'll be an
easy self-defense. Judge, the crazy sonofabitch was trying to protect
a killer." He cocked the gun. "Do yourself a favor. It's my sister we're
talking about."

"Yeah, I seen him," Hank said reluctantly. "He was in here a little
while ago. Bought a bottle of pop and some cigarettes."

"What was he driving?"

"I didn't see no car."

"So he was walking?"

"He might have been, I guess."

"Which way did he go when he left here?"

"I don't know," Hank said. "I wasn't paying attention."

"Don't lie to me. What did he have to say?"

Hank looked over at the pop case where the boy had stood and drank the root beer. "He mentioned something about the old house where he used to live, that's all."

Bodecker put the gun back in his holster. "See? That wasn't so hard, was it?" He started out the door. "You'll make a good little rat someday."

Hank watched him get in the cruiser and pull out onto Black Run Road. He placed both hands flat on the counter and bowed his head. Behind him, in a voice faint as a whisper, the radio announcer sent out another heartfelt request.

53

AT THE TOP OF THE FLATS, ARVIN STARTED SOUTH. The brush
was thicker now along the edge of the woods, but it took him only
a couple of minutes to find the deer path that he and his father had
walked on their way to the prayer log. He could see the metal roof of
the barn, and he hurried on. The house was gone, just like the storekeeper had said. He set his bag down and walked in where the back
door used to be. He continued on through the kitchen and down the
hall to the room where his mother had died. He kicked at black cin-
ders and charred pieces of lumber, hoping to find some relic of hers
or one of the little treasures he had kept in his bedroom window. But
except for a rusty doorknob and his memories, there was nothing left.
Some empty beer bottles were arranged in a neat row on one corner of
the rock foundation where someone had sat and drank for an evening.

The barn was nothing now but a shell. All the wood siding had
been torn off. The roof was rusted through in spots, the red paint
faded and peeled away by the weather. Arvin stepped inside out of
the sun, and there in a corner lay the feed bucket in which Willard
had once carried his precious blood. He moved it over to a spot near
the front and used it as a seat while he ate his lunch. He watched a
red-tailed hawk make lazy circles in the sky. Then he took out the
photograph of the woman with the dead man. Why would people do
something like this? And how, he wondered again, did her bullet miss
him when she wasn't more than five or six feet away? In the quiet,
he could hear his father's voice: "There's a sign here, son. Better pay
attention." He put the picture in his pocket and hid the bucket behind
a bale of moldy straw. Then he started back across the field.

He found the deer path again and soon arrived at the clearing that
Willard had worked so hard on. It was mostly grown over now with

snakeroot and wild fern, but the prayer log was still there. Five of the crosses stood as well, streaked a dull red with rust from the nails. The other four lay on the ground, orange-flowered trumpet vines curled around them. His heart caught just for a second when he saw some of the remains of the dog still hanging from the first cross his father had ever raised. He leaned against a tree, thought about the days leading up to his mother's death, how Willard wanted so much for her to live. He would have done anything for her; fuck the blood and the stink and the insects and the heat. Anything, Arvin said to himself. And suddenly he realized, as he stood once again in his father's church, that Willard had needed to go wherever Charlotte went, so that he could keep on looking after her. All these years, Arvin had despised him for what he'd done, as if he didn't give a damn what happened to his boy after she died. Then he thought about the ride back from the cemetery, and Willard's talk about visiting Emma in Coal Creek. It had never occurred to him before, but that was as close as his father could get to telling him that he was leaving, too, and that he was sorry. "Maybe stay for a while," Willard had said that day. "You'll like it there."

He wiped some tears from his eyes and set his gym bag down on top of the log, then walked around and knelt at the dog's cross. He moved away some dead leaves. The skull was half buried in loam, the small hole from the .22 rifle still visible between the empty eye sockets. He found the moldy collar, a small clump of hair still stuck to the leather around the rusty metal buckle. "You were a good dog, Jack," he said. He gathered up all the remains he could find on the ground— the thin ribs, the hipbones, a single paw—and pulled off the brittle pieces still attached to the cross. He laid them gently in a small pile. With the sharp end of a tree branch and his hands, he dug a hole in the moist, black dirt at the foot of the cross. He went down a foot or so, arranged everything carefully in the bottom of the grave. Then he went over to his bag and got the painting of the crucifixion that he'd taken from the motel and hung it on one of the nails in the cross.

Going back to the other side of the log, he knelt down in the place where he had once prayed next to his father. He pulled the

Luger out of his jeans and set it on top of the log. The air was thick and dead with the heat and humidity. He looked at Jesus hanging from the cross and closed his eyes. He tried his best to picture God, but his thoughts kept wandering. He finally gave up, found it easier to imagine his parents looking down on him instead. It seemed as if his entire life, everything he'd ever seen or said or done, had led up to this moment: alone at last with the ghosts of his childhood. He began to pray, the first time since his mother had died. "Tell me what to do," he whispered several times. After a couple of minutes, a sudden gust of wind came down off the hill behind him, and some of the bones still hanging in the trees began to knock together like wind chimes.

54

BODECKER TURNED ONTO THE DIRT LANE that led back to the house where the Russells used to live, his cruiser rocking gently in the ruts. He cocked his revolver and laid it on the seat. He eased slowly over flimsy saplings and tall clumps of horseweeds, coming to a stop about fifty yards from where the house had once stood. He could just make out the top of the rock foundation above the Johnson grass. The little that remained of the barn was another forty yards to the left. Maybe he would buy the property once this fucking mess was over with, he thought. He could build another house, plant an orchard. Let Matthews have the damn job of sheriff. Florence would like that. She was a worrier, that woman. He reached under the seat and got the pint, took a drink. He would have to do something about Tater, but that wouldn't be too difficult.

Then again, the Russell boy might be just the thing he needed to win another election. Someone who would kill a preacher for getting some young pussy had to have a screw loose, no matter what that hick cop in West Virginia said. It would be easy to make the punk out to be a cold-blooded maniac; and people will vote for a hero every time. He took another hit off the pint and stuck it under the seat. "Better worry about that stuff later," Bodecker said out loud. Right now he had a job to do. Even if he didn't run for office again, he couldn't bear the thought of everyone knowing the truth about Sandy. He couldn't put it into words, what she'd been doing in some of those pictures.

Once out of the car, he holstered his revolver and reached in the rear for the shotgun. He tossed his hat in the front. His stomach was churning from the hangover, and he felt like shit. He flicked the safety off the shotgun and started walking slowly up the driveway. He stopped several times and listened, then moved on. It was quiet, just a few birds chirping. At the barn, he stood in the shade, looked out past the remains of the house. He licked his lips and wished he had another drink. A wasp flew about his head, and he smacked it down with his hand, crushed it with the heel of his boot. After a few minutes, he proceeded across the field, staying close to the tree line. He walked through patches of dry milkweed and nettles and burdock. He tried to recall how far he had followed the boy that night before they came to the path that led to where his daddy had bled out. He looked back toward the barn, but he couldn't remember. He should have brought Howser with him, he thought. That fucker loved to hunt.

He was just beginning to think he must have passed it by when he came upon some trampled-down weeds. His heart revved up just a little, and he wiped the sweat from his eyes. Bending down, he peered past the weeds and brush into the woods, saw the outline of the old deer path just a few feet in. He looked back over his shoulder and saw three black crows swoop low across the field cawing. He ducked under some blackberry brambles and took a few steps, and he was on the trail. Taking a deep breath, he started slowly down the hill, his shotgun at the ready. He could feel himself shaking inside with both fear and excitement, the same as when he'd killed those two men for Tater. He hoped this one would be as easy.

55

THE BREEZE DIED DOWN and the bones stopped tinkling. Arvin heard other things now, small, everyday sounds traveling upward from the holler: a screen door slamming, kids yelling, the drone of a lawn mower. Then the cicadas stopped their high-pitched buzzing just for a moment, and he opened his eyes. Turning his head slightly, he thought he heard a faint noise behind him, a dry leaf cracking under a foot, maybe a soft twig breaking. He couldn't be sure. When the cicadas began again, he grabbed the gun off the log. In a crouch, he made his way around a thicket of wild roses to the left of what remained of the clearing, and started up the hill. He had gone thirty or forty feet when he remembered his gym bag lying next to the prayer log. But by then, it was too late.

"Arvin Russell?" he heard a loud voice call out. He ducked behind a hickory tree and stood up slowly. Drawing in his breath, he glanced around the trunk and saw Bodecker, a shotgun in his hands. At first, he could just see part of the brown shirt and the boots. Then the lawman took a few more steps, and he could make out most of his red face. "Arvin? It's Sheriff Bodecker, son," the sheriff yelled. "Now I ain't here to hurt you, I promise. Just need to ask you some questions." Arvin watched him spit and wipe some sweat out of his eyes. Bodecker moved a few feet farther, and a wood grouse flew out of its hiding spot and across the clearing, its wings beating furiously. Jerking the shotgun up, Bodecker fired, then quickly jacked another shell into the chamber. "Damn, boy, I'm sorry about that," he called out. "Goddamn bird scared me. Come on out now so we can have us a talk." He crept on, stopped at the edge of the brushy clearing. He saw the gym bag on the ground, the framed Jesus hanging on the cross. Maybe this sonofabitch really is nuts, he thought. In the shadowy light of the woods, he could still make out some of the bones hanging from wires.

"I figured this might be where you would come. Remember that night you brought me out here? That was an awful thing your daddy did."

Arvin eased the safety off on the Luger and picked up a chunk of dead wood at his feet. He tossed it high through an opening in the branches. When it bounced off a tree below the prayer log, Bodecker fired two more rounds in rapid succession. He jacked another shell into the chamber. Bits of leaf and bark floated through the air. "God-damn, boy, don't fuck with me," he yelled. He swiveled around, looking wild-eyed in all directions, then moved a little closer to the log.

Arvin stepped out silently into the path behind him. "Better lay that gun down, Sheriff," the boy said. "I got one pointed right at you."

Bodecker froze in midstep, and then let his foot down slowly. Glancing down at the open gym bag, he saw a copy of this morning's *Meade Gazette*, lying on top of a pair of jeans. His picture on the front page stared back at him. From the sound of the voice, he judged the boy was directly behind him, maybe twenty feet away. He had two shells left in the scattergun. Against a pistol, that was pretty good odds. "Son, you know I can't do that. Hell, that's one of the first rules they teach you in law enforcement. You don't ever give up your weapon."

"I can't help it what they teach you," Arvin said. "Set it on the ground and step away." He could feel his heart pounding against his shirt. All the moisture suddenly seemed sucked out of the air.

"What? So you can kill me like you did my sister and that preacher down in West Virginia?"

Arvin's hand began to tremble a little when he heard the sheriff mention Teagardin. He thought for a second. "I got a snapshot in my pocket of her hugging on some dead guy. You turn loose of that gun, and I'll show it to you." He saw the lawman's back stiffen, and he tightened his grip on the Luger.

"You little sonofabitch," Bodecker said under his breath. He looked down at his likeness again in the newspaper. It had been taken right after he was elected. Sworn to uphold the law. He almost had to laugh. Then he raised the Ithaca and started to whirl around. The boy fired.

Bodecker's gun went off, the buckshot tearing a ragged hole in the wild roses to Arvin's right. The boy flinched and pulled the trigger again. The sheriff gave out a sharp cry and fell forward into the leaves. Arvin waited a minute or two, then cautiously approached. Bodecker was lying on his side looking at the ground. One bullet had shattered his wrist, and the other had gone in under his arm. From the looks of it, at least one of his lungs was pierced. With every heaving breath the man took, another spurt of bright red blood soaked the front of his shirt. When Bodecker saw the boy's worn boots, he attempted to pull his pistol out of his holster, but Arvin bent down and grabbed hold of it, tossed it a few feet away.

He set the Luger on top of the log and, as gently as he could, pushed Bodecker over onto his back. "I know she was your sister, but look here," Arvin said. He took the photograph out of his wallet and held it for the sheriff to see. "I didn't have no choice. I swear, I begged her to put the gun down." Bodecker looked up at the boy's face, then moved his eyes to Sandy and the dead man she held in her arms. He grimaced and tried to grab the picture with his good arm, but he was too weak to make anything but a halfhearted effort. Then he lay back and began to cough up blood, just like she had.

Though it seemed to Arvin as if hours went by while he listened to the sheriff fight to stay alive, it really took the man only a few minutes to die. There's no way to turn back now, he thought. But he couldn't go on like this, either. He imagined the door to a sad, empty room closing with a faint click, never to be opened again, and that calmed him a little. When he heard Bodecker expel his last, soggy breath, he made a decision. He picked the Luger up and walked around to the hole he had dug for Jack. Getting on his knees in the damp dirt, he rubbed his hand slowly over the gray metal barrel, thought about his father bringing the gun home all those years ago. Then he laid it in the hole alongside the animal's bones. He shoved all the dirt back in the hole with his hands and patted it down flat. With dead leaves and a few branches, he covered all traces of the grave. He took down the picture of the Savior and wrapped it and put it in his gym bag. Maybe someday he'd have a place to hang it. His father would have liked that. He stuck the photograph of Sandy and the two rolls of film in Bodecker's shirt pocket.

Arvin looked around one more time at the moss-covered log and the rotting gray crosses. He would never see this place again; probably never see Emma or Earskell either, for that matter. He turned and started up the deer path. When he came to the top of the hill, he brushed aside a spiderweb and stepped out of the dim woods. The cloudless sky was the deepest blue he'd ever seen, and the field seemed to be blazing with light. It looked as if it went on forever. He began walking north toward Paint Creek. If he hurried, he could be on Route 50 in an hour. If he was lucky, someone would give him a ride.

ACKNOWLEDGMENTS

I am extremely grateful to the following people and organizations, without which this book would not have been possible: Joan Bingham and PEN for the 2009 PEN/Robert Bingham Fellowship; the Ohio Arts Council for a 2010 Individual Excellence Award; Ohio State University for a 2008 Presidential Fellowship; my friend Mick Rothgeb for advice on firearms; Dr. John Gabis for answering my questions about blood; and James E. Talbert at the Greenbrier Historical Society for information about Lewisburg, West Virginia. I owe a special debt of gratitude to my agents and readers, Richard Pine and Nathaniel Jacks at Inkwell Management; and lastly, for his faith, patience, and guidance, I want to thank my editor, Gerry Howard, along with all the other wonderful people at Doubleday.

off the sho